THE CLEANSING

THE CLEANSING

ROBERT PUGH

CITIOFBOOKS, INC.
3736 Eubank NE Suite A1
Albuquerque, NM 87111-3579
www.citiofbooks.com
Hotline: 1 (877) 389-2759
Fax: 1 (505) 930-7244

Ordering Information:

Quantity sales. Special discounts are available on quantity purchases by corporations, associations, and others. For details, contact the publisher at the address above.

Printed in the United States of America.

ISBN-13:   Paperback   979-8-89391-872-4
                  eBook   979-8-89391-874-8
                  Hardback   979-8-89391-873-1

Library of Congress Control Number: 2025916870

This novel is a work of fiction. Names descriptions, entities, and incidents included in the story are products of the author's imagination. Any resemblance to actual persons, events, and entities is entirely coincidental.

TABLE OF CONTENTS

DEDICATION

This novel is dedicated to my wife, Cindy, who was there when the story began and has been my encourager through it all. Thank you.

CHAPTER 1

Wednesday, April 3, 2013, early morning

Howard shifted his weight for the second time in less than five minutes. "Sitting on stakeout was never one of my strong suits." He and his son William had been sitting in the car for four straight hours, waiting for something to happen. "It's funny, but somehow I forgot about this part of the job."

William took another sip of his now cold coffee. "You used to tell me that it was all about putting in the time."

"Yes, but it was different back then. My butt could handle sitting four hours in one place, and coffee didn't give me indigestion like it does now."

They had been sitting in Howard's car, since three o'clock that morning. Everything pointed to a meeting they believed would take place that morning pointing them toward Max's killer. Every lead directed them this house. They learned of this meeting the hard way: solid investigative journalism work by case-hardened, old-fashioned, in-your-face newspaper reporters. Like Howard always said, "Nothing comes easy."

They sat there for three-or-four more minutes watching as the rising sun slowly peeked out from between the clouds. Their vigilance, however, paid off one minute later.

"William, is your camera ready?" he asked quietly as he pointed at a dark blue sedan pulling into the driveway. "It's time to do your thing."

With steady hands, William began taking pictures in rapid-fire fashion. He captured the images of the driver and a second man as they emerged from the car and began walking toward the house. When the front door opened, several frames of film caught their suspect shaking hands with the unknown visitors, before entering the house. The second man, tall and muscular-looking, wearing a black leather jacket with a dark brown turtleneck sweater, remained on the front steps where he assumed a sentry-like posture.

Howard tapped William's shoulder and pointed toward the sedan. "Wait. There's someone else in the car."

He swung the telephoto lens to his left and started the rapid-fire snapping, zooming in while trying to improve the picture resolution.

"I don't see anyone."

"She's in the back seat on the right-hand side."

"What makes you think it's a woman?"

He couldn't resist. "Maybe her profile and the large hoop earrings might be a clue."

Training his camera on the back seat, he snapped several more pictures. Just as he finished, the first bullet fired in their direction slammed into the left rear panel of their vehicle.

William was startled. "What was that?"

"Somebody's calling card. Get down!"

Howard started the vehicle, hurriedly dropped the gear lever into drive, and smoked the tires as he sped off. Two more bullets smashed into the rear trunk lid, before they had gone fifteen feet. The next round shattered the passenger's side rearview mirror.

"Are you okay?"

William was visibly upset. The look on his face testified to that.

"Dad, what's going on? Why would anyone want to kill us?"

"Maybe it has something to do with what they think we know." He wheeled the car around the corner and floored the accelerator.

"We don't know anything – and that's the problem. All we've got are a bunch of ideas and a loosely woven theory."

"They don't know that and now maybe it's not just a theory anymore."

He slowed the vehicle not wanting to attract attention. For the next several seconds, he checked his rearview mirror to make sure they weren't being followed.

"Right now, I think we need to get these pictures to Randy. Maybe he can figure out who we're dealing with here. It's obvious that we've gotten too close for somebody's comfort."

"They tried to kill us."

"Son, the game's changed – and so have the rules. Now, we earn our stripes."

XXXXX

From his very first day on the job for a now retired journalist like Howard Ewing, it was always about the story – and there were no short cuts. The instinctive skills, which had been sharpened for thirty-five years doing what he knew, now spoke to both a relevance and relationship with the industry he had made his life's work. He struggled with the coming technology before retiring, but he believed the story always would be center front.

Lately, he started to make a conscious effort to keep up with the younger generation. He uses Facebook®, but that was only because his son William managed to stop by the house occasionally to show him how to make it pertinent in his life. He had started to follow the blogs of journalists who wrote extensively about this newer, fast-paced world of twenty-four-hour news cycles and digital reporting. Still, there was something special to him looking at what was printed above, or below, the fold of a newspaper and the feel of it in his hands.

He and Carla, his wife of thirty-four years, spoke often of how much the business had changed over those years, even to the point where several papers had closed their doors. They both agreed, however, there were some things that newspapers were better at doing than a website. Nowhere was that more evident to him than how and when he learned about the death of his friend and long-time co-worker, Max Leopard.

Two months earlier on Saturday evening, February 2, 2013, Howard Ewing was at home relaxing in his easy chair and reading the newspaper. Carla was in the kitchen fixing them both a quick snack of popcorn.

"Oh my God," he said in a raised and disbelieving voice, "Max Leopard was killed in an automobile accident."

"Did you say that Max Leopard died? What happened?"

"According to this article, he died last night in a one car accident on U.S. Highway 27, south of Avon Park."

"Wasn't he about to retire? He started about the same time you did."

"No, but he was thinking about it. I spoke with him and Eileen briefly two weeks ago at the mall. We talked about a lot of stuff, including how well their daughter was doing." He put the paper down. "Come to think of it, he did mention something he had been working on for several weeks, but it was just in passing. He seemed perfectly happy even telling me how they were looking forward to spending some time traveling and seeing the mountains out west."

"I wonder how she's doing. I haven't seen her since we all got together at the park last summer."

His cell phone alerted him that he was receiving a call. He picked it up and connected the call.

"Hello."

"Mr. Ewing?"

"This is he."

"You probably don't remember me, but I started with the paper about a week before you retired. My name is Arthur Golden – and I work the metro desk. Mr. Lasko asked me to call you to make sure you knew about Max Leopard's death and that it was ruled accidental."

"Yes, I just saw the article. Do you know if there's any additional information released by the police surrounding the accident?"

"No, I don't. I was told to tell you that they have closed the investigation."

"Do you know who was in charge of it?"

"No sir, I do not. All Mr. Lasko told me was to make sure you got this information." Somewhat polite about it, he abruptly ended the call and hung up.

"That was weird. I haven't heard from Arthur Golden, since I left the paper." He looked at Carla. "Out of the clear blue, he calls tonight to tell me that Marty Lasko instructed him to tell me that Max's death was ruled accidental and that they've already closed the investigation."

She offered him some of her popcorn. "Marty? I thought he wasn't working for the paper any longer, since his last heart attack."

"No, he's semi-retired – at least he's supposed to be doing less stressful stuff now. Why would he ask Arthur to call me? Why wouldn't he call me himself?"

"Maybe he's following the doctor's orders and doing less stressful stuff. You don't suppose that Max was in some sort of trouble do you?"

"Max? He was about as tame and shy as any person I've ever known. He was the walking definition for the word saint. I never heard him say a bad word about anyone."

They knew they needed to make a visit to pay their respects, but they also knew it wasn't going to be easy.

While driving toward Eileen's house the next morning, there wasn't much conversation. They looked at each other occasionally, smiled, but neither had much to say.

As they approached the driveway, he realized they weren't the only ones who had decided to pay their respects to Eileen. Howard immediately recognized two others who were standing near the front door.

He turned to Carla. "That's Bob and Emily Kiser. He's with the circulation division."

Carla turned to him, as she pointed toward another car. "Who's that?"

"I know that's Nora Chester, and I'm guessing that must be her husband. I think she's still in the finance department."

After getting out of the car, they walked to the front door, rang the doorbell, and waited. It was Bob Kiser who opened the door.

Once inside, they took off their coats, and went into the living room. There were six others in the living room who were sitting and socializing.

"Eileen just went into the kitchen," one of the guests said, while pointing to a hallway.

Carla excused herself and headed that direction. Howard walked over to where Bob and Emily Kiser were seated and extended his right hand to shake hands.

"Bob, it's good to see you." He then turned his attention to Emily. "It's good to see you, too. How have the two of you been?"

While he was trying to play nice with the other guests in the living room, she found Eileen who was making a fresh pot of coffee. Seeing Carla out of the corner of her eye, she stopped what she was doing, leaned forward, and steadied herself against the counter.

Carla walked up to her and put her left arm around her shoulders and gently hugged her.

Eileen turned and hugged her as well. That's when the tears started.

She wasn't exactly sure what to tell her or say to her. They just stood there hugging each other as two old friends would do under those circumstances. After a minute, Carla urged her to sit down, while she finished making the coffee for her.

Eileen, whose eyes were reddened and swollen from the crying, looked at her and thanked her for coming.

"I wouldn't be anywhere else."

"Is Howard with you?"

"Yes, he's in the living room talking with Bob and the others." After she finished making the coffee, she sat down at the table with her.

"What can we do to help right now?"

Eileen shook her head and shrugged her shoulders. "I don't know. The people at the funeral home have been wonderful and are taking care of all the arrangements. Max's boss has been very kind."

"What about the kids? How soon will they be here?"

She paused and let out a sigh. "Jessica's flight gets into Orlando this afternoon at three. Little Max is driving in and should be here later this morning. He called last night from Augusta to let me know."

"Would you like for us to pick up Jessica?"

"Thank you, but she said she's getting a rental at the airport."

Carla reached out and took Eileen's left hand into hers. "I'm so sorry –," she started, but was interrupted by Eileen.

"No, I'm sorry Carla. I know I haven't been much of a friend lately. I don't know what else to say, except that I'm sorry."

For the next several minutes, they sat – each sharing memories and how their children were the light of their lives. It was as if a long-lost friend had come home.

When they were back in their car and headed home, Howard had a lot more to say than he did on the drive there.

"When I was speaking with Bob, I got the impression that no one at the paper knew why Max was near Avon Park. Whatever he was doing there apparently wasn't work related; at least that's the skinny at the office."

"We didn't talk about that at all. Instead, we spent our time catching up on the kids. Did you know that Jessica is engaged to a young man from Virginia? Little Max is almost finished with dentistry schooling and he's expected to graduate next spring."

He chuckled slightly. "That kid always was fascinated with teeth. I'll never forget when he saw Eileen's mother's false teeth in a glass. Remember that? He was maybe three of four when that happened."

The trip home went quickly as they both shared about their visit. They were relieved to the point that they were glad they went.

Later that evening, while sitting at the kitchen table and eating dinner, Howard looked at Carla with a curious expression on his face.

She saw it. "What's running around in that mind of yours?"

He put his fork down and leaned back in his chair. "I've been thinking about something Bob told me this morning: No one seems to know what Max was doing near Avon Park. I know you didn't ask Eileen about it, but maybe we should. I've been thinking that since no other vehicles were involved, maybe the police investigation can tell us more about it. Maybe I should contact them first and then speak with Eileen."

"See, there you go again – looking for an angle – as if there is something to investigate. The funeral hasn't even been planned. It might be best if you wait until after it."

"It won't hurt for me to check with Randy. He might be able to find out more from his perspective than I could right now. Besides, wouldn't you want to know if that was me?"

She leaned forward slightly. "Of course, I would. I just think it's probably best for you to wait until after the funeral. She didn't ask you to do this did she?"

He reached out and took her right hand into his. "No, but my gut is telling me that there's something more to this."

Just saying those words helped him to feel relevant, again. Now, he just needed to be patient with the process.

CHAPTER 2
February 19, 2013

Two weeks had gone by since the funeral. Howard's inquiries into Max's accident had not turned up any more answers than when he first started his mini-investigation. No one, including Eileen, seemed to know why Max was in that part of Florida – or where he was going or where he had been. There was nothing that indicated any suspicious activities or wrongdoing, but that didn't stop him.

He managed to get a copy of the police report but found no drug or alcohol related issues connected to the accident. He studied the photos that had been taken at the scene, but nothing of any consequence was revealed in them. He spoke by phone with the officer who had arrived first on the scene, but that led nowhere. Still, the haunting questions of why Max was on that road and at that location when he died remained.

He was sitting at the kitchen table eating breakfast, when Carla put down her coffee cup and spoke directly at him.

"You've been sitting there for ten minutes pushing those eggs around on your plate. Is there something wrong with them? I made them the way you like them."

He shook his head. "It's not the eggs. I'm stuck on this thing surrounding Max's death. There's something that just doesn't add up and I can't put my finger on it."

"Maybe, there is no reason other than he died in an accident that has no explanation. That's why the police called it an accident."

Howard shook his head, again. "Tell me something Carla, in all the years we knew Max what was the one thing that stood out about him more than anything else?"

She thought for a few seconds. "He was a team player."

This time, after he shook his head, he put both of his elbows on the table and leaned forward. "I'll grant you that, but what one thing about his character jumps out at you? You've said it before about him."

"Oh. You mean the comment I made about his conservation of energy?"

"Yes. No matter what it was that he was doing, he was always doing something with a purpose behind it."

"Yes, I remember saying that, but that was so long ago. That was long before he and Eileen even moved to Charlotte."

"From what you remember of him, would you say that he was still the same Max after they moved back, and he came back to work at the paper?"

"He wasn't the one who had changed. Eileen was the one who seemed to be less than cordial. Max was still the same old Max." She chuckled briefly. "Where are you going with this?"

"I don't know. I just know that I'm having a hard time accepting the fact that his death seemed so useless. It would be so out of character for him to leave this world that way."

She saw the expression on his face and heard the sadness in his voice.

"What else is there to do?

"I wish I knew. I am glad that you and Eileen have rekindled your friendship. She needs that right now."

"It's hasn't been easy. I've felt at times when the two of us are sitting in her kitchen drinking coffee that she's miles away. She's struggled at times keeping focused and her conversation with me seems more like rattling on about nothing."

"Still, she needs you."

"I know that, but it's been difficult."

They say that time can heal all wounds and that coping with the loss of someone you've known for years can become easier. Although the reasons behind Max's death continued to nag at him, life began to get back to some sense of routine for Howard. Each Tuesday, he would meet up with old friends for coffee at the diner that was only two blocks from his former work place. There, they would talk about whatever seemed to be making headlines and whatever was on the television news programs that morning. On the second and fourth Thursday of each month, he and two of his closest friends, Randy Tomlin and Calvin Rolle, would meet for lunch at Harry's Place.

He met Randy, who retired from the paper a year before he did, when they were assigned to cover a bank robbery story in DeLand in April 1979. Initially, Randy had been hired as a photographer for the daily newspaper. His extensive and impressive portfolio came about at a very young age working as a freelance contractor. Their collaborative efforts and the work they did on that case were well received. They were both recognized with commendations and citations from the Governor. Even in retirement, Randy continued to have many of his photos and written articles published in several magazines and journals.

Howard decided to try his hand at writing, once he decided finally to retire. He won a few awards for his efforts in short stories, but getting novels published was another thing entirely. He had finished two manuscripts, but no literary agent proved interested.

Calvin Rolle, also a newspaper veteran who retired two years before Howard, decided to try his hand at writing novels the day after he walked out of his office. After a year of writing efforts and eighteen rejection notices from several different literary agents, he turned his attention to painting, instead. Several of his early pieces received recognition at local fairs and festivals. Major recognition came his way for his interpretation on canvas of the construction sites of downtown Orlando. He had entered one of his works in a national competition and walked away with a third-place finish and a ten-thousand-dollar award. Since then, many of his works have been displayed in galleries throughout Florida.

On this Thursday, their conversation was more than just the usual reminiscing about how "kids" had taken over the world and were running it into the ground. It was more than their usual banter about how the newspaper industry had changed and that the good old days would never return. As they enjoyed their meal together that Thursday, the conversation became pointed. It allowed for the inquisitive and fact-finding nature of their former selves to emerge. During that hour they spent together, not one of them finished their meal because of the topic of conversation. For Howard, it was exactly what he needed.

"It's been a month since his accident and there's nothing you can do to change the fact that it was an accident," Randy said. "I went through the same files you did and came up with nada."

"I know. I know." Howard took a sip of his sweet tea. "Randy, I can't get this idea about his being on that road out of my head. Why was he there? Nothing makes sense to me. You know how he was. If someone can give me a good reason for why he was there, then maybe

I could walk away from this and let it rest. I'm telling you something's not right."

Calvin looked at Randy, smiled, and then turned and spoke directly to Howard.

"I think I know what you're saying, but no one seems to have the answer to your question. Remember that story we did about that guy who was convicted of multiple murders? Remember that one? He was the guy who lived in Apopka, worked in Orlando, but partied in Oviedo on a regular basis? Nothing in that story broke until a lead was developed by that lieutenant from Orlando who approached the evidence with a different premise about the motive for the killings."

Randy believed that was his cue to reenter the conversation.

"I remember that one because I was at the second crime scene taking shots of the carnage. That was evidence for sure." He leaned forward, then leaned to his left so he wouldn't have to raise his voice, and looked Howard directly in his eyes.

"But Howard – we don't have any evidence. Each of us has looked at the photos and came up with zilch. If there was something in those photos, don't you think one of us would have seen it?"

Howard nodded in agreement. "Look guys, I know you're probably right about all of this. It's something that I can't shake. It isn't about the evidence we've seen, it's about the evidence we haven't."

They sat there for a few seconds realizing that he wasn't going to give up on this until there was some sort of closure for him. Calvin, knowing that Randy was right about not seeing anything in the photos that would provide any kind of lead or advance the story, also knew exactly what Howard meant by the unseen evidence. Over the years, all three of them had covered stories that had remained dormant until a fresh pair of eyes began looking deeper into the background of the stories.

Calvin, also lowering his voice to barely above a whisper, leaned toward the center of the table.

"Suppose we look at this from another angle. Instead of asking why he was on that road that day, maybe we should be looking into what he was doing a week-or-two before his accident." He looked directly at Howard. "Have you? I mean – have you asked Eileen if you could look through his personal stuff? Who knows? We just might find something that will help us one way or another."

Howard was somewhat surprised by his question. "No, I haven't because I didn't want to cause her any further distress."

Randy, intrigued by Calvin's comment, spoke up. "As far back as I can remember Max was really good at keeping notes. He once showed me his collection of notes that he stored in his basement. There had to be fifteen or twenty good-sized storage containers full of all those handwritten notes. Maybe if she'll let us look through those things, who knows what might pop?"

"Just how do you propose we do that?" Howard asked.

"We need something that will not raise suspicion about what we are doing."

Calvin sighed. "Oh – you mean lie to her?"

"No, we need to agree on a reason that the three of us need to look through those note pads. Is there anything current that all of us are involved in that Max was a part of?"

They sat there thinking for several seconds, before Randy spoke up.

"What about that story we started back in June about how so many of our local churches had been vandalized? We never finished that story, and I remember all of us agreed to be mutually involved in the project – especially Max. I know he called me about that at least on two separate occasions. That wouldn't be lying now would it?"

Howard chuckled. "No, it wouldn't, but it does require us to write that piece and submit it to the paper."

"It'd be like getting back onto the horse and into the saddle, again."

They all looked at each other for a few seconds.

Howard spoke first. "I'm game."

Calvin looked at the other two. "I'm in."

Randy put his napkin down into the middle of his plate. "I say all for one – and one for all. Let's do this thing."

XXXXX

The week-end came and went, and Howard had not yet approached Eileen about looking through Max's personal notes. As he sat on his porch thinking through the possible opening lines for how he would carry this out, Carla came in and sat down next to him on the sofa.

"Okay, you want to tell me what's bothering you?"

"I agreed to approach Eileen to ask her if Randy, Calvin, and I could look though Max's old steno note pads. We're working on a story we started last June about all those break-ins at the churches"

"Are you serious? The three of you want to write a story that Max was involved with a month after his death?" She smiled at him. "What do you really think you're going to find in his notes?"

He smiled back at her. "Is it that obvious? We thought we had a pretty good cover story."

"What's really going on?"

"The three of us think that Max's death didn't fit his lifestyle. We all believe that if we can determine what he was doing, where he had been, and who he might have been seeing a week or so leading up to the day he died, we might be able to find out why he died that day and why it appeared to be an accident."

"Do you think that Eileen is going to buy into this?"

"If you help us, then yes she will. If you show any signs of doubt or indecision about what we're trying to do, then she'll figure it out and probably resent our actions. The last thing we want to do is to give her any sense of false hope or a belief that his death was something other than an accident. We don't know a lot about the back story, but you've heard me tell you before that there's always a back story. The three of us agree that this situation is no different."

Chapter 3

March 5, 2013

The diner was busier than he had expected that morning. Fortunately, Howard had arrived early enough to save the corner booth where the three of them liked to sit. As he sat there waiting for Randy and Calvin, an early morning spring rain started. For the first few minutes, it was something welcomed and pleasant. It didn't take too long for it to develop into a wind-driven, nasty morning storm that soaked everything, and everyone caught without cover for more than a few seconds.

He watched as the wind blew the rain onto the window panel near the booth. He watched as the cars threw waves of rain drops out of the way, while their headlights gave it an eerie look. As he sat there looking out the window and occasionally taking a sip of hot coffee, he recalled the time he was working a story with Max that occurred during the spring in 1986. They had just been given the assignment by their editor, Marty Lasko.

"I want the two of you to go to Melbourne and find out what's happening at the insurance meeting this morning at eleven o'clock. Here's a voucher that should cover your expenses for the day."

Howard took the voucher and they both started walking toward the exit.

"By the way," Marty said in a louder voice, "make sure that one of you gets the names of all of the companies that bid on that contract. Stop by city hall and check out their business licenses as well. I want four hundred words on this before deadline tonight."

It was unusual to send two experienced reporters to cover a routine commission meeting and to be given a voucher for the day's expenses. Max started whistling as they approached the car.

"Why are you so happy?"

"It's a nothing assignment. On top of that, we've got money in our pocket and a full tank of gas in a company car. What's not to be happy about?"

"What's a nothing assignment? I think Marty wants us to split up on this and get all the angles for the story. He must think something's going on that's out of the ordinary."

"He's always like that. It is strange, though, for the two of us to share this assignment. How about I stick around the meeting, while you go into town and dig up those business licenses?"

"We can draft the copy on the way back. If we're going to make deadline, we won't have any time to dilly-dally around. It'll take about two hours to get there, two hours to get back, about three hours for the meeting, and you should be able to get whatever you can get on those licenses in the meantime. All total, we should be back by four o'clock. If we have the intro ready, we can get that into copy and on his desk before he leaves at five o'clock. We'll be able to call it a day and go home. What do you think?"

Max started whistling, again.

As Howard pulled the car out of the parking lot and onto the street, Max stopped his whistling.

"What happens if the meeting runs longer than expected?"

"We'll just make up the time on the highway. I'll let you drive home because the way you drive, it'll save us an hour." They both smiled.

Unaware that he had come in and sat down opposite him, he hadn't heard anything that Calvin had said to him. Finally, Calvin reached out and tapped his hand. That got his attention.

"I didn't see you come in. I'm sorry."

"Man, wherever you were, you were at least a thousand miles from here. Has Randy shown up?"

"He called. He said he's running late but should be here in another five minutes or so."

The waitress came over, took his order, and refreshed Howard's coffee cup.

"What were you thinking about when I came in? The look on your face was like you were in another world."

"I was thinking about a piece Max and I did back in the eighties. We found out about the bidding irregularities for insurance that cities and other incorporated communities had been using. The Legislature ended up changing a lot of the guidelines and passed several laws that tightened the statutes."

"I remember that one. The Lieutenant Governor rolled over, pled out and resigned."

"Actually, it was Max who found the connection that blew up the story. By the time State Attorney Joseph Curtis finished with that case, three other notables ended being locked up as well."

They saw Randy drive up, get out of his car, and make a dash for the front door. He made his way to the booth and gave the waitress his order as he walked toward them.

"I'm sorry I'm late guys. I had a little bit of a problem at the house. It seems that there's a leak in the garage. It just happens to be directly over the washing machine. Of course, it was discovered just as I was getting ready to leave. I called the roofers only to be told that the first they can get to my house is next Wednesday. Roofing business is apparently not impacted like a lot of other businesses have been lately."

After he sat down, the waitress brought him a cup of coffee.

"So, where are we? What's the status of contacting Eileen?"

"I called her yesterday afternoon. Carla and I are going over later this morning to talk with her. I'll approach the subject and see what she says."

Randy grabbed the sugar container and began pouring sugar into his coffee cup.

"What happens if she says no and won't let us near those things?"

"Frankly, I hadn't considered that. My intention is for us to get a good look at them and anything else that he might have kept around the house."

Calvin raised his hand, as if to ask permission to speak. "Are you considering asking her about us boxing them up and taking them out of there? It might make it easier on her if we did."

"That's the plan at the moment."

They spent the next forty minutes talking, eating, and making sure they all had their stories straight. The rain hadn't let up at all which gave them an excuse to not be in any hurry. After another round of coffee, however, they each paid their bill and headed home.

When Howard got home, Carla was in the kitchen making more cookies she planned to take with them. "How'd your meeting go?"

"Well, the plan is in motion." He sat down at the table and grabbed one of the cookies and ate it. "These are really good."

"Thank you. What time did you want to leave?"

"I'm thinking about ten-thirty. How's that fit your baking schedule?"

"That should be just about right, but I'll need another thirty minutes for this last batch and to clean up." She opened the oven door and peeked at the progress of those she had put in several minutes before. "These are just about done."

By ten-thirty, they were in their car and on their way to see Eileen.

The rain had begun to let up a little, and like the other times they had visited her, the conversation during the ride over was light – until Carla changed the topic of conversation.

"I think this is a good thing you and Randy and Calvin are doing. If for nothing else, it'll help to keep your skills sharp."

"I hadn't thought about it that way. No matter what happens, good, bad or indifferent, at the very least I'll sleep better at night knowing we tried."

When they reached the house, Eileen welcomed them and hung their coats in the hallway. They followed her into the kitchen where she had been baking cookies, too.

Carla handed her the container. "Here, how about we swap a few?"

They both laughed. Once they were seated, Eileen poured each of them a cup of coffee. When she was finally seated, she looked at Howard.

"This isn't just a social call is it?"

"Eileen, I've come to ask a favor of you. A few of us were working with Max on a story a while back that we never finished. We want to finish it. To do that, we'll need his notes. Is it too much to ask to allow us to gather them and take them with us so that we don't have to travel ground already covered?"

"Take what you need. In fact, there are boxes of those things in his workroom and in the basement that are doing no one any good. Take those, too, if you'd like."

He let out a long sigh.

Eileen looked at Carla, then at Howard. "What's wrong? Did I say something that was wrong?"

Carla spoke up. "No Eileen, you didn't. That was his way of thanking you now."

"I don't understand."

Howard reached out and grasped her left hand into his. "These notes will help us pick up the story where it left off. Plus, it will help us piece together his thoughts and whereabouts when he collected the information. It will help build the story quicker and fill in the pieces that are missing."

She stood up. "Where are my manners? I've got freshly baked cookies sitting here on the counter and I haven't even offered either of you one of them." She placed a plate of chocolate chip cookies on the table in front of them. "The chocolate is still kind of sticky, but that's when I like to eat them. Max liked them that way, too. Please, help yourself."

The remainder of the visit they spent talking about their children and her grandchildren. During the discussions, he felt as if a heavy burden had been lifted from his shoulders. So much so, he excused himself from the table for a few minutes to call Randy and Calvin. He couldn't keep quiet about this any longer.

Before they left, he had decided with Calvin to bring his trailer and to help with the boxing and loading of the notepads on the following Monday morning. After Eileen showed him where they were stored, he took a quick look in a few boxes. In total, he counted seventeen boxes dating back to 1973. Each box had no less than thirty note pads in it. Some of them had as many as forty.

As they were riding home, Carla voiced a concern for the first time. "Does this mean all of these boxes are going to end up at our house?"

"Yes, for the time being. I think we need to be able to keep a close eye on them. I told Randy and Calvin that we'd be able to do our work on the porch, but that we'd store them in our utility room for now."

Just then his cell phone rang. He connected the call and put him on speaker phone.

"Hi, Randy what's up?"

"I just got off the phone with Louis Velazquez. He's agreed to let us look through the storage bins at the office. He thinks Max might have left a few of his notes there."

"That sounds great. Calvin and I are moving the boxes next Monday. Unless there are any objections from you, I planned to store them at my house so that we can work there."

"Okay. That works for me. Right now, I'm headed toward the office to look around. Louis said to meet him there."

"Tell Benson I said, 'Hello.'"

Chapter 4
March 11, 2013

Moving the boxes of note pads went off without much fanfare. Eileen was gracious throughout the whole process and vacuumed the carpet after all of them had been carried out. When the last of them had been loaded and Calvin had secured them, she invited them inside for coffee and a snack. She felt overwhelmed at times thinking about how her life had changed in the last month. She was grateful for friends who helped her to face what some would think to be simple tasks, but the prospects of having to let go of her now late husband seemed daunting. This morning, it was as if she had literally turned a corner and left much of that behind.

As she poured coffee for each of them, she felt and sounded content. "I can't thank you guys enough for what you're doing. I really had no idea what I was going to do with all that stuff, but now with all those boxes out of the way I can fix up that room for the kids for when they come to visit."

"Eileen, would you like an advance copy of the story when it's ready?" Howard asked.

"That would be nice. I thought that I'd start putting together a scrapbook of things that Max kept. It would make a nice thing to start my first book with that on page one. You know he kept a lot of those kinds of things in his workroom closet."

"You don't suppose that he might have kept any of his notes in there do you?"

She stood up. "Now would be a great time to take a look, I mean since you're already here." Both could hear the confidence growing in her voice. "There might be something of use to you for your story."

As if rejuvenated and energized, she waved at them to follow her.

Max's closet was not what the ordinary person would think of as a closet. It took up the entire length of the east wall of the room and was comprised of three sets of bi-folding doors. It was in line more with what one would consider to be a tribute. When they first glanced at its contents, they could tell it was something that Max had done. It was not just organized; it was systematized, categorized, and alphabetized where each item had been clearly marked with the date and location of the event.

She stepped back to let them get a better look. "He would spend hours in here remembering with great fondness about what he called, 'the back story'. He knew there was always something going on in the background that influenced or brought attention to the main part of the story." She paused for a few seconds. Her voice became quieter. "What is it that you are really looking for?"

Howard approached her, put his right arm around her shoulders, and let out a sigh.

"We've got a job to do. I just hope that you know how much we care about you and how much we cared about Max."

"So that's a non-answer answer. Let me put it this way: Just what do you hope to learn from all this research? There's something you haven't told me."

Calvin looked at Howard and then at her. "Since you've breached the subject, maybe we should tell you the bottom line." He looked at Howard again, hoping for some sign of approval for what he was about to do. Fortunately, the phone rang, and she excused herself to go answer it.

"What are you thinking? We agreed not to approach that issue."

"Man, she's on to us in a big way. You heard her. I think we owe it to her to tell her the complete truth and not skip around it anymore."

"If you do this, we've got to tell Randy right away. I don't want him blindsided by any of this. Whatever you do, don't get caught up in the details. Just stay on the surface issues for now. If anything comes up later, that'll be the time to let her in on the deal."

Eileen returned apologizing for the interruption.

"Now, where were we? Oh yes, Calvin you were just about to tell me what's really going on – and don't tell me anything about some cockamamie story about finishing a project. What is it about all of Max's things that are so important?"

Howard decided to jump in at that point. "We're struggling with the fact that Max died near Avon Park. It was out of character for somebody like him and makes no sense."

"Are you telling me you think that he was murdered?"

Howard looked at Calvin, but it was Calvin who spoke next.

"We don't think so, but we haven't had time to look at all of the details. We don't even have a theory. Worse, all we've got is pure speculation and certainly no proof."

"That's a non-denial denial if I ever heard one."

They both shook their heads. "Calvin and I, along with Randy, know enough not to jump to conclusions. We didn't want any of this to come up right now unless, or until, we found something that was substantially more than speculation. You've kind of forced our hands on this today. We don't want to lie to you or mislead you. We just want to learn the truth about the entire incident."

She stepped back and then walked over to the window. She asked them to stand there and to look out the window with her.

She pointed at the large oak tree in their back yard. "Max and I didn't plant that tree, but we have taken care of it because it gives great relief from the sun in the late afternoons. It's strong and stands firmly rooted. If you look closely on the north side of the tree, you'll find where he carved our initials in it five years ago. It was his way of saying not just that he loved me, but that I could always count on him."

She paused and faced them both. "This thing you're about to do is not just for yourselves. It is for Max and for me. As much as I want to know everything as soon as you do, it scares me to think of the possibilities. Just promise me one thing: When you know the truth, you'll tell me right then and not a minute later." They both agreed.

They went back to the closet and began opening drawers, containers, and small storage boxes. They found two more note pads that were kept in plastic storage bags. They found a black leather briefcase which contained several loose news clippings from local and national news organizations as well as articles from several magazines. Some of them were less than two months old. They collected these things and put them in the car.

After another round of coffee and cake, they excused themselves and walked out to the car preparing to leave. She accompanied them to the driveway. As they walked together, they promised to not leave anything unturned during their efforts. She thanked them for what they intended to do and waved at them as they got into the car and then drove off.

When they reached Howard's house a little less than an hour later, they began carrying the boxes into the utility room. As they did, they were careful to make sure that they aligned them by date. They knew they would want to start with the most recent material and work back from there.

Calvin, beginning to feel the wear-and-tear on his back, told Howard that he would be back in the morning to help.

"Since it's on my way, I'll pick up Randy in the morning. There's no sense in spending anymore on gas than we need to."

"That'll save a few bucks. I'll call Randy right now and let him know what happened. Let's try to start around eight in the morning."

They shook hands, said their good-byes, and Calvin got into his car and drove off.

Howard went into the utility room, sat down in an old wicker chair, and stared at the boxes for several seconds. As he did, Carla walked in, put her hands on his shoulders, and began to massage them.

"How's your back?"

"Sore. Calvin thinks he might have pulled a muscle in his. You know we're not as young as we used to be; and right now, I feel every bit of my age."

She continued massaging. "There sure are a lot of boxes here. Are you sure this is what you really need to do?"

"No, were not sure, but we know we have to do something – and this seemed like a good idea when we first thought about it. Max was the kind of guy who was thorough. If there's anything here, I just hope we don't glance over it. That's why I felt we needed a place where we wouldn't feel rushed or inconvenienced in any fashion."

"You're right about working on this here." She stopped massaging his shoulders, leaned down, and kissed the top of his head. "I'm not sure what it is you want me to do, but I know how to make coffee. Would you like a cup right now?" She turned to walk toward the kitchen.

"I would, but first I need to call Randy and tell him what's going on."

He got up from his chair and followed her into the kitchen. "You know, she saw right through us. I mean, she knows we're working on trying to figure out what really happened to Max. She was so gracious how she handled it this morning."

While reaching into the cabinet next to the sink to get two clean coffee cups, Carla smiled. "When I was over there last Friday, we talked about how she was afraid that she might forget things about Max that were special to her. She mentioned things like still being able to smell his aftershave on some of his shirts that he had hung in the closet, seeing his toothbrush in the glass in the bathroom every time she walks in there, and sitting in her chair in the living room watching television and realizing he wasn't with her. I got the feeling she's coping, but it's been difficult for her."

"She's stronger than I thought she was."

"Have you ever thought about those kinds of things? You know – if I were to die before you?"

"No, I haven't – and right now I'm not planning on having to anytime soon."

He took out his cell phone and selected one of the numbers from his phone log and then waited for the connection.

"Hey Randy, I wanted to let you know everything went fine this morning. Calvin said he's going to pick you up on the way in, and we're going to try to get started around eight o'clock. By the way, Eileen knows. She suspected all along what we are trying to do."

Just after he hung up, he turned to Carla. "I hope we're doing the right thing."

"You are honey. You definitely are."

CHAPTER 5
March 12, 2013

When there's something important on your calendar, especially something you have wanted to do or so expectantly spectacular, it's hard to sleep the night before because of the anticipation and excitement surrounding it all. So, it was for Howard. He tossed and turned most of the night, thinking about what it was he and his friends might find as they began to launch their journey into what they considered important. His mind wandered through many of the journalistic twists and turns a story can take, while wondering how the event would unfold. He was excited about the opportunity, but at the same time he was concerned over how the journey could end. It wasn't Christmas, but it might as well have been.

Sometimes, the anticipation of something so inexplicably wonderful can be so high, that impatience becomes your worst enemy. Sometimes, however, things just go sour and head south in a hurry.

The three of them spent the better part of that morning talking and working on a plan to deal with the size of the project. Three professional, experienced journalists took over an hour trying to determine a likely successful approach, before they finally agreed each one should take a different box to start with. It seemed like such a milestone had been achieved, especially once they started delving into the contents of each box. Calvin quickly saw the inevitable, if not the proverbial handwriting on the wall, and decided there was a greater, more pointed and immediate issue to overcome.

"Let's suppose that we think we find something in one of his note pads. What do we do with it? I mean, how should we keep track of it and any others we find?"

Howard pointed to the table on the porch. "We'll put anything we think might be important over there for us to discuss."

Randy, already flipping through the pages of one of the note pads, spoke up.

"Listen to this: Max was interviewing somebody named MC. According to his notes, M.C. indicated that someone named TW flew to Copenhagen last August. The rest of his notes read almost as cryptic as that. What do you think that meant to him? What should it mean to us? How do we know if that has any bearing on what we're looking for?"

"That's a lot of questions about a question. What's the date on that?"

"December 12, 2011."

"What box did you start with?"

"It was marked number three. You guys took numbers one and two."

Calvin asked to see the actual entry. Randy stood up and walked over to pour himself a cup of coffee, handing the note pad to him as he walked by.

"Obviously, we need to think through this in more detail." Howard leaned back into his chair, took a sip from his bottled water, and then continued. "What we need is a story board that allows us to pin up these items so we can put them in order. That should help us establish a time line and time frame."

Randy, while stirring sugar into his coffee, turned to Howard.

"I don't think Carla would appreciate our sticking pins in these nice walls – or us even using scotch tape for that matter."

"We need to be able to visualize these things – at least I do."

Calvin was still flipping through the note pad he had just gotten from Randy. "These same initials MC show up in two or three other places, but they're maybe a month or two apart. He must have been working this MC person for some reason."

When Howard got out of his chair and headed for the living room, he reiterated an earlier statement. "That's the problem. Does it have anything to do with what we're looking for?" he asked, as he started to exit the room.

"Where are you going?" Calvin asked.

"I think I have a solution to our problem. If you two will give me a hand, I have just what the doctor ordered."

The three of them went into the garage where Howard pointed at three pieces of wooden paneling that were left from his project for one of the spare bedrooms.

"If each of you will grab one of these, we can lean them up against the wall and use them for the back drop of our story board."

Ten minutes later, they were seated and once more poring over the note pads. There was the occasional distraction by each of them reading something out loud to each other and their light-hearted banter about some of the misspelled words. Before they knew it, Carla called from the kitchen to remind them that it was lunch time.

"Here," she said, as she put some sandwiches down on the table, "start with these. I've got some fruit and chips for you as well." She noticed the paneling. "Howard, are you planning on paneling the porch?"

"No, we're using this to pin-up anything that might be of interest to us."

She tried not to sound too terribly sarcastic. "It's kind of blank at the moment."

Randy had already started eating one of the sandwiches. In between chews, he commented. "It's early and we're just getting started."

"I get it – you want me to leave." She turned to Howard. "Just let me know if there's something I can do."

Calvin started to make his way to the table. "You're right. This might take a while."

For the next three hours, all three of them diligently and thoroughly went through several pages of notes hoping to find those same M.C. initials, anything that might point them in a direction. Calvin thought he had found that elusive first clue, only to realize that it was the beginning of a shopping list. Howard stood up each time he thought he had found something.

"What is it? What did you find?" Randy asked.

Recognizing that his standing was causing a distraction, Howard decided to take a break.

"I'm going outside to get some fresh air. I'll be back in a couple of minutes."

"It's probably a good thing for us all to step away for a minute or two," Calvin said.

The three of them went outside and on to the patio. Calvin stretched his arms and arched his back. He turned to Randy. "Sitting in that room made me feel like I was facing a deadline, again. You know what I mean?"

"I do." He, too, stretched his arms and took in a deep breath. "It feels good, doesn't it?"

When Howard stretched his arms and arched his back, he yawned deeply. "There's one thing for sure, this is going to cut in to my nap times."

They laughed and each one commented about how they had become accustomed to their daily nap. Randy went so far as to inquire about his being able to bring his own chair just so he could be comfortable. "Well, I just thought I'd ask."

Howard nodded in agreement and pointed at Calvin. "What about you?"

Calvin's grin was from ear-to-ear. "No thanks. But if you don't mind, I think I'd rather just borrow the use of your spare bedroom each day around one o'clock."

They spent the next ten minutes walking around the back yard talking about the weather, how much they were looking forward to the coming baseball season and wondering how certain friends from the paper were doing. Howard was the one who suggested they get back inside before it started to rain. The wind had picked up and the temperature had dropped slightly during their breather.

When they were finally seated again and back on task, Howard looked at the clock.

"It's three-thirty right now. How about we try to finish the day around five?"

All three agreed that five o'clock would be their quitting time for the day.

Fortune sometimes has a way of artfully insinuating itself into events by unfolding slowly. It creeps innocently and cleverly into conversations where participants are lured into notions and suppositions that sound not just logical, but likely. When you're tired, fortune may be as close as the tip of your nose. Sometimes, it is not only the last thing you can see, it often eludes even the most notable of philosophical gurus. When you're tired, words that point to fortune may sound as if you're hearing them while seated at the bottom of a barrel. At first, nothing sounds clear. Then, after they've had enough time to echo and bounce all around you, you realize their importance. The context becomes understood and things then become clearer.

This time it was Calvin who stood up. Before he said anything, the excitement on his face was telling. He started pacing in front of this chair. "Guys let me read this to you and then tell me what you think: 'Must talk with Mr. B about Austin clip. GR's death ruled accident.' What do you think about that?"

Howard leaned forward. "What's the date on that?"

"It is August twenty-fifth, last year."

Randy shot back. "I've got those GR initials in my notes, too. I've seen them in maybe four or five different places – in multiple places."

Howard leaned back into his seat and put down the notes he had been reading. "What's really important here is that we have our first lead and follow-up."

Calvin decided to sit back down. "What do you mean?"

"It means," Randy interrupted, "we've got a warm body to talk to."

"That's right. Mr. B." He paused for just a second. "Good old Mr. Benson."

The room became strangely quiet as they sat their looking back-and-forth at each other with a sense of unspoken satisfaction.

Carla walked into the room just then and saw that the paneling was still empty. She saw the looks on their faces and the subtle grins they tried to conceal from her.

"All of you look like the cat that just swallowed the canary. Somebody spit him out and tell me what's going on."

Howard leaned forward and cleared his throat. "First, you must promise, and I mean promise not to say a word to anyone about what we tell you. You can't share any of this information we put on this paneling with anyone. From this point forward, what we say and do in this room stays in this room."

She could sense the intensity with which he spoke. She heard what he said, but she wanted more clarity. "Does this mean I can only speak with the three of you about this?"

"That's right – not even Eileen. We aren't saying anything to anyone about nothing. Especially Eileen – got it? It's that important. It doesn't matter how innocent it may sound or how innocuous you may think it to be; we speak only with each other about what we discover or consider for now."

She sat down next to him. "What have you found? It must be something or you wouldn't have sworn me to secrecy like you just did."

He shook his head. "We're not sure. We're really not sure, but we think we have our first lead – and it's a doozy."

"Well if I'm supposed to keep secrets, somebody's going to have to tell me one."

Howard hesitated. Both Randy and Calvin nodded their heads as if granting their consent. He looked directly at her. "Our first lead happens to be with Mr. Benson."

"Mr. Benson? You mean the General Manager of our newspaper?"

"Yes. Mr. Rudy A. Benson, our former boss."

"What's he got to do Max's death?"

"That's a pretty big leap, don't you think?" Randy asked.

Calvin spoke up. "Carla, we're not accusing him of anything. His name popped up in one the notes Max wrote concerning something else. This lead means we'll have someone to talk to about what Max had written. He might be able to make sense of it for us."

She thought for a moment, sat back slightly, and slowly rubbed her hands on her blue jeans just above her knees. "He's a pretty tough customer, if you ask me."

Randy, who appeared to be taking all of this in, agreed. "She's right." He looked at Howard first, then Calvin, and then back at Howard. "We've got something that might mean nothing. Then again, it might be something that could set off bells and whistles and create a problem we don't want. We need to think this thing through carefully, before we do anything else. At least we now have a starting place."

Howard agreed. "A bigger problem is how are we going to approach him without raising any suspicion on his part about what we're doing?"

They sat there for several seconds thinking through the possibilities. Carla, in the meanwhile, had walked back into the kitchen. When she returned, she was carrying a bucket of ice, three glasses, three bottled waters and a package of chocolate chip cookies on a tray, which she set down on the table. Then, she went over and sat back down.

"Has anyone come up with any ideas?"

Howard smiled and even chuckled a little. "You know, we might want to sleep on this one and start fresh in the morning."

Randy stood up and thanked her for the refreshments. Calvin did as well. As they were standing around the table eating cookies, Howard hinted at Carla to leave the room so they could discuss a few other items.

"I've got an idea about what we can do about Mr. Benson, but it's going to require one of us to stick his neck out a mile long."

Randy raised his hand. "I'll do it."

"You don't even know what I've got planned."

"It doesn't matter. I've got the least to lose. Besides, he was a real jerk, and I'd like to squeeze him just a little and see what comes out of him."

"Okay, but you'll need a story to get you in to see him."

Calvin pointed his finger at Randy. "I've got your back."

"Then it's settled. Let's meet back here in the morning around eight and we'll get a fresh start."

They all agreed, shook hands, and said their good-byes.

Carla closed the door behind them as they walked to their cars, and then walked back onto the porch.

"Do you really have a plan?"

"Yes," he said, as he pointed at the note pads on the table. "It's one that even Mr. Benson won't see coming. Right now, I'm ready for dinner."

CHAPTER 6
March 13, 2013

Sometime after midnight, something woke Howard abruptly from a sound sleep. When he sat up onto his side of the bed, he realized that he must have been dreaming. He eased into his slippers, put on his robe, and walked around on the inside of the house checking doors and the windows in all the rooms. Satisfied that everything was as it should be, he went and sat down on the sofa on the porch. He reached to his right and turned on the lamp on the end table that put a soft, golden hue on everything in the room.

He sat there for a few seconds staring at the empty panels that were staring back at him. He got up, went over to the table and picked up the note pad that Calvin had been searching through, and found the page he had marked. He walked back into his office area where his computer and copier were located. What he had forgotten was how loud the copier could be in a very quiet house. It didn't take long before Carla joined him.

"What are you doing? Are you okay?"

"Yeah, I'm fine. I couldn't sleep and I woke up thinking about all of this. So, I got up, went through my routine again, only I realized I wasn't going back to bed anytime soon."

She followed him as he walked back onto the porch. "This thing's really got you concerned doesn't it?"

"Let me show you something." He walked over to the middle piece of paneling and pinned the copy he had just made of that page from the note pad onto it. Then, he stepped back.

"This is the first bit of information we've found that could lead us to another, that may lead us to another, and then to another, until we know the truth about what really happened to Max. Maybe then, we'll at least be able to bring peace to Eileen. When Calvin identified that information this afternoon, it was like I was a kid again and just getting started in the business."

"You may feel that way now, but you're not going to be worth much to the guys in the morning if you don't get a good night's sleep." She walked over to where he was standing and hugged him. "You may have felt like a kid this afternoon, but you're going to feel like an old man when the alarm goes in a few hours." She nudged him and pulled slightly on his right arm. "Let's go get whatever sleep we can. Staying up at this hour of the night will not help the bags under my eyes."

She was right. After he turned off the clanging, irritating noise of his alarm at six o'clock that morning, he rolled over and sat up on his side of the bed. He felt as if he hadn't slept much at all. But after his first cup of coffee and remembering the challenges that awaited him on his porch, he was wide awake and couldn't wait to get started.

After Calvin and Randy arrived and had poured themselves some coffee as well, they saw where he had pinned the copy of Max's notes to the paneling. Calvin was the first to speak.

"Somebody's been up early this morning and got a head start on us."

Randy, who had just finished stirring a good amount of sugar into his coffee, commented about how symmetrical it appeared. "This is center ground?"

"For now," Howard said, "but that might change." Pointing to the opposite wall, he showed them a three by four white slate board that he brought in and hung on the wall just before they arrived. "I think it's important for us not to clutter up the paneling. Let's use the white board to put up initials or names of unidentified people. Perhaps, we might even use sticky notes on one side of it to include dates and locations along with the initials. That way we can check our work as we go along without having to interrupt each other as much. What do you think?"

"I think the more we get into this, the more we're going to need to make up the rules as we go along," Calvin said, before chuckling slightly. "Right now, I want to get back to what we talked about yesterday. What about this thing with Mr. Benson? What's the plan?"

He hadn't figured out all the details, but Howard laid out the strategy and the necessity of a cover story Randy would need to gain access to Mr. Benson's office. To begin with, he proposed for Randy to call and make an appointment with Mr. Benson to discuss his coming out of retirement. The story he would lay out for him was that after having lost his wife less than two years ago, he was beginning to feel like he was not useful to anyone or any organization. He would explain that going back to work would be good for him and give him purpose in his life. He was to sell the idea that it would also be great for the newspaper because he would be willing to make himself available at a considerably lower salary. They all believed that Mr. Benson would see the win-win situation in front of him and bite on it. Randy was a little uneasy about the proposition, however.

"This means I've got to go back to work every day. When will I have a chance to work with you guys on these note pads? Besides, Benson didn't even show up for my wife's funeral."

Howard knew he had touched a nerve. "I'm sorry, but it was the only thing I could think of. I'd understand if you don't want to do this. Maybe we just need to think through this a little more."

"It's not that. It's just that I was really looking forward to spending a lot of time with you guys on this. The idea might work because that scrooge knows when he's getting a bargain. Have you worked out all of the details?"

"Some of them, but there are a few things we need to consider. Remember how we thought about using an uncompleted story that we had started with Max to get Eileen to go along with us? I think the same idea using that same uncompleted story would be perfect because it might even open up the technology we can't get to. You know how tight and closed-in the access is to those computers at the paper. If they start snooping around, Eileen can back up our story, since she thinks she knows what we're doing. With you on the inside and able to access the technology without drawing attention, it only helps us that much more. What do you think?"

He nodded his head. "I think this might be crazy enough to work. If we make sure we've checked all the details with Benson first, then the rest of it should fall into place. You know how he's a stickler for details. When we're finished, I'm quitting for good."

Howard smiled. "Who knows? You might want to stay on for a little longer. You might end up liking the money."

"There's little chance of that."

They sat and talked a few minutes more. The three of them agreed there shouldn't be any unnecessary delays and that he should go ahead and make the call right away.

Calvin, as he walked over to the table to retrieve the note pad, he had started with, confirmed the idea. He looked right at Randy. "Sooner is better than later."

There was a renewed energy in the room that morning, as the three of them went through the material that Max had unknowingly prepared for them. It was as if with each word or notation, on the pages of those note pads, might be the answer to the question they all wanted answered. As the morning dragged on an entire pot of coffee was consumed. Needing a break, Randy stood up, stretched his arms, and stepped onto the patio for a few minutes.

It was just before noon, when he decided it was time to make that call to Mr. Benson. He came back inside; picked up a piece of paper he had placed on the coffee table, took out his cell phone, selected a number from his contacts, and then tapped the touch screen. The other two put down their note pads, sat back in their chairs, watched and listened to what happened next.

He stood there for a few seconds. It became obvious to them that he had reached an automated directory and was working his way through it. After several selections, his demeanor changed considerably. His eyes lit up like those of a child when he sees his presents under the tree for the first time on a Christmas morning. He raised his hand, put his right index finger over his lips gesturing for complete silence, sat down, and then finally spoke.

"Good morning. This is Randy Tomlin calling." He paused listening to whoever was on the other end of the call. "Well, thank you very much. That's very kind of you. I am calling to make an appointment with Mr. Benson. Is he available Friday morning around ten o'clock?"

The other two were watching closely, almost hanging on every word. The wait time seemed like forever. Howard stood up and started pacing. Calvin leaned forward in his seat.

"He'll see me at nine-thirty? That will be fine. Thank you very much, Mrs. Morrel. I'm looking forward to meeting you then on Friday morning at nine-thirty. Good-bye."

He tapped his phone once more and walked over to where Howard was standing. It didn't take very long before high five's and fist bumps started among them.

It was obvious that he was pleased with the result, but quickly reverted to high fives. "Fist bumps may not be my cup of tea." He paused for just a second. "Now, let's go through the dress rehearsal. Who's going to be Benson?"

Calvin jumped at the chance.

Chapter 7
Friday, March 15, 2013

The word retire should be used to describe only the action when one elects to go to bed. At some point or event in the past, the idea of retirement came to be used in conjunction with deciding that going to work each day was no longer a viable option, or you became someone who just got in the way at the work place. At that stage in life, someone fashioned the notion that it would be more appropriate to categorize what happens to a person, figuratively speaking, as being put out to pasture. Not only does that seem practical, somehow it seems just and an honorable thing to do. In Randy's case that would have been closer to the truth two years ago – not so much lately.

When Michelle, his wife of thirty-one years, was taken from him on April 16, 2011 by the slow, excruciating cruelty of cancer, he pretty much decided to quit working, took up fishing, and would sit on his porch most evenings and wait for sundown. He would go to church on Wednesday nights because that's what the two of them had done all of their married lives. He wasn't much of a church-goer at a younger age. Although his mother would take him with her most Sunday mornings, he would rather have been fishing with his dad, instead. Now that the memory of his late wife's funeral had eased, he was beginning to get out more frequently – other than just Wednesday evenings.

When his first pension check showed up, he and Howard made a point of it to meet on every Tuesday morning for coffee at the diner they used to go to for lunch when they worked for the paper. They were both known there as regulars by the waitresses. Randy was best known for the amount of sugar he would put in his coffee. Howard was known for the amount of cream he would put in his cup before the waitress would pour the coffee into it. Calvin joined three months after he had retired.

Most Tuesday mornings, Max would join them. He'd order coffee as well, but he always wanted a stack of pancakes to go with it. He was known for the amount boysenberry syrup he would use to smother his pancakes, often flowing off the edge of his plate.

Eight o'clock at the diner on Tuesday mornings had been well established as the place where world problems were debated with great conviction and solutions were as easy to come by as seeing right from wrong. A deep and steadfast friendship developed over a few short years in that diner that had been mostly conventional for over fifteen years at the office. While they were all still working at the paper, their work schedules didn't allow for them to meet too often. Since they were no longer obligated to go to work each morning, they nicknamed the diner "The Water Cooler." It became the place for their clandestine-like meetings where they also could pick-up on the latest town gossip.

They had planned to meet at the diner that Friday morning, but not until after Randy's appointment with Mr. Benson. Aside from the excitement of launching the first step of their loosely designed plan to learn more about Max's death, they acted more like high school kids who couldn't wait to share some piece of juicy gossip between classes.

Howard was the first to show up at ten o'clock. Calvin arrived fifteen minutes later. They each ordered their usual coffee and sat there staring out the window anxiously waiting for Randy's car. Every minute or so, Howard would take a sip of his coffee. Calvin would shift his weight from one side to the other about every two minutes. It didn't go unnoticed.

Their waitress, Chloe, came over to refill their coffee cups. "You two haven't said one word to each other since you've arrived. Is everything okay? Is there something wrong with the coffee?"

"Nothing's wrong, and the coffee's just fine. We're waiting for our friend."

"You mean Randy? Randy Tomlin?"

"Yes. He should be here any time now."

Just as he had finished responding to her, Randy drove up, parked his car, got out and started walking toward the front door.

Chloe had just walked away from their table. As she passed Randy on her way to her work station, she took his order for coffee and a donut as he walked toward the table.

"Guys, you aren't going to believe this, but Mr. Benson hired me on the spot. The interview wasn't much. He's assigned me to work directly with Jerry Locker who is now the City Editor – and you know what that means.”

Howard put his coffee cup down. “It means you’ll be doing his work and yours. He’s notorious about how he gets away with that.”

“It gets better. He was in on the interview and told me to oversee a part of the layout division. That means I will have the access to the computers we’ll need.”

Chloe brought his cup of coffee, a glazed donut, and a silver-domed, glass container of sugar to him. “I know how you like your sugar, Sugar.” She smiled at him, flipped her long, red-haired curls with her right hand, and walked slowly and suggestively away from him.

Howard looked at him. “Have the two of you got something going on that you’d like to tell us about?”

“No, I wouldn’t like to tell you about it because there’s nothing to it.”

“Are you kidding me? She was flirting with you and encouragingly so.”

“So, what’s that have to do with anything?”

“She’s half your age – that’s what.”

“She is not. She’s less than half my age.” They all laughed.

It took a few more minutes before conversation returned to business and the reason they had agreed to meet that morning in the first place. Randy began by telling them a few details about his work station, the new equipment he’ll have to work with, and how Mr. Benson had related his excitement about having someone with his experience joining the team.

“Apparently, they’ve had to lay off a few of their last hires. Things must be kind of tight right now.”

“In other words,” Howard began, “your salary offer was a deal he couldn’t refuse.”

“It was like taking candy from a baby.”

After telling them about the actual twenty minute interview, he told them how one of the assistants in Mr. Benson’s office gave him his identification badge and how it worked, a folder full of paperwork that had to be completed and to be returned to her by Monday, and then how they escorted him on a brief tour of the new facilities located on the second floor.

"You guys won't believe what they've done to the place. There's a pretty good-sized cafeteria on the second floor that serves more than just sandwiches. There's a small gym, but it's well equipped – at least what I could see of it. And by the way, see this identification badge?" He took it out of his pocket to show them. "It's that new digital thing and there are scanners required on most doors now."

He went on for another ten minutes helping them to understand that the place where the three of them had retired from was no longer the same. "It's changed considerably. It's been updated and renovated to bring it into the twenty-first century. It's really gone high-tech."

"That's a good thing," Calvin shot back. "We wouldn't want it any other way. Most of those guys are well versed on this high-tech stuff. What they don't know about is the low-tech stuff we used throughout our career. That might work to our advantage."

Howard agreed. "Not only that, if we play our cards right, we might actually be able to pool our resources. As Max used to say, 'They'll never know what hit them.'"

They finished their coffee and decided to reconvene at Howard's house to continue their efforts with the notepads.

They spent the rest of the day combing through Max's scribbling. At one point, Calvin dropped the pad on the coffee table, leaned back into his chair, and sighed. "He must have gotten lousy grades in penmanship when he was in school."

Howard, who had just returned from using the bathroom, concurred. "There are a lot of entries and notes that you just need to back away from for a while – and then try again."

Randy stood up and went to the white board. "Have either of you seen these initials in any of the notes you've looked through?" He wrote the initials WE with the date of August 5, 2012 next to it. "These have popped up three times beginning in August 2012."

Howard chuckled. "Those are my son's initials. You know – William Ewing. Those are the only ones I can think of."

Calvin thought for a moment longer. "What about William England? He used to work directly for the business editor back around 2008. There was Warren Epstein in accounting, but didn't he move to Pennsylvania a few years back?"

"I believe he did," Randy said.

"I wonder if Max made contact for some reason with my William." He put the note pad down, grabbed his cell phone he had set down on the end table, and selected his son's phone number.

"William? This is Dad. Got a minute?" He paused. "Good. I'm putting you on speaker. Mr. Tomlin and Mr. Rolle are in the room with me. We're working on an article that Mr. Max Leopard started with us several months ago before his death. We think we came upon your initials in one of his notes with an August date next to it. Does any of this ring a bell to you?"

After a moment's silence, he replied. "Yes. He called and hired me to take some pictures of him in two different locations. I did; and then, I gave them to him two days later."

"What two different locations?"

"The first one was of him standing right outside City Hall in Orlando. The other was of him standing in front of the State Attorney's office in Orlando as well."

"Did he say why he wanted those?"

"Only that he needed them to work on his scrapbook. He paid me for them – and that was that."

"Is there anything else you can remember about those two locations?"

There was silence for a few seconds. "The only time he wanted me to photograph him was when he raised his right arm – and then he wanted me to rapid shoot until he dropped his arm. The funny thing was that his back was to me in most of the pictures."

"Do you still have those pictures?"

"I'll have to make copies for you, but yes I have them."

"How soon can you take care of this for us?"

"I'm in Ocala right now doing a shoot but should wrap up here in about thirty minutes. I could probably have them ready by six-thirty tonight."

"Can you bring them with you when you come over for dinner tonight? I'll throw some pork steaks on the grill and ask your mother to fix some of that creamed corn you like so much."

"Sure, Dad; but, what's this all about? What are you working on?"

"I'll tell you about it over dinner, when you get here."

They said their good-byes and disconnected the call.

The three of them sat there for a few seconds, before Calvin spoke up.

"What does that sound like to you?"

"It sounds like Max was either going fishing or he thought he might have been on to something and wanted documented evidence as proof," Randy said.

Howard didn't say anything right off. Instead, he got up, went over and stood next to the sliding glass door. He stood there for a few seconds and then turned to face the other two.

"It still doesn't explain why he was on U.S. Highway 27 near Avon Park.

"It doesn't have to right now," Calvin said pointedly. "It tells us something about a part of the story that takes place at least six months before he died. This could be the pivot from which the story will either gather momentum or not." He looked at Randy and then back at Howard. "You don't suppose there are enough pork steaks for the rest of us, do you?"

Randy stood up and stretched his arms. "I don't want you to think we're imposing on you, but I don't want to wait until tomorrow morning to take a look at those pictures."

Howard smiled and shook his head. "I don't think Carla would mind, but I have to warn you about William and creamed corn. If you don't get any before he does, you won't get any of it. That boy can eat some corn – especially if his mother creams it for him.

CHAPTER 8
Friday evening, March 15, 2013

William Tyler Ewing was born September 14, 1980. When he was nine years old, Howard introduced him to the world of photography through a contest that was being sponsored by a magazine – and he was immediately hooked. At ten, he had won two separate competitions for his age group. By the age of sixteen, he had begun working professionally for the newspapers in the area and worked part-time for a magazine that featured pictures of landscapes and wildlife, and as well as part-time employment at a local photography studio.

When it came time for him to go to college, the Ewing family agreed that his needs might best be served if he stayed near home, work on his two-year degree, and then seek a major school where he could finish his studies. William had other ideas. He had saved enough money that he could afford to spend six months in Paris, France where he wanted to gain some life experience and to, as he put it, 'live life without strings attached.'

At the end of those six months, he returned home without a penny in his pocket and no prospects of gainful or meaningful employment on the horizon. He went back to his part-time job with the same magazine, but successfully started a freelance career for most of his work with regional and national newspapers. Within a year's time, he had gained a considerable reputation within the publishing circles in Florida, which ultimately landed him a prestigious position that allowed him to travel once more.

This time it would not be overseas, but on assignments for a national weekly magazine in the United States. For five years, he never knew one week to the next where he might be working, and he seemed to enjoy that – that is until he met Joyce Keplinger. She turned his world completely inside out and him upside down on April 7, 2009. After dating for more than eight months, he decided it might be best if he stayed closer to home and not have to travel as much. She agreed to do the same and took a position with a national newspaper that had a major office in Orlando, Florida.

A year later, he proposed to her one evening while the two of them were walking on the beach in Daytona. Because of uncertainty in both of their schedules, they decided to put the wedding on hold, until July 2011.

Joyce's family's circumstances caused another delay, when her mother and father decided to divorce in March that year. William understood the need for her to deal with the family issues first and patiently waited until things had calmed down some four months later. They finally agreed on a wedding date of April 1, 2012 – which proved to be more than a forewarning. Two weeks before their wedding, William received a text message from her that she was taking a three-day assignment covering a news story in New York City and had to leave immediately. She told him it was one of those last-minute things that just came up, but that she would be right back.

Two days later after landing in New York, she called him from New York City and told him that the wedding was off because she was going to marry some guy named Ted. The news was devastating to him.

Howard and Carla did what they could for him, but what do you do to help a grown man get over a broken heart? Howard's answer was for him to get back into the dating scene. Carla advised him to take a little time off from dating and to concentrate on his work. William's answer was to return to Paris, France for a two-month vacation.

When he returned, he seemed refreshed and renewed. His work load picked up quickly. By that July, his schedule had become such that he hardly had time to think about Joyce. He had managed to get beyond that heartache. In fact, on the flight home he met a young woman named Karen Travis who knew absolutely nothing about photography. She was an accountant who worked with an insurance agency. He knew very little about accounting or the insurance industry. It seemed like the beginning of a perfect match.

When he arrived that evening, Randy met him at the front door. They shook hands. "Man, you have filled out pretty good," he said, as he patted William on the back. He thanked him. "Come on. Your Dad is on the patio grilling those pork steaks."

They made their way through the kitchen where William stopped to hug and kiss his mother. "I'm glad you came tonight. I've made creamed corn just the way you like it."

"That wasn't necessary, but I'm glad you did." He put his satchel on the end of the counter and walked toward the patio.

Calvin saw him and extended his right hand to him. They shook hands and all three of them went outside.

"Son, how's your project in Ocala going?"

"Slow, but I think it's going well. I brought those pictures with me. They're in my satchel on the counter."

"They'll keep until after dinner. I hope you're hungry."

"Dad, what's all this about a story you're doing for Max?"

"It's a project we started with him, before he died. Initially, we wanted to finish the story about the number of churches that have been vandalized in our area lately."

"I remember taking a few shots of those in Orlando and Clermont."

"They might come in handy to help with the background for the story."

Randy, who had been standing quietly next to William and drinking sweet tea, got William's attention. "There's more to it than that."

Howard jumped into the conversation. "Son, we think there are some unusual circumstances surrounding Max's death."

"What do you mean unusual?"

"No one seems to know what he was doing on that road and why he was near Avon Park the night he was killed."

"Does Eileen have any ideas?"

"No, she doesn't – and what we tell you from this point on must be kept among us and told to no one else. We don't know what the truth is right now, but we intend to find out."

"What about Mom? How does she fit into this?"

"She knows we're working on it but doesn't know much of the details. Her job has been pretty much feeding us and staying out of our way. I think it's better if it stays that way."

Dinner conversation stayed focused on William's work and his recent promotion. He wasn't at liberty to tell them all the details, but he did relate that his new job will allow him to display much of his photographic work in a couple of local galleries. He was excited about the opportunities that it presented to him.

When dinner was over, they all helped to clear the table, while Carla finished cleaning the kitchen. "Will you boys need a pot of coffee tonight?"

"Maybe so," Howard said. "Now William, where are those pictures? We'd like to see what it is that was so important to Max."

He spread all the pictures on the dining room table. There were twenty-six of them in total. Certain pictures were printed on eight-by-ten glossy paper. The others were mostly five-by-sevens.

"What are we looking at here?" Howard asked.

"These on the top row were taken at the State Attorney's office in Orlando. The ones on the bottom row were taken at City Hall."

They studied them carefully for a few moments, before Calvin spoke up. "Howard, do you have a magnifying glass? It might help."

He reached into the drawer of the end table nearest to them and retrieved the magnifying glass he often used to read exceptionally small print. "They're handy. What can I say?" He handed them to him.

Randy looked at the pictures on the top row and realized all were pictures of well-dressed men exiting the building. "Do any of you know who these guys are?"

"I haven't a clue," Howard said.

Calvin nudged William's elbow, offering the magnifying glass to him. "Take this and look carefully at the fifth guy from the left on the top row. Tell me if you think he's the same person on the bottom row, second from the right."

William studied the two photographs carefully. "I believe it's the same person in each photograph. The only difference I see is that in the one on the top, he's carrying a leather briefcase. The one on the bottom the same guy is carrying a metal case of some kind. Who is he and why did Max want me to take these pictures?"

Howard moved closer to the table, picked up the magnifying glass that William had just put down, and examined the same photos.

"Max wanted these photos to prove a point. Whether it was this guy or any of the other guys in these photos, these photos answered a question Max had been seeking an answer to."

William saw one of the notepads on the end table. "Is this where you found my initials?"

"Yes, it is." Howard picked it up and handed it to him.

"I took those pictures on the seventeenth of August." He started flipping through its pages, until he stopped on one of them toward the front. "Listen to this: 'With W.E. Event involves contacts with P.T. and J.H.'"

He handed it back to him, and Howard immediately started for the hallway to the kitchen. "I'll be right back. I want to make a copy of this."

When he returned, he pinned that copy of the page to the first of the three pieces of paneling. "This is definitely before the accident." He took a step back.

"When you went with him that day, how did he seem?"

"What do you mean?"

"Was he anxious? Was he quiet? What did he act like during your time with him?"

"He was as calm as a cucumber. He drove and hardly said one word. On the way home he asked me about how I was doing, did I plan to travel abroad soon, and that kind of stuff."

"When he contacted you, what exactly did he tell you the reason was for wanting these photos to be taken?"

"The only thing I remember was his asking if I would help him take care of this. He said he didn't have the equipment to take the rapid shots – and admitted that he knew very little about getting the right kind of shot. He just needed my professional help and offered to pay me."

The next thirty minutes was filled with each of them speculating about Max's motives or his intended use of these photos. That's when Randy created another can of worms.

"When Eileen let us take a look around, we didn't see or find these photos at the house. You don't suppose that he put these in a safe place somewhere do you? You know how deliberate he was about things. I'm willing to bet these and other documents are hidden – and for good reason."

They all looked at each other. Howard said it, but the others were thinking it. "First thing in the morning, we need to visit Eileen."

CHAPTER 9
Saturday, March 16, 2013

Carla walked onto the porch and noticed Howard sitting on the sofa. "You're up early."

He was looking at the two pieces of information he had pinned to the paneling. "I think we've finally got this thing off center ground."

"Would you like some coffee?"

"Thanks. That would be nice." He got up and followed her into the kitchen.

"William showed us some pictures last night that Max had him take last August. None of us recognized any of the men in the pictures, but the real oddity was that those pictures should have been at Max's when we looked through his things. We didn't see them because we didn't know they existed. Now we're wondering where they are and maybe what else might be hidden with them."

"Since we're going over to Eileen's this morning, what are you planning on telling her? From the way you're making it sound, he's been hiding things – maybe even from her."

"I wouldn't say that. I would say that he put them somewhere for safe keeping."

"That may be all well and good, but she didn't know any of this was going on, until the three of you started poking around."

He sat down at the kitchen table. "See, that's exactly what we don't want to happen."

"What's that?"

"We don't want her to be offended by thinking that he was doing something behind her back – even though it appears that he was. I'm sure it was work related."

While the coffee brewed, she sat down at the table next to him. "Just be careful how you approach this because if these things are hidden in the house, she's going to wonder what else he might have been up to. Are you prepared to tell her what you know so far?"

"We agreed not to do that until the truth was known."

"Whose truth are you talking about?"

"When we know the truth about Max's death, that's when we'll tell her the whole story."

"How long do you think that's going to take?"

"I don't honestly know. What I do know is that we have a plan and we have all agreed for now to stay within its design."

"Did you want some cookies to take to her this morning?"

He chuckled slightly. "Sure, why not? The guys have nicknamed me the 'Cookie Man.'"

It had been several weeks since the two of them had sat in the kitchen, early on a Saturday morning, drinking coffee together. The time they spent together like that was special to her because it brought back memories of when William was little. He would still be asleep on Saturday morning and neither of them had to go to work. It was a time when she didn't have to share Howard with anyone, especially his work, even if it was only for an hour or so.

There was a period in their lives when Howard's work consumed most of his waking hours. If he wasn't at the office, he was in the field interviewing witnesses or following up one lead after another. To her, his work at that time was a necessary evil which she had to tolerate.

Once the reality of retirement set in, they had found a great deal of time on their hands. Since they both loved being outdoors, Howard suggested that get away occasionally. After years of saving for their retirement, they decided to purchase a small cabin near Dillard, Georgia that would allow them to do just that.

They closed the deal in late August 2011 and spent a week-end figuring out what they wanted to do to fix up the place. They spent four days in early September cleaning and painting it. They refurbished the bathroom and kitchen a week later. It wasn't much, but it offered them the opportunity to enjoy the fresh air, the quietness of the forest, and a place where they could enjoy just being by themselves. It was to be their home-away-from-home, and they decided to keep its existence unknown to anyone but themselves. "You can't escape, if people know where you are," Howard argued. They didn't even tell William.

They went back in January to check on it and to open it up for a few days. It snowed heavily that week-end, enough to keep them inside for three days. They talk often about that week-end when they're by themselves – and only to themselves. They began to see the cabin as another world and became protective of what it offered and represented.

While they were sitting quietly in the kitchen that morning, they both kidded each other about that week-end. It was the first time in a long time that she began to feel at ease with Howard's retirement situation.

She took a sip of coffee, then put it down in front of her, and leaned toward him. "Have you ever thought about going back to work? I mean I know that Randy is only doing this because of this thing with Max. But, have you?"

He smiled at her. "Actually, yes, I have, but that was over a year ago – before we bought the cabin. I wouldn't change what we have now for anything in the world."

For the next forty-five minutes, they talked about a lot of things. He spoke about the improvements to the cabin he would like for them to do. Carla approached the possibility of taking a trip to Texas to visit relatives she hasn't seen in several years. The time they spent just talking with each other that morning was, as Carla would often say, "like money in the bank."

The drive to Eileen's was always easier on Saturdays than any other day of the week. When he arrived, he saw that Randy had parked his car in the driveway near the garage. He pulled into the driveway and parked behind it. Armed only with a container of a two-dozen cookies in his right hand and the pictures that William had brought the night before in the briefcase he was carrying in his left hand, he started walking toward Eileen's front door. He made it half-way up the sidewalk, when Eileen stepped out from the house and waved for him to come in.

"Look at you," she said, "you're all official looking this morning with that briefcase. Should I be worried?"

"Actually – no, I bring you cookies from Carla's bakery and an alliance formed by old friends." After he handed her the container of cookies, he entered the house and followed her to the kitchen.

Randy and Calvin were sitting at the kitchen table. "I see the two of you are up bright and early this morning."

Randy, after taking a sip of coffee, stood up and they shook hands. "I couldn't sleep last night thinking about this."

"About what?" she asked.

Howard had barely had a chance to sit down, before she had poured him a cup of coffee and placed one of her strawberry cheesecake muffins on a plate and placed it in front of him.

"Now I know why the two of you got here so early," he said.

She looked at Randy. "What was it you were thinking about that kept you awake last night?"

"Eileen, would you join us at the table? We have a question and we think you're the only one who knows the answer."

"I remember you told us not to get you involved in any of this until we know the whole truth. I wish that could be true, but this morning we need your help on something." Howard cleared his throat and took another sip of coffee. "Is there some place that Max would store things that maybe he didn't want others to find – you know sort of like a private place?"

She thought for a moment. "You guys really haven't figured this thing out, have you?"

They all shook their heads. "We know enough now to believe that Max put some things out of sight for safe keeping." He took the photos out of his briefcase and put them on the table directly in front of her. "Have you ever seen these before?"

She looked at them, thumbing through them quickly. "Who are all these men? And, why is Max in these pictures?"

"Eileen, we don't know, but we do know that when you let us look through his things, we didn't find these or any other photos like these." He paused, looked at Randy and then Calvin, and then continued. "We know that Max has these photos somewhere because they were taken for him by my son William."

She sat there not saying a word.

"Could there be some place that Max kept work-related information other than here at the house? What about a safe deposit box?"

"No, I would have known about that." She sat back in her seat. "What are you really asking me? Do you honestly believe that he's hidden these and other things?"

"It's the only answer we can come up with at the moment."

Calvin stood up, went over to the coffee pot, and refilled his coffee cup. "We know that these photos were important to him. We also know that he was in possession of them by last August. I don't think any of us want to invade your privacy over this matter, but we do think that Max put these someplace to safeguard them – and maybe you."

She stood up and retrieved the coffee pot. "Would either of you like your cup refreshed?"

"Eileen," Howard began, "let me ask you this: When Max wanted to hide things from you like presents for anniversaries or birthdays, did you ever learn about those places after the fact?"

She smiled. "He once put a pair of diamond earrings in the ice cube tray in the freezer. I discovered them quite by accident, but I never did tell him."

Calvin sat back down. "That's exactly the kind of thing we're talking about, only these items would be more along the lines of photos and documents."

"Listen, you're welcome to go through this house with a fine-tooth comb, if you –," she started, but was interrupted by Howard.

"I'm not sure that is necessary. What about somebody else? Who is it he trusted with work-related material when he needed to keep it hush-hush?"

She couldn't think of anyone. "He would go to the office quite a bit when he felt he needed privacy, but he hasn't been back there in several months. I'm sorry, but I guess I haven't been much help to you this morning." She leaned forward in the chair. "Maybe something will come to me later."

Calvin wasn't ready to leave. "Let me change the subject for a minute. Where are Max's keys? You know the key ring he would carry with him."

"It's in the top right drawer of his desk."

"Do you mind if we have a look?"

"Of course not. Why do you ask?"

"It's just a hunch."

They followed her into the room that was just off the kitchen.

"I know we've looked through this room before, but we haven't looked at his keys. There might be one on that key ring that doesn't belong there – and it just might open what we're looking for."

Randy sat down in front of the desk, opened the drawer and pulled out the key ring. He handed it to her. "Can you tell us what each of these opens?"

She began first with the house keys and then the alarm control box key. Their safe deposit box key was the next one. Next to it was the starter key for the golf cart he liked to use when working outside. There was a small key that opened a cash box he stored in the closet, but Eileen knew all about that. There were his two car keys and a skeleton key that unlocked a small container in the attic. She knew about that one, too.

As she was going through the keys, Randy noticed something unusual about the desk. He pointed at Howard to look at the bottom right drawer.

"What am I supposed to be looking at?" he asked.

Randy pointed at the apparent depth of the drawer on the inside. Then he closed the drawer and asked him to look at the apparent depth of the drawer on the outside. When he pulled open the drawer again, they looked at each other. "They're not the same," Randy said.

"Eileen, do you mind if we check on something here?"

"Of course not, what it is you want?"

Randy pulled the bottom drawer out and removed the contents that had been neatly stored in it. "Watch this," he said, and then removed a false bottom cover to reveal two large manila-colored envelopes.

Eileen gasped and put her right hand over her mouth. "I'd have never thought to do that."

Randy reached in, pulled out the envelopes and handed them to Howard. "Let's go sit down and see what's in here."

The first envelope contained the pictures they had learned about from William. Also, there were news articles, several documents that he had placed into vinyl sleeves to protect them, and more pictures. The second envelope contained a list of names and addresses that none of the three recognized. There were more newspaper articles, clippings from magazines, and toll receipts he had been collecting, since October 2012.

"He spent some time on this," Calvin concluded. "It's going to take us a while to figure out what all of this means," he said, and then looked at Eileen. "But we will get to the bottom of this. I'm sorry you've had to learn about this in this manner."

"On the contrary, I'm glad you found this. If this will help you get to the truth, then that's what needs to happen. Believe me; I'm as surprised about all of this as you are – for sure."

They put everything back into their respective envelopes, thanked her for her hospitality, and headed toward their vehicles.

While walking, Randy whispered to Howard and Calvin. "Are we meeting this afternoon?"

"Yes, and I better call Carla to let her know we've got guests for lunch."

CHAPTER 10
Saturday, March 16, 2013

The first thing Howard did, when he got back home, was to make copies of everything that was in those envelopes. He kept the originals but gave a complete set of the copies to Randy and Calvin. They spent the next three hours pondering over every piece of paper and every photograph. Howard was preoccupied with the news clippings. Randy stayed focused on looking through the additional photographs. Calvin started putting the documents in chronological order by using whatever identifying date he could find for each one.

"Whatever it was that he was involved in started last April. From the looks of things, he was traveling a great deal to Orlando."

"And," Howard began, "he was watching someone with the initials F.S. carefully."

"That could be Frank Scott," Calvin said. "There was an article in the first envelope about him." He started searching through the stack of documents in front of him. "Here it is. It's about him visiting someone in the hospital. There's a picture attached." He handed it to Howard.

He looked at it and then handed it to Randy. "Do you know this guy?"

"No, I don't; but I'll bet you all the tea in China we'll come across his name again." He looked at Calvin with a puzzled look on his face. "Calvin, take this and see if you think this Frank Scott person is one of the guys in those pictures that William took."

While Calvin began that process, Howard made another copy of both the article and the picture of Frank Scott and pinned it on the center piece of paneling. Then, he took a piece of string and attached it to the pins of the two documents now on the paneling. "Remember how we were taught this? Finally, all those years of training are paying off," he said while smiling.

Randy looked at the documents that were now pinned on the center panel. "How do we know they're connected?" he asked, while pointing at the string.

"We don't. When we connect the two, I'll replace the string with one of a different color. Red would be easy to follow, don't you think?"

"You actually were taught this in journalism school?"

"No, I learned this from Carl Pinotti."

"Wasn't he the reporter who broke that story about all those bank robberies in 1984?"

"Yes, and I attended a training he did a year later at the Philadelphia conference. It was fascinating to watch him develop this strategy. His presentation described the development of the story, and how he used this technique throughout. He said it took longer than he wanted, even becoming frustrated at times because of how long it took. He told us that if we chose to use this method not to rush ahead with assumptions. That's why he'd change the string color. Red meant evidentiary value. White was an assumed connection without proof. For him, it was easier to follow red that ultimately tagged several documents, connecting them by dates and locations, and eventually led him to the person who not only organized and masterminded the robberies, but who was responsible for the two murdered guards."

"But, we don't know what we're looking at here in the long run."

"I believe we do. We know that Max is dead. We also know that he died in a very unlikely location that makes no sense to any of us. We now know that he had begun to connect certain individuals to whatever it was he was working on. What we don't know are who they all might be, how they are connected, and to what end they each played in this story. Whatever that story is, the bottom line is that we are looking into Max's death." He turned and made eye contact with Randy. "I believe his death was the result of his having uncovered something that someone wanted to keep quiet."

Randy seemed confused. He stepped away from the paneling and started rubbing his chin with his right hand. "What are you saying here? Are you saying we could be next?"

"I don't know what's in store for us, but I do believe Max's death was not accidental." He pointed at all the documents and photos that were on the table and then to those he had pinned on the paneling. "We have an advantage that Max didn't. My guess is, for whatever the reason, he didn't or couldn't see the big picture. We need to put that picture together, before we make too many more assumptions. It's important for us not to leap off the proverbial cliff, until it's time to leap."

"If what you're saying is true, then the big picture probably includes some big dudes who are not interested in who our favorite baseball team is. Do you hear what I'm saying?"

"I hear you. But, we need to take our time with this, so we don't stumble into a hornet's nest, which is what probably happened to Max. We've got as much of the information that he compiled that we know of, and we need to take advantage of that. Let's do our due diligence with what we've got first, make our list of questions from that effort, then set our priorities and see where we go from there."

Randy walked over to the sliding glass doors and stood there looking outside. Howard walked over to where he was standing and put his right hand on his shoulder.

"With your going back to work on Monday, you'll be at the office every day. That's the same access that Max had. Now there are four of us, if you include Max and all the work he has already done. He was trying to work this by himself, and that certainly was not an advantage for him." He turned and faced Randy. "And, I think it cost him his life."

Calvin stepped back from the table where he had been looking at the pictures and pointed at one of them. "Hey guys, come look at this."

When the other two were within viewing distance of the photographs, he picked up one of them and handed it to Randy.

"This is the photograph of Frank Scott you asked me to take a look at." He handed the magnifying glass to him as well. "You tell me what you think, but I think this is the same guy in one of the photos that William took outside of the State Attorney's office." He pointed to the photograph nearest to him.

Randy studied it for a few seconds. "It is definitely him."

Howard couldn't pass up the opportunity. "Now the question is: How are Frank Scott and someone whose initials are G.R., and whose death was ruled accidental, connected?"

Randy saw what he was doing. "Okay, I get it."

Calvin joined them at the center panel. "Get what?"

Randy pointed at the picture of Frank Scott. "They share a common entry date of August 25th. Max's note said the G.R.'s death was ruled accidental on the same day that he saw Frank Scott at the State Attorney's office. The notes referred to Austin, which is probably Austin, Texas. This is where the research begins, and the speculation must end. We must now connect these two by finding out who G.R. was and how did he know Frank Scott."

Calvin nodded in agreement. "Once we do, the rest of those pictures should take on a whole new meaning." He reached for the notepad he had been working on. "I've still got several pages left in this one."

Randy shook his head and then looked at Howard. "Didn't you say this guy Pinotti told you that this whole thing could take a while?"

"He did. And, something else he said was that when we connect more than two or three items, we should use a high-lighter on it so we can see what it says from a distance. He said that it helps to step back from the boards every so often just to see what jumps off of it – kind of like looking at the trees and the forest at the same time."

Calvin shook his head. "If we stand back too far, we'll miss what we've got up here so far. It looks kind of hopeless at the moment."

Randy started to clean up the area where he had been working. When he was done, he carried his glass to the kitchen and put it in the sink. Howard was right behind him with his half-empty cup of cold coffee. Calvin stayed behind and sat down at the table.

Randy let out a sigh. "I'm going home. I've got a big day ahead of me on Monday. I'm no longer going to be retired. I think I'm going to rest most of tomorrow."

"Just don't be late for work in the morning. Would you like a wake-up call?" Howard asked. "Make sure your cell phone is fully charged before you go to bed."

He thanked him. They shook hands, just before Randy went out the front door and headed for his car.

When Howard went back to the porch, Calvin was seated at the table holding one of the photos.

"I heard what you told Randy. Do you really believe that Max was murdered?"

"It sounds ludicrous to think that someone like Max would end up being murdered, but from the very beginning I've had a very uneasy feeling about this whole thing."

"If that's the case, then we're in dangerous waters. Do you remember the story that McCluskey did on that random shooter near Jacksonville? He ended up dead because that story got leaked to the wrong person, was published and ended up going national. They found him dead on the side of the road with a .38 caliber bullet in his brain three days later." He leaned forward. "If what you believe to be true actually is true, then when whoever we're dealing with figures out we're on to them, they won't even as much as blink an eye when they come after us. Are you ready for that?"

Howard sat down in the chair next to him. "What I know is that we are going to have to be a lot smarter about this than it appears Max was. We've got to go slowly and double source our facts when we can. I'm certain the three of us can keep this under our hats. My concern is for Eileen and Carla. That's why we need to keep them in the dark and out-of-the-loop on this thing. Not that they would intentionally tell someone about any of this, but they're going to have to be super careful when getting their hair done or going grocery shopping. Your fears are understood and appreciated. Let's back away from this tomorrow and start fresh on Monday"

After shaking hands, Howard followed him as they walked toward the front door. Calvin opened the door but turned to face him before exiting.

"We've got ourselves smack in the middle of what could be a story that most journalists would volunteer to cover in a heartbeat; and, it seems like no one else cares about it or may even know about it. To do this at our age; going slow is our only option."

They said their good-byes; then, Howard closed and locked the door behind him.

As he walked back to the porch, he couldn't help thinking about Randy. He believed Calvin would be up to the challenge, but he wasn't sure about Randy.

This could become personal to him, he thought. *I just hope he can keep his focus. The last thing we need is for one of us to go rogue and get hurt — or worse.*

Chapter 11
Sunday, March 17, 2013

It had been over six weeks since Max's death. Howard had become the energy behind the inquiry who believed what they were doing was not only right, but just. Randy had found a renewed sense of purpose whose energy proved to be compelling. Calvin was quickly becoming the pragmatist in the bunch who not only saw the big picture but was the only one with military experience.

They all agreed on one basic notion: Each believed they had been united years ago for this journey. Also, they could see and agreed that their lifetime of collective experiences prepared them for what was in front of them. They already started to feel the collective pressures of developing a story from almost nothing, and it was weighing on their supposedly retired bodies.

The three of them took Sunday off. They agreed to not meet again, until Monday evening after Randy was able to leave work. He agreed to call them an hour ahead of time to let them know when he was leaving and that he was planning on bringing dinner.

Sunday was a day of rest around the Ewing household. It had always been that way. Church was at eleven followed by a scrumptious lunch which Carla had started long before leaving for church. With very few exceptions, that's exactly what happened on this Sunday, except the weather turned warm and the sun decided to shine most of the day.

When they returned from church on that Sunday, they changed their clothes, ate lunch, and then decided to go for a drive. He wasn't too excited about it, but she had wanted to go to the beach. Since the weather helped both of them feel more like it was spring than winter, a walk on the beach was exactly what she thought was needed.

Their trip to Ormond Beach was a forty-minute car ride for them. When they got there, the tide was on its way out and parking was plentiful. They took off their shoes, secured the car, and started walking toward the south so that the wind would be at their backs on the return trip. The surf was noisy and kind of soupy, but a few surfers had decided to brave it and the very chilly Atlantic waters. The seagulls and other shore birds seemed to float in the air, before they decided to land and forage for food. It was an ideal day to visit the beach. Carla, however, had other things on her mind.

She reached out with her right hand and took his left hand into hers. They hadn't walked hand-in-hand on Ormond Beach or any beach, since the summer of 2001. He looked at her and smiled.

"What's bothering you?" he asked, while squeezing her hand slightly.

"Why does something have to be bothering me?"

"You've been awfully quiet today. You hardly spoke at church. You didn't say anything during lunch either."

She looked straight ahead as they continued walking. "I heard what you said to Randy and Calvin yesterday. Do you really believe that Max was murdered?"

He slowed his pace. "Right now, I believe he was. I don't know all the facts about what happened or why. What I do know is that Max had no reason to die where he did and when he did. It makes no sense."

"The Coroner ruled it as an accidental death because there was only his vehicle involved in the accident."

"That's true, but nobody has seen the blood evidence or tissue samples."

They walked a few more feet. "You also told Randy that you think there could be serious trouble the more you dig into this story."

"It's possible."

"What about all of those documents you found in Max's desk and all of those notepads you've got to go through? Surely you could use my help with those."

"There may be things in there that weren't meant for other eyes."

"Is that why you want to keep me and Eileen in the dark and out of the-loop on this because you think we might learn something that might threaten us?"

"Yes."

"I realize you think you're trying to protect me, but I think you're really shutting me out of this. I know I can help. I've watched you for almost thirty-five years develop your trade."

"And so you have, but –," he started, before she interrupted.

Her voice increased in intensity. "I want to help. Eileen is my best friend, even though at times we haven't acted like it. At the very least, I can help with things that require a little more finesse – you know, like a woman's touch."

He smiled at her, again, but didn't respond right away.

She looked at him. "What's to think about? I just offered my help, and you know I'm good help. I promise to not get in your way. I just want to help you with this."

They took a few more steps before he decided to respond. "For now, you must stay behind-the-scenes so to speak. Obviously, you're going to see the information that goes up on the panels. That's part of the problem. We can't have any of this going outside the house until all of us agree on a strategy beforehand. When you were listening last night, did you hear Calvin talk about the McCluskey story?"

"Yes, I did. I understand the consequences and the need for privacy and certainly secrecy. I want to help you catch whoever is responsible. If that means I cook and clean, I can do that. If it means making copies or typing summaries, I can do that, too. If it means helping by listening or being a sounding board, I do that extremely well. You know this." She stopped walking and turned toward him so she could face him. She looked up at him. "I have been your life partner for almost thirty-five years. Let me be your partner now."

He hugged her and kissed her on her forehead. He nodded in agreement.

"When we get home, there are a few things you need to know about before this goes any farther. I'll explain them to you after dinner tonight."

"You're not just saying that to get me to be quiet?"

"No, there are things about this story that are more complex and sensitive. Your greatest challenge will be in not talking with Eileen about these things even though you feel her knowledge of them might bring comfort to her. We've got to stay focused on the end game."

"I understand all of that."

"Keeping things quiet and among ourselves will be a challenge for all of us. She insists that she doesn't really want to know until it's the right time, but she could end up resenting what's done because of being purposely kept-in-the-dark all along the way."

She nodded in agreement.

As they walked, they talked more about how to deal with Eileen. He began to understand what she meant when she spoke earlier about the 'woman's touch' approach. She had an insightful manner about hers and Eileen's friendship that he didn't. He saw that now.

Their walking on the beach that Sunday afternoon proved more than beneficial to both of them. For Howard, it was a dose of tonic for his soul. For Carla, it was absolution.

CHAPTER 12
Monday, March 18, 2013

Just as he promised, Randy showed up with pizza less than an hour after calling from the office. Calvin had arrived fifteen minutes before him and went directly to the porch. After fixing a cup of coffee, he started studying the same notepad he had been looking through on Saturday.

Howard already had started reviewing a couple of the documents from the envelopes they had found in Max's desk. Once the others arrived, he put them down, and announced that dinner was being served in the kitchen. "We're sitting at the kitchen table tonight. Carla has fixed a salad to go along with the pizza, and there is sweet or unsweet tea for you to drink. She also made some more cookies for us for dessert."

Dinner conversation focused mainly on how Randy's first day went. They kidded him about some of his comments but were excited to hear the news about his first disagreement with the City Editor, Jerry Locker.

"I'm telling you this guy is an air head. How he ever got as far as he has is a mystery for sure. He doesn't know which end is up."

"What did he do that's got you upset?" Carla asked.

"He gave me an assignment to edit some copy that a first-year journalist student could do. Then, he had the audacity to tell me to do it over because it wasn't to his liking."

Calvin, fighting back laughter, looked at him. "Did you do it?"

"Of course I did; then I went upstairs and took a coffee break. That's when I saw Mr. Benson."

"What happened with him?"

"Nothing much; he just nodded like he was trying to say 'hello' and kept walking."

"Anything else happened today that was exciting?"

"Not really – unless you include the three hours I spent at a grocery store helping a newly hired, young, wet-behind-the-ears reporter cover the opening of the store."

Howard tapped Calvin's shoulder. "Makes you want to just jump back into it, doesn't it?"

Calvin laughed. "Randy, are you sure you're going to get through this okay?"

"I'll be fine. What happened with you guys today?"

Howard finished the last of the salad on his plate, put his fork down, and looked at him. "Carla and I did some advance work knowing the two of you would be here tonight. As soon as we're done eating, I'll bring you up to speed." He paused and looked at Randy. "What time are you planning to leave tonight?"

"I'm thinking around eight-thirty. I've got to get my beauty sleep."

"In that case, you better leave now." They all laughed.

The next two hours were spent looking through the documents trying to find something they could call a lead. Howard gave Carla a notepad to start going through, while he and Calvin scanned the remaining photographs from the envelopes. Randy continued scanning the same notepad that he had started on last Saturday, when something caught his eye.

Randy leaned forward in his chair. "Have any of you come across 'aggravated battery' in any of your notes?"

No one responded.

Randy cleared his throat. "On August twenty-eighth, Max made a note about an article from a Miami paper about a banker being attacked by someone named Jeffrey Holdren. He circled Holdren's name and connected it to the initials P.T. with a notation of JAX next to it. What do you think that means?"

"JAX is probably Jacksonville," Carla said matter-of-factly.

Howard was the first to see it, but Calvin was the first to speak it. "Those are the same initials we have on that document on the left panel." He walked over to it and pointed at the paper. "These are connected to the pictures that William took."

Howard pointed his index finger at Calvin. "There's the first link to a possible chain." He turned to Randy. "Who wrote that article?"

"It doesn't say."

"Calvin, how long will it take for you to access this story?"

"It depends on whether or not the paper's access to their files is password protected."

Howard's laptop was sitting at one end of the table. Calvin sat down, opened it, and turned it on. "It'll take a while, but I think I can get this even if it's not the originating paper. Hopefully, this story went state-wide."

Carla stood up and walked over to the panels. "Is it me or does it seem strange that everything we picked up on so far is connected to those few days in August?"

Randy's face lit up. "I think it's time for me to take advantage of my access to the computer storage system at the paper, first thing in the morning."

"You'll need a cover to make sure you don't raise any suspicions. Are you still going with the vandalism storyline?"

"Yes – for now; I think it's best."

"Once you're in, just what is it exactly you're going fishing for?"

"These initials might produce a hit on a search connected with this story. I know you said not to jump to any conclusions, but J.H. is probably Jeffry Holdren."

Just then Calvin spoke up. "It is Jeffry Holdren. Here's the article that came out on August twenty-seventh last year. It was written by somebody named Susan Leeds."

Howard sat down at the table next to Calvin. "I think I know of her. She's a reporter working for one of the Tampa papers – at least she was three years ago." He turned his attention to Calvin. "See if you can search Holdren's name with the initials P.T. But before you do that, print that page so we can post that article."

Carla saw Howard take out his cell phone. "Who are you calling at this hour of the day?"

"I'm searching Susan Leeds phone number. I'm pretty sure she'll remember me from that conference in Tallahassee three years ago. She went on-and-on about how our paper was willing to fully support our reporters to participate in things like that. I remember her saying that it was all she could do to get her editor to pay for a two day stay at a four-day conference."

"Here it is," Calvin said. He pointed at the laptop's screen. "Those initials belong to a Peter Theron who used to be a news reporter from Atlanta."

"What do you mean 'used to be?'" Carla asked.

"The search hi-lights an article indicating that he died from a heart attack, while he was jogging on the morning of August twenty-fifth. It says he was fifty-three years old."

"Is there a picture?"

"Yes – and, I'll print that too.

Carla retrieved the printed copies and handed them to Howard.

"Randy, check out this picture of Peter Theron against those that William took on August seventeenth."

Then he turned to Calvin. "See if you can find a phone number for Susan Leeds. I'm getting nothing here."

Randy spoke up. "If you guys strike out tonight, I'll just add that to the list for my little adventure with the computer at work tomorrow."

Calvin raised his hand and smiled. "That won't be necessary." He had Howard copy down the phone number he found through a search on the computer.

"Are you serious? You're calling her tonight?" Carla asked.

"Yes," he said, as he connected the call on his cell phone.

The room became curiously quiet, as the others focused on him standing near the sliding glass doors with the cell phone to his right ear. Carla went over to the sofa and sat down. Calvin stopped his work on the computer, and Randy put down the notepad he had been thumbing through and watched.

It didn't take long for him to begin a conversation with her. He explained who he was and that he had read her piece on Peter Theron.

"You indicated that he died from an apparent heart attack while jogging. Did the autopsy confirm that?"

As he stood there listening, his gestures indicated he was becoming frustrated with her lack of brevity.

"So, he was cremated?" Again, there were several seconds before he spoke.

"He's divorced? Did you do any follow-up with her about that?" Again, several seconds went by as the three others watched him begin to pace in front of the sliding glass doors.

"And, where will I find that?" He smiled at Carla, while he wrote down what he was being told. Then he responded. "You will? That would be great."

He gave her his email address, thanked her, and then disconnected the call.

"Well, that was interesting," he said. He went over to the sofa and sat down next to Carla. "She's sending an electronic file on Peter Theron's most recent articles. She had been helping him with developing the background on a story for a couple of months. Apparently, she was his partner of sorts – albeit from a distance."

"What was the story he was working on?" Randy asked

"She didn't say. She just said she'd send the file via email first thing in the morning, and she said she was glad someone else was interested."

"What's this about his being cremated?" Calvin asked.

"His brother decided that. She told me there's a family feud of some kind that's been going on for several years. His brother won the argument over his ex-wife's wishes. She had wanted him to be buried in Bushnell, along with other veterans. Instead, his brother had him cremated and spread his ashes somewhere in the foothills in North Carolina. He had a Power of Attorney that Peter had given him several years ago. I lost part of what she was saying because she just rambled so much. What I did get was that his ex-wife is now fighting the brother in court for part of the estate."

Carla turned to Howard. "How is any of this going to help us find out what happened to Max?"

Randy got her attention. "This picture of Peter Theron looks a lot like this guy in the one William took on the seventeenth in Orlando." He handed it to her. "Take a look and tell me what you think."

While she was comparing the two pictures, Howard went over to the table and sat down.

"Peter could have been a contact or a source. At this point, all we know is that he was a reporter who was in Orlando on the seventeenth and died the same day someone did with the initials G.R. from Austin, Texas. Is that a coincidence? What we know is that Peter Theron had a portfolio of articles that we should get to see tomorrow. This may not take us too far down the road, but he is a player – so to speak."

She turned and faced him, then pointed at the picture on the table. "That's the same guy William saw on the seventeenth; and eight days later after being in Orlando at the State Attorney's office, he ended dying of an apparent heart attack while jogging. So, who is this guy with the initials G.R.? And, what's his connection in all of this?"

"Hey, Guys! When I did a search on Peter Theron, Jeffrey Holdren, and included the initials G.R. nothing comes up to identify him. I guess we'll have to dig into the Austin data base and do a search there to learn more."

Randy stood up and stretched his arms. "I've got to get home and get some sleep. Five thirty is going to be here before you know it."

They all agreed to stop what they were doing and to call it a night.

After saying goodnight and closing the door behind them, Howard went back to the porch and found Carla sitting on the sofa staring at a photograph she held in her right hand.

"This was taken eight days before he was found dead. I wonder if he knew he only had eight days left to live on the face of this earth. I wonder what I would do if someone told me I only had eight days left to live."

"I'd spend those eight days someplace with you," he said, and then sat down next to her.

His comment must have been amusing. She chuckled and then responded.

"Is that the best you have for me? I thought maybe we would get snow bound again at the cabin"

"That's a great idea."

She put the picture down on the coffee table and leaned forward slightly.

"We've been at this for over a week now and we don't even know what we're really looking at. When are we going to see the big picture?"

He stood up and then walked over to the paneling. He pointed at the document about the person with the initials G.R. "If we can figure out who this person is –," he started, and then stepped away from the paneling, "we may not know the big picture, but the puzzle will take on new meaning. Right now, we have facts and information. We need to take those and turn them into a story for people to understand and grasp. It appears as if Max had been working on this for several months and he never went out-of-town to do his research. We may end up having to travel to Austin to learn the real story behind all of this."

"We've never been to Texas, unless you count the time we flew over it."

He didn't respond. Instead, he stood there looking at the document on the paneling with Jeffry Holdren's initials on it.

He turned toward her. "Are you up for a trip to Jacksonville tomorrow?"

Chapter 13
Friday, March 22, 2013

Their trip to Jacksonville proved uneventful, but they did not come home empty handed. They spent the better part of their day searching through data bases that they had hoped might prove worthwhile. The rest of the day, they spent shopping in a nearby mall. Howard's contacts with the local newspapers hadn't produced any substantive results toward advancing the story, but going to the mall provided him with decent prices on new pairs of socks and underwear.

The rest of the week was filled with the mundane things of everyday life like grocery shopping, cleaning and dusting, and taking care of the yard. It took him until late Wednesday afternoon, but he managed to go through the articles he had received from Susan Leeds concerning Peter Theron. There was one that reported on the death of a senior executive at a local television station, but there didn't seem to be anything out of the ordinary about the circumstances surrounding his death. Howard made a copy of it, however, and pinned it to the third piece of paneling.

The work week was drawing to a close. Randy had not been able to join them on Tuesday or Thursday evening because of work-related obligations. Calvin, who had come down with a really bad cold on Tuesday, was advised to stay away until he was over it because nobody wanted any of what he had. They cancelled their usual Thursday luncheon date at Harry's Place, and everyone agreed to wait until Friday evening and to meet at the usual time.

By the time Friday arrived, they felt as if their research had taken two huge steps backward. Randy was starting to remember why he decided to retire in the first place, and Calvin had grown tired of sitting in his house with a box of tissues within reach. Both Howard and Carla had been busy that afternoon going over the documents and photographs. They spent three hours scanning and analyzing. By the time four-thirty rolled around, they put things down and began their preparations for that evening.

While she was preparing dinner, Howard vacuumed and straightened up the porch. When he was done with that, he decided to spend a few moments before his guests arrived to rearrange the information that they had already accumulated, hoping it might give everyone a fresh perspective. When he was done with that, he decided to make copies of the emails he received from Susan Leeds. Each of the articles had been sent as an attachment in the email, and he wanted to make sure there was a paper trail that could be followed by all of them.

While he was working on printing one of the attachments, another email came in from Susan, only this one was marked urgent. When he opened it, she had written to inform him that she had located two other articles written by Peter Theron. One of them was a story about a young woman named Sarah Wright who was found dead in her apartment in Atlanta on August 26, 2012. The police were unable to determine who killed her, but they had ruled her death as a homicide. The case had since gone cold.

"Carla, would you come here for a minute?"

"Can it wait? I'm in the middle of something."

"You've got to see this. This may be what we've been looking for."

She put down her spatula, turned the burner off under the frying pan, and then walked onto the porch. Standing to his immediate left, with her hands on her hips, she looked at the document Howard had printed.

She read through it quickly. "Okay, who is this Sarah Wright and what does her death have to do with this thing?"

He handed the document back to her. "Read the next to last line, again."

She did, but her expression did not change. "I guess I'm just dense tonight. What's so important about this?" She handed it back to him.

He got up from the table, walked over to the three pieces of paneling, and pinned the document on the far-right panel.

"Do you see any connection with these other documents?"

She shook her head indicating she didn't.

For the next five minutes, he explained what he thought were the similarities those articles shared and why this last bit of information was important. She took a step away from the paneling and began asking questions trying to poke holes in his reasoning. Another five minutes went by, and they were still on the porch going over what he had explained to her when he first began ten minutes earlier. By that time, she had stopped asking questions and began making assumptions. That's when he first believed that his arguments were not only right, but by being able to hear his arguments and forced to defend them, it helped to kick start their thinking that would lead to a plausible understanding about Max's death. More importantly to Howard, it was his first glimpse at the bigger picture.

Carla went back into the kitchen to resume dinner preparations; while he opened the second attachment sent to him. Realizing it was a story Peter Theron had clipped from a newspaper; he printed a copy of it and included it in the portfolio of stories that had been forwarded to him earlier. It was about a news station owner, Robert Clements, who had gone missing for more than three months. The FBI had been called in to investigate what the local authorities called a suspected kidnapping. The date which was in a handwritten note in the left-hand margin of the document was November 12, 2012. Someone had underlined a portion of the story that told of an eyewitness account about the last known whereabouts of Mr. Clements. He had been last seen by a hunter at a nearby wood processing factory twelve miles east of Athens, Georgia. Since then, the case had gone cold and the FBI had no further leads to act upon.

He made another copy of the article and pinned it immediately under the story about the television executive on the far-right panel. First, he connected each of them with a piece of white-colored string, and then he connected both of them to the story about Sarah Wright. When Carla came back in and saw what he had done, she stood there quietly for a few seconds, taking in the information now on three separate panels, and then smiled.

"Max certainly wasn't alone was he?" she mused.

"No he wasn't. What's more disturbing is that we're only really looking at a few solid leads with plausible supporting details. There's bound to be more, and we're going to have to be patient with this process."

"You know between the documents Max had compiled and the articles Peter Theron accumulated, I can see this is more than just state-wide events. We're talking about Florida, Georgia, probably Texas, and who else knows how many more states are involved."

"What does that tell you about what we're looking at here?"

She thought for a few seconds. "We may not have enough paneling."

Twenty minutes went by before Calvin arrived. Fifteen minutes later, Randy showed up bearing a file folder filled with copies of newspaper clippings he had collected over the course of the week. While Howard and Carla finished getting dinner ready and on the table, Randy and Calvin started looking through the clippings.

An outsider, who might have listened to or observed typical dinner conversations among these four well-educated adults, would have identified them as dull or ordinary people – perhaps even boring. On this night, they were anything but boring. Although Carla only sparingly contributed to the substance of the conversation, she did provide the one meaningful supposition that captured the group's attention.

"After listening to the three of you and the ideas you've mentioned in between your gulps and lip smacking, I think somebody out there doesn't like news reporters."

The other three, almost as if they had choreographed their actions, put down their utensils and simultaneously leaned back into their seats. They all looked directly at her.

She wasn't bothered by their actions or their intense stares. "Well, it seems kind of obvious to me that if we're reading about the deaths and disappearances of people who work for newspapers or news stations, then something or someone has a thing for them."

Randy, after taking a drink of his sweet tea, looked at Howard and then at her. "What do you mean when you say, 'a thing for them'?"

Calvin drew his own conclusions. "You think that there's a war on reporters?"

"I didn't say that," she responded. "This 'thing' could be a serial killer."

Randy looked at Howard. "Let's suppose for just a minute that what she thinks is right. The problem with her assumption is that the killer's locations, method of killing, body disposal, and the many more signature parts of a serial killer are unlike any we've covered. I'm not sure we're looking at a serial killer here."

Howard agreed. "Let me show you something."

They all got up from the table and followed him onto the porch. He stood next to the paneling, while they observed.

"Each of these clippings and documents deal with newspapers or news stations as part of the storyline. Photographs substantiate that we're literally looking at news reporters and political issues. Stories that we've managed to uncover so far have been geographically limited to deaths that have occurred primarily in the southeast region. To date, the information we have that connects these individuals is that their deaths occurred within a relatively short time period. The oddity appears to be the disappearance of a news station owner whose case is being treated like a kidnapping. The others were involved in accidents or died from seemingly natural causes."

Calvin interrupted. "If it's not a serial killer, what do you think it is?"

Howard continued. "Some of these accidents, like Max's, don't make much sense to either the families or friends. We all know about how death can be caused by almost untraceable drugs that might speak to that problem. I don't know a lot about that stuff, but what I do know is that we're not looking at a serial killer here. I think we're looking at a person or a group of persons with a grudge or bear some kind of resentment toward people involved in the news industry."

Randy's eyes widened. "Are you thinking conspiracy?"

"It takes more than one person to do what we've seen so far. We just don't have enough information yet to make that bold of an assertion."

"Let's use that as our new starting point," Randy suggested.

Calvin agreed.

Carla wasn't so sure. "If we think there is a conspiracy, then what is the end game of those conspiring? What's their point?"

"If we make this our new starting point, then we need to come up with an idea we can work toward."

"Suppose these reporters," Calvin started, "were working independently of each of other, but didn't know they were working on a storyline that would lead to a similar conclusion. If all four of us looked at this, then we'd have something easier to identify and our conclusions would more likely be in synch and focused toward a plausible ending. Personally, I like the conspiracy concept of a group of persons who have more than just a grudge against news reporters. Suppose by eliminating those reporters they aren't making a point, but achieving some kind of goal."

"Yeah," Howard said, "but to what end? What happens after they're all dead or go missing? Is it murder for murder's sake? Or is it murder for what purpose and for whose advantage?"

Carla went back into the kitchen, picked up her plate, and put it in the sink. "What happens when those reporters die?"

Randy chuckled slightly before responding. "They get buried and there's a lot of slow walking and sad talking afterwards."

"Seriously, what happens at the work place when you lose someone?"

"If the business can afford to, they hire a new person to fill the void," he said casually. Then he repeated what he said, only this time more slowly and with greater emphasis on the 'new person' as he said it.

Calvin understood exactly what he meant. "Our next focus should be on who replaced these people. We'll need to be careful because poking around stuff like this can get you into trouble in a hurry."

Howard went and carried his plate to the sink as well. "We haven't talked about this, but some of the things we're going to have to do will require funding. Since we don't have expense accounts at the moment," he said and then looked at Randy, "we'll have to agree to chip in to help defray expenses."

"What expenses are you thinking about?" Carla asked.

"For starters, the expenses for the trip to Austin someone will need to make."

"We're also looking at Atlanta, Tampa, and probably Miami, too," Calvin added.

"Austin should be first, unless we split up and tackle this in pairs."

"I guess that lets me out," Randy said, "unless it's on the weekend."

Howard pointed his finger at Randy. "Don't worry, we'll figure this thing out. What's important is that we need to follow-up on a couple of these articles pretty quick. If what we are suggesting is true, every day that passes is a lost opportunity."

The next hour was spent establishing a calendar that everyone agreed upon. They planned their meeting dates, trips, and worked out how they would finance their activities. Howard and Carla agreed to take the trip to Texas, while Calvin promised he would go to Tampa to visit with Susan Leeds by the end of the coming week. Randy knew traveling was out of the question, but he said he'd help offset some of Calvin's expenses.

Howard reviewed his notes. "Then it's settled. Our next meeting will be here on the twenty-ninth, Friday evening, at six o'clock. Carla and I will be back from Austin by then, and Calvin will have visited with Ms. Leeds. Randy, you've agreed to search the data bases for Miami and Fort Lauderdale. We'll all be ready to report on what we've found by then."

CHAPTER 14
Tuesday, March 26, 2013

The last time Howard and Carla had flown together was in 1993 when they went to visit her mother. Flying wasn't one of his favorite things to do, but he managed enough courage to get on the plane in Daytona Beach, flew to Atlanta, and changed planes. When he finally put both feet safely on the ground in Austin, Texas on Tuesday morning, he breathed a sigh of relief. With all that behind him, they rented a car and drove to their first destination: The Public Library.

Traffic was light, and the local drivers seemed a forgiving bunch to two out-of-towners. Their thirty-minute trip ended with both of them wondering if they were looking at a library or some executive's corporate headquarters. By contrast, it dwarfed most public libraries either of them had even visited. Still, they managed to find a parking spot within easy walking distance, secured the car, and went inside.

They located the information desk which was manned by a lady with a telling Texan accent and a whisper-like voice. Even Carla commented later on how she had to lean forward to hear what they were being told, and then had to translate her words into something other than Texanese. Still, they learned of the whereabouts of the newspaper files and how to access them. Armed only with their information from Max's notepad about a person with the initials G.R. from Austin on August 25, 2012, and whose death was ruled accidental, they separated, and each went to different computers.

The first thirty minutes went by and neither of them had found anything that remotely connected them to a person whose name had those initials.

"I've been through two of the local papers and even expanded the date search information and came up with nothing," Carla whispered.

"Keep trying. I'm expanding the search to newspapers in surrounding cities. According to what I just found, we should be searching Dallas and Houston as well. You take Dallas, I'll go look at Houston."

Another ten minutes went by without any promising results.

"I'll try El Paso and you take Lubbock."

Another three minutes went by. This time Carla got his attention by standing up and pointing at her computer screen. "Come look at this," she whispered.

What he saw was a newspaper article she had found about the death of a prominent station owner named Gerald Reinhart who died in a one car accident early on the morning of August 25, 2012.

"Locate the obituaries and see if there's more information about him there."

He brought a chair and put it next to her, before he sat down. He leaned forward and watched as she skillfully went through screen-after-screen until she had found it.

"Print this and the article," he said. "We'll need these for Calvin and Randy."

"What do we do now?"

"It says here in the obituary that his wife and two sons are still living. How long do you suppose it will take for us to get to Lubbock from here?"

She checked a website that provided a mile's calculator. "We're looking at roughly a seven-hour drive from here. If we left right now, we could get there before dark, get a fresh start tomorrow, catch a plane back no later than Thursday, and be ready for the meeting on Friday."

He didn't hesitate. "Let's go."

They wasted no time getting things wrapped up in Austin and headed out for Lubbock. They made exceptional time as they traveled toward what they thought would be their next nugget. Back in Florida, the storyline was beginning to take on a new perspective.

Calvin arrived in Tampa at nine-thirty in the morning. He had called ahead and made an appointment with Susan Leeds who decided it would be best if they met somewhere other than her office. He agreed to meet her at a restaurant which was tucked in behind a clothing outlet off of Dale Mabry Highway.

When he arrived at the address she had given him, he wondered if she had misled him on purpose because it looked more like a vacant alley than a parking facility for a restaurant. He stopped the car, looked around for a few seconds, and then decided to try to reach her again on her cell phone. He waited for a few seconds, listening to the ringing of the phone. Finally, his call was connected.

She told him not to move or drive off and that she would be right out. That's when he saw a woman exit one of the doors about thirty feet in front of him, stop, and then started to walk toward him.

"Are you Calvin Rolle?" she asked.

He leaned his head slightly out the window. "Yes. Are you Susan?"

"Yes, I'm Susan Leeds. Come with me."

He got out of his car, locked the doors, and followed her through the doorway from which she had just appeared. It led to a short, poorly lit corridor that made its way to the back end of a kitchen. She motioned for him to join her at one of the tables that lined the south wall.

"I thought it best if we meet here because I'm not sure why it is you wanted to know more about Peter. Grant you, this place is a little off the beaten path, but I know and trust these people, and what we talk about here will not be heard by anyone else."

Calvin cleared his throat. "This seems kind of hush-hush for a simple follow-up to the information you sent Howard."

"The information I sent you was intended to provide you with the answers to your questions. What you've started looking into will require answers that won't be easy for either of us to come by."

"It answered some of our questions, but it created more than it answered."

For the next fifteen minutes, they talked about Peter and her relationship with him, about Peter's family and how difficult it had been dealing with his brother, as well as how Peter's ex-wife was now locked in a complicated legal battle over the remainder of his estate.

"How much was Peter worth?"

"I'm not actually sure, but I know it's somewhere in the eight figures."

"How does a reporter come into that kind of money? Was it his family's?"

"It was his mother's side of the family, and they've been quarreling for years."

"Where does all of this stand now?"

"It's in the courts at the moment. There's a hearing in June of this year, but my guess is that it will never happen. I think his brother is going to make a deal with the ex-wife just to get her out of the picture."

"What picture would that be?"

"I thought you knew. It's all about the control of where the money comes from – the business enterprise. His brother owns fifty percent of the business and he's been wanting to buy-out Peter to gain full control of the company – that is until Peter's untimely death. The family's got money in real estate, television, radio, and several printed publications as well. They're beyond filthy rich."

He sat back trying to take all of this in, when he noticed she had started to look over her right shoulder on more than one occasion.

It sparked his curiosity. "Are we being watched? Is there a problem with us talking about this?"

"I wasn't sure if I could trust you or not. I did my own research on you and Mr. Ewing. You guys seem to be on the up-and-up, but a girl can never be too sure about those things. You know what I mean?"

He noticed she had become more focused on who might be behind her than the conversation between the two of them.

"You seem to be preoccupied with the possibility that someone might come crashing in here at any moment. Is there someplace else we can meet to finish this because I get the idea that you're feeling a little uncomfortable at the moment? I need to leave by tomorrow morning, but I can meet you whenever or where ever you say this afternoon or this evening."

She thought for a few seconds. "There's a park just up the road a few miles. I'm in the middle of writing a piece about it, and I have a two o'clock appointment there today. We can meet there after I'm done. It's a public place, but it will give us the privacy we need."

He agreed. "What kind of car are you driving?"

"It's a 2010, dark blue Mustang." She wrote her license plate number down and handed it to him. She had barely finished doing that before she got up, walked out of the kitchen area, and headed for the front door of the restaurant. He went back out the way he had come in.

When he got back to his car and had sat down in the driver's seat, he called Howard.

"You aren't going to believe this."

Meanwhile, Randy was in his office working on a story with a three o'clock deadline, when an interoffice email popped up on his computer screen. It was from Lisa Jacobs a longtime employee of the paper and former colleague of Max's. She was inviting him to meet her for coffee in the break room in thirty minutes. He was hesitant at first about accepting the invitation, so he thought about it for a few seconds.

Lisa Jacobs had been with the paper for thirty years, but was too young to retire. Now fifty-eight and not looking for advancement or transfers within the organization, she was not interested in traveling and living out of a suitcase. She was happy with what she was doing and enjoyed going to work every day. She never became that jet-setting, world-wide news reporter she once hoped to be when she first started in the business. Instead, she fell in love with the central Florida area. That was thirty-five years ago.

She flew to Daytona during the summer of 1978, right after graduating with a degree in Journalism from the University of Illinois. She interviewed with the paper four hours after landing at the airport, and she was hired on the spot.

Over the years, it was not just her journalistic skills that endeared her to the paper and the people. She was great at understanding the underlying feelings of the local and surrounding communities. Through all of the good times and bad, she had gained the respect and admiration of the leaders of those communities, and when something was happening in the area, she knew about it. If she didn't, then she knew someone who did who couldn't wait to tell her about it.

In 1996, she won recognition for her story on pesticides and their connections to the food industry. The story was picked up by the national news industry and her work became center stage for more than two weeks. That story and her work ethic caught the eye of one of the producers for a major national television company, based in New York City, who offered her a job as an investigative reporter. She wasn't interested. Ten years later in 2006, she was offered a similar position with a national cable news show, but she turned that down as well.

She and Randy had worked together on a few assignments, but mostly she spent her time assigned to the metro news division, while he spent his time on the state and national news scenes. When he decided to retire, she attended the party that had been thrown in his honor. During that gathering, the two of them shared a quiet moment where they spoke of how much they respected each other's work.

Ever since he left on the afternoon of his last work day, he regretted not having spent more time working with her. In the few times they had shared a by-line or collaborated on the research for a back story, he left each experience feeling as if he had grown professionally. They were both team players and their work ethic enhanced the public's image of the newspaper. It wasn't any kind of special chemistry between the two of them. It was more like knowing what the other person was really good at and then staying out of each other's way on purpose.

He shrugged his shoulders. "What the heck," he whispered, as he typed in his response to her email.

He leaned forward, put his elbows on the arms of his chair, and looked at the clock. He was still waiting for a return call from a contact he had made earlier with a reporter with one of the Miami-based newspapers. While researching one of the databases for articles from one of the leading newspapers in the Miami area, he read about a story, dated September 1, 2012 how the wife of one of the more prominent local attorneys had been found dead in her vehicle four blocks from her home. The police were not sure what caused her death, but they described the circumstances surrounding her death as "suspicious." As he read through the story, his eyes locked in on an item the reporter had included as part of the background. Over the last six years, many of his clients had been news agencies and journalists. He had defended them on several occasions and now was the lead attorney in a current, multi-million-dollar lawsuit brought against one of the papers for slander.

Before leaving to meet with Lisa, he printed a copy of the story, put it in the file he had started for the others to look through when they got together, and locked it in the bottom drawer of the filing cabinet behind his desk. He picked up his cell phone and headed for the elevator.

As he walked by Jerry Locker's office, he could hear him shouting at someone over the phone. His secretary, seated to the right of his office door, appeared nervous and upset.

"Are you okay?" he asked.

"I think he's going to have a heart attack."

"What's got him so upset?"

"It's somebody from corporate and they didn't like something that happened yesterday."

"Listen, I'm on my way to the break room. If you need me, call me. Okay?"

He continued walking toward the elevator, and he could still hear him shouting. It wasn't until the door closed behind him after he had gotten onto the elevator that the soft background music coming from the speaker helped to drown out Locker's voice.

After exiting the elevator, he turned right and headed for the break room. The corridor, lined with window panes on his left, allowed the sun's rays to warm the hallway. He could see the tree-lined parking lot below and watched as one of the eighteen wheelers slowly backed its way into the receiving bay of the adjacent building.

When he reached the entrance to the break room, he didn't see Lisa at first. He walked over to the coffee pot, poured himself a cup of decaf, and then set it on the counter to search for the sugar. After looking in the cabinet to his right, he heard a voice from behind.

"I knew you'd be looking for this," Lisa said, holding out the sugar dispenser toward him.

He took it from her and thanked her. "This stuff will probably kill me one day, but right now it's what seems to help."

"How have you been Randy?" She walked over to the coffee pot and refreshed the cup of coffee she had fixed prior to his arrival.

"I've been doing okay, I guess. How have you been doing?"

She smiled and took a seat at one of the tables near the refrigerator. "It's been busy around here." She put her coffee cup down in front of her. "I'm really sorry about Michelle. How are you holding up?"

He thanked her. "Coming back to work has been a good move for me right now. It's helped with the quiet times at the house."

"I think I know what you mean. You know I hesitated about sending you that email because I didn't want you to think I was being forward or prying, but I'm curious about why you really came back to work. Sometimes when I get home, all I can think about is quiet and putting my feet up."

"Sometimes while sitting there in the comfort of my home with my feet up, I would turn the television on and the volume up as loud as it would go just to try to drown out the quiet."

She leaned forward. "Are you working on anything of significance? I figured by now you would have published a bestselling novel about the ins-and-outs of the newspaper business."

"I thought about it, but I just couldn't muster the interest. Instead, I've taken up crossword puzzles as a hobby, but that only goes so far."

She smiled at him. "I'm crazy about those, too."

It was something about the way she said that which caused him to let down his guard.

For the next forty-five minutes, they sat there talking about everything from work to vacations, travel, foods they both liked, people whom they had worked with over the years, and then back to work-related topics. He hadn't sat and talked with or listened to another person – especially an attractive woman – like that in forever. It was energizing, and this opportunity was appealing to him.

"Wow," he said, as he pointed to the clock on the wall, "Do you think we'll be docked pay for this long break?"

"I'll cover for you."

He stood up as if he were planning to leave. She looked up at him.

She stood up. "Are you doing anything for dinner tonight?"

He shook his head. "Where would you like for me to take you?" He couldn't believe what he heard himself just say. He hadn't been on a date in years.

She noticed he was blushing. "I apologize. I just wanted to talk with you more about things. I have so enjoyed this time."

"There's no need to apologize. I think it'd be great. I'll be happy to pick you up at six – or we could meet some place."

She gave him her address, and they exchanged cell phone numbers.

"I'll be ready by six," she said.

I hope I am, he thought, as he stepped onto the elevator.

Chapter 15
Tuesday, March 26, 2013

The afternoon went quickly for Randy. By the time he arrived at Lisa's apartment to pick her up, Howard and Carla were just driving into the outskirts of Lubbock, Texas. They had made exceptional time, especially once they cleared Abilene. They had to stop once for gas and once for a bathroom break. Other than that, traffic had worked in their favor.

When they found the motel they planned to stay in for the evening, they decided to stop for dinner first before checking in. They were tired and hungry, but they wanted to eat before going to their room. They drove beyond the motel for another mile and found a small restaurant that served meals family style. There, they learned that the Gerald Reinhart's family lived a few miles northeast of town. The waitress not only knew Mrs. Reinhart, she knew both sides of her family.

"She's had it pretty rough since Gerry died," she said, as she poured them both a cup of coffee. "Apparently the insurance money's been held up because they thought it might have been suicide."

Howard continued to press for information. "Did you know Mr. Reinhart?"

"Oh yes, he used to come by here a lot, when he was in town. His business took him out of town – mostly Austin, from what I heard."

"He was a regular here?"

"I guess you could call him that."

"There's a place like this back in Florida I go to every week where a bunch of us guys meet for coffee every Tuesday morning. Did Mr. Reinhart meet with other guys here like that?"

"No, he'd come in with Mrs. Reinhart occasionally for dinner, but usually he was alone, and it was just for lunch."

"Was he from around these parts?"

"Yes, he was born just up the street in a little tiny house. His momma used to take in wash and clean houses to help make ends meet. She was a sweet, sweet lady. When he came back from going off to school, he moved her into the house where they live now – only she died a year later from pneumonia. That was a pretty rough winter."

"What happened to his dad?"

"Oh, he died a few years after he got back from Vietnam. He's buried in the cemetery not far from where the family still lives. I didn't know him, but I heard that he was a very generous person."

Howard looked at Carla and then at the waitress. "You've been very kind. Thank you."

"It's been my pleasure." She started to walk away. "Your food will be right up."

Howard smiled. "There's something to be said about living in small towns."

Carla smiled. "Lubbock's no small town."

"It is in this restaurant," he said, before he took another sip of his coffee.

Once they each finished eating a slice of peanut butter pie for dessert, they decided to call it an evening and went to their motel room. About the time they were entering their room, Randy and Lisa were sitting down at a table in her favorite restaurant.

Randy wasn't exactly sure what to expect. He hadn't dated or been out with another woman in several years, and apparently his worrisome look told Lisa as much. After being seated, the waiter filled their water glasses and left a basket of piping hot yeast rolls for them.

"This is nice," she said, before taking a sip from her water glass. "They've always had great food here and even better service."

All he could manage was a smile back at her and to nod his head in agreement. She could sense his awkwardness about being in public with a woman who wasn't his wife, and it was making her uneasy just thinking about the whole idea of his being uncomfortable.

"If you'd rather not be out in public right now, I'd be happy to cook dinner for you."

That got his attention. "It's not that. I'm a little nervous – that's all."

"Randy, you've got a bad case of anxious and it's making both of us uncomfortable. I'm beginning to think it might be better if you really would let me fix dinner for you. Do you like pork chops? How does that sound to you?"

"Like a turkey being pardoned at Thanksgiving."

He made their excuses to the waiter, paid whatever they owed, got back into his car and then drove to her apartment.

It was as if the weight of the world had been lifted from his shoulders. The conversation on the way to her place was light-hearted, open, and it lasted the entire thirty-minute trip. He even managed to laugh a little at himself, especially when she said he looked like a lost puppy sitting across from her at the table in the restaurant.

"Come on in and I'll get dinner started," she said, after she opened the door to her apartment.

When he walked in earlier that evening, he really hadn't noticed the view from the sliding glass doors in the living room that opened onto a small balcony.

"Take your coat off. Would you care for some coffee?" she said, with a raised voice from her kitchen.

"Yes, thank you – that would be nice." He could hear her moving about the kitchen, cabinet doors opening, and the water being run.

"Is there something you'd like for me to do to help?"

"I can manage. Just make yourself at home."

He walked over to the sliding glass doors and stood there for a few moments taking in the scenery. "This is quite some view you've got here."

"I enjoy it almost every evening."

That's when he saw the eight-by-ten picture frame hanging on the wall to the left. Under it were two other pictures in smaller frames. All three of them were pictures of the same man, except in the other two, she was in each picture standing next to him.

He didn't hear her come into the room, while he was looking at the pictures.

"That's Leonard," she said. "He died fourteen years ago. She paused for just a second before continuing. "These over here," she pointed to the picture frames on the end table, "are our children, Fredrick and Samantha."

"I must apologize to you. I had no idea you lost your husband so long ago." He turned to look at the pictures of her children. "That would have been about the time you came to work for the paper."

"Actually, I met him just before I came to work here. My children, however, still live in South Carolina. They still want me to move back there, but I have resisted that notion as long as my work stays challenging and rewarding. It's tough not seeing the grandkids as often as I'd like, but they come here every-so-often."

She walked back into the kitchen and he followed her.

The aroma let him know the coffee had finished brewing.

"Help yourself. You'll find the coffee cups and the sugar in the first cabinet on the left." She pointed to the cabinets behind him.

Dinner was ready forty minutes later, but the rest of the evening lasted until almost ten-thirty. For a few minutes before dinner, they sat on the balcony and watched the sun set. After dinner, he helped with the dishes. For most of the evening, however, she sat at one of end of the sofa with her feet curled up under her listening to him talk about himself, and he sat near the other end, listening to her talk about herself. During this time, as he sat there enjoying her company, he came to realize how lonely he had become.

He looked at his watch. It was getting late, and he had reached that moment wondering what would come next.

"I really should go. It's late and we both have to go to work tomorrow." He stood up, reached for his coat, and then started toward the door.

She stood up and followed him. "This has been nice. I'm glad you let me cook for you."

They stood at the door for a few seconds looking at each other. He wasn't sure whether to kiss her goodnight or what to do. Fortunately for him, she knew exactly what to do.

She extended her right hand to him. With great relief, he shook her hand.

"Thank you for a wonderful meal. The best part of the evening though was the company." He opened the door to leave, only to be stopped by her for just a moment.

"Thank you for a wonderful evening. I guess I'll see you tomorrow at the office?"

"I'm looking forward to it."

XXXXX

Calvin's afternoon meeting never happened. Susan called him, after he had sat in the park for over an hour, and explained that her previous meeting ended up going longer than she had expected. She extended an offer that if he still wanted to meet with her, they could meet at a restaurant of his choosing, but it had to be in St. Petersburg and not in Tampa.

He agreed, but decided to let her pick the place and meeting time. He jotted down the address and the name of the restaurant, and then drove to the motel he had planned to stay in for the evening. After a quick nap, he took a shower, changed clothes, and got directions to the restaurant from the night manager at the front desk.

It took thirty minutes to find the restaurant and another twenty minutes waiting in his car before Susan showed up. He was beginning to think he had made a mistake to meet with her for dinner. While waiting for her to arrive, he kept thinking about how much drama had already played out during his brief encounters with her and how it made him feel.

Almost at the point of deciding to leave, he saw her drive into the parking lot and into a parking place. Once he was certain it was Susan, he got out and began walking toward her. They were about twenty feet apart, when a vehicle entered the parking lot at a high rate of speed. To him, it was no mistake. The driver of the vehicle was aiming directly at her.

He yelled at her to get out of the way. Luckily, she was not hurt. She had a few abrasions on her left knee and broke a heel on her left shoe when she dove to get out of the way. She was sitting on the pavement, by the time he reached her, and tried to help her to her feet.

The car did a U-turn at the end of the parking lot and came back heading directly for both of them. It swerved back-and-forth as the driver aimed the vehicle at them both, but Calvin quickly got her to safety near the front door of the restaurant. Within seconds, the vehicle disappeared into the night by exiting the parking lot as quickly as it had entered.

One of the waitresses saw what happened and came running outside.

"Are the two of you all right?"

Calvin nodded that he was okay. "Are you okay, Susan?"

She sat down on one of the benches near the front door. Her expression told it all.

The waitress recognized it. "That person tried to kill you. Are you sure you're okay?"

Susan was shaking so badly, she could barely speak. He reached down and picked her up, with her broken shoe dangling from her left foot, and then carried her inside. He put her down gently on one of the cushioned seats in the foyer, took out his cell phone, and started to call the police.

"Please, no police. It will only make matters worse." She reached up and tried to grab his phone from him.

"Susan, whoever that was just tried to kill you. Of course we're calling the police. There are witnesses who saw exactly what happened and, besides, I got the license plate numbers."

Against her wishes, the police arrived within a few minutes of his calling. They took statements from both of them, three other witnesses, and then took pictures. When asked to sign the complaint form, she refused. He didn't. An hour later, things had calmed down enough that Calvin thought staying for dinner seemed like the right thing to do.

He made arrangements for the two of them to be seated in a quiet area where the lighting was dimmed, and others were not seated too closely.

"See? Isn't this better?"

"You shouldn't have signed that complaint." He wasn't exactly sure how to read her, but the expression on her face could easily have been taken for one of irritation mixed with fear.

"Susan, would you mind telling me what's really going on? First, we meet in some clandestine location and all you can do is to keep looking over your shoulder. Then, our meeting in the park ends up not happening. I'm still not sure exactly why, but now this and I've only been in town for nine hours. That person was not messing around. What's this all about?"

She leaned forward slightly. "I guess you've earned the right to know."

Dinner was served to them at eight o'clock. By ten o'clock, the waitress told them the restaurant was closing in a half-hour. During those two hours, he listened while she explained what she knew about the circumstances around Peter's death. She was brutally honest with him about how she believed there was something big about to happen, and it wasn't just something that was going to happen in Tampa or even just the State of Florida.

"Peter told me a few months before he died that he had heard about some kind of alliance between three-or-four high stakes people, who were scheming something so massive and unthinkable to most people, that even he thought he sounded crazy just talking about it."

As he sat there listening to her, he started wondering what he and the others had gotten themselves into. That's when the investigative reporter in him resurfaced. "You're only one source. My friends are going to think I'm crazy, if I present this to them as evidence. There's got to be more. What else are you not telling me?"

"You're right, but I don't have that with me right now."

"What are you talking about and where is it?"

"It's a CD that Peter made two days before he died. The problem is I don't know where it is either."

"Who else knows about this?

"I think maybe we've over extended our stay here tonight," she said, as the waitress approached them for the third time with their bill in her hand.

"You can't go home tonight," he said, as he handed the waitress enough cash to pay for the dinner. "You're coming with me tonight, and we can figure this out in the morning. Right now, I think discretion would be the better part of valor. Don't you?"

She didn't argue with him. "I'll need a few things from my apartment."

"No, we can get whatever you need at the store near the motel. The thing is to make sure that you're safe and off the grid, so to speak, for the evening."

As they got up to leave, the abrasions on he left knee had caused her knee joint to swell making walking difficult and painful. She looked up at him.

"Okay, but let's not make a habit of this." He picked her up into his arms and carried her to his car.

"What about my car?"

"We can come back for it later. I think it's best if we leave it here and go somewhere safe."

"I've got to go to work in the morning."

"You need to call in sick tomorrow morning."

He started the engine, pulled out of the parking lot, and eased into oncoming traffic.

"My room at the motel has a bed and a sofa in it. You can take the bed, I'll take the sofa. In the morning, we can get a fresh start on this. Right now, I want you to tell me what it was that you couldn't tell me back there. Who else knows about the CD?"

The thirty-minute car ride back to his motel took forty minutes. He wanted to make sure he wasn't being followed and that he gave her every opportunity to be forthcoming. During those extra ten minutes, she provided an earful of disquieting information that confirmed his earlier suspicions. She wasn't just in trouble; she was trouble waiting for a reason to happen.

CHAPTER 16
Wednesday, March 27, 2013

Sleep was not an option for Calvin. He stayed up watching Susan fall asleep, while he made sure no one came crashing through their motel room door during the night. Howard and Carla woke up at their usual time, only to learn that as a result of their being in a different time zone, it would be another hour before they could venture back to the restaurant where they had learned so much about the Reinhart family the night before. Randy slept like a baby; that is until Calvin called him at six o'clock that morning.

"Listen Randy, I'm sorry to wake you, but you need to know what I've learned so far."

For the next several minutes, Calvin told him everything that had happened and everything that Susan had told him, especially about the CD Peter had made before he died. Randy told him to slow down because he couldn't take notes that fast.

"Maybe you need to record this and send it to us via your phone email. Have you talked to Howard yet?"

"No, I thought it was too early to call him"

"Wake him up. We can hook up on a conference call later this morning to catch up each other on all of this. My suggestion to you is that you keep a low profile today and get out of town as soon as you can. Make sure you're not followed."

"What about Susan? Somebody's after her. They tried to kill her last night."

"What are you thinking? Let the police deal with that."

"I just can't leave her here by herself."

"Talk with Carla about this. She'll know what to do."

They said their good-byes and he disconnected their call. Susan overheard what he had said about not leaving her alone.

"Why are you doing this? Now you're the one being less than above board."

He decided to level with her and told her how he and the others had started working on Max's death as well as the unlikely circumstances surrounding it.

"This Max person must have been a really good friend of yours."

"He was. His wife, Eileen, just wants to know the truth like we do. Right now, I'd settle for understanding just what's at stake here. For some unknown reason, someone tried to kill you, and I think it has everything to do with this Peter Theron person."

She sat up in bed. It was then he remembered that she had slept in her under garments. He reached for her clothes. "You really need to get dressed," he said, as he tossed her blouse and skirt to her that she had thrown over the back of a chair.

She laughed. "I think that's sweet. You're quite the gentleman."

He turned around, until she said she was completely dressed, broken shoe and all.

"How's the knee feeling this morning?"

"It's sore, but I think I can walk on it," she said, while gingerly trying to stand.

"The toiletries we picked up at the store last night are in the bathroom. I'll wait until you're done."

Meanwhile, Randy had gotten out of bed, went to his desk, and rewrote his notes trying to make sense out of all that Calvin had told him. Once he was sure he hadn't left out anything, he put them in his satchel that he carried to work each day, got dressed, and headed for the office. He knew it was earlier than usual, but it didn't seem to matter.

As he drove, his thoughts went back-and-forth between his evening with Lisa and Calvin's bombshell-of-a-phone-call that woke him so abruptly. He was worried about Calvin's situation and the dilemma he was in, but he believed he could handle it. What worried him more was his insistence on watching over Susan.

I hope he knows what he's doing, he thought.

By the time he got to his office and was seated at his work station, the sun had just begun to peek over the horizon. He spent a few minutes rechecking the notes he had taken from Calvin's phone call, checked his calendar of events and his emails for any assignments he had been given for the day, and then decided to go to the break room to search for some coffee.

On his way to the elevator, he heard Jerry Locker calling him from his office.

"What are you doing here so early Tomlin?"

"At the moment, I was going to go get a cup of coffee." He stopped and leaned on the door frame of Locker's office. "Are you okay? I thought you were about to break a blood vessel in your forehead when I went by here yesterday."

"Oh – you heard that?"

"Who didn't? Your secretary was almost in tears worrying about you."

"Isn't she sweet?" He stood up behind his desk and motioned for him to come in.

"Do you have a moment?"

He smiled. "Of course I do. What's on your mind?"

He pulled a chair over to the front of the desk for him, pointed as if to invite him to sit down, and then he closed the door.

"That phone call I got yesterday was from corporate headquarters. Somebody's got the idea up there that they need to tell us what we should be printing. I have never had an editorial rejected like I did yesterday. They said they'd review it again out of deference to me, but they never called back. What I saw in the copy this morning was written by someone who doesn't even live here – and I don't know him either. Whoever it is has the unmitigated nerve to take a position for this paper that does not reflect what we've tried to do in our community for more than thirty years. Imagine us taking a posture against developing our parks and, instead, wanting to turn them into shopping centers."

"How long has this been going on?"

"It's going on six months, as best as I can remember, maybe seven."

"What happened six months ago that would bring any of this on?"

"Our company had a big change at the head office. The managing editor was replaced by someone from the outside who never had worked a day in his life setting print or having to sell advertising. All our departments have seen budgets slashed and trying to hire somebody around here seems like it takes an Act of Congress. How you got on board is a mystery to me. The gods must have been smiling on you that day."

"Am I to understand that Mr. Biederman, who helped to grow this company for the last twenty-five years, was let go? How did that happen?"

"He was pushed out the door with some kind of packaged deal. It's sad because he died within two weeks of his forced retirement."

"How did he die?"

"That's the strangest thing. He died when he fell from his roof cleaning the leaves from the gutters. The hospital said death was caused by severe internal injuries from the fall."

"Were there any witnesses?"

"His wife was home at the time, but she didn't see it happen. She's been a wreck since that day. Her sister has come to live with her temporarily, but that hasn't helped much."

"You know I remember that story now. It seemed odd to me at the time, but I had been away from the paper for well over a year at that point."

"It's more than odd, if you ask me." He lowered his voice to barely above a whisper. "The other members of the management team all seem to be walking on eggshells around this place. It's amazing. It's really sad, too." He shook his head.

He sensed his reluctance to be specific, and he recognized his apprehension to talk about this in greater length.

"I remember Mr. Biederman was pretty well liked by most of the folks around here. He actually came to my retirement party. Who's the new managing editor?"

"His name is Mitchell Rayner; Mr. Mitchell Rayner."

Randy stood up and headed for the door. "Can we continue this at another time? There are a couple of things I need to get done this morning, and I really would like a cup of coffee. Can I bring you one on the way back?"

"No thanks, I'm still working on this one," he said, as he pointed at a tall, disposable cup sitting on the corner of his desk. "It's cooled off enough for me to drink it now."

As he exited the office and continued walking toward the elevator, it was clear that the conversation they just had was supposed to mean something to him. *Jerry Locker doesn't just sit and chit-chat to waste time,* he thought. *Reading between the lines is exactly what he'd want me to do.*

When he reached the break room, he was disappointed because no one had made any coffee. He searched through the cabinets and eventually found everything he needed to brew a pot. *It'll only be another five minutes,* he thought. *I think I'll just wait on it to be done.*

While waiting for the coffee to finish, he stepped into the hallway and looked out one of the windows that lined the hall. He noticed a woman running from the adjacent building carrying a rectangular package wrapped in what he thought looked like brown paper. As she ran, he saw something fall out of her coat pocket. Within a few seconds, she had reached her car, got in, and drove off.

As he watched, he could hear the coffee pot going through the last stages of its brewing cycles. He was just about to go back into the break room, when he saw one of the security guards walk out of the adjacent building, stopped ten feet from the door, and began looking in every direction. He walked toward the parking lot and, again, looked in several directions. It became obvious that he had given up his search, when he started walking back toward the door.

Struck by what he considered to be a mystery, he observed the security guard attempt to reenter the building, but the alarm sounded until he used his key to shut it off.

"That's more than strange," he mumbled.

"What's strange?" Lisa asked. He hadn't seen or heard her approach.

"I just saw something that doesn't make any sense." He then realized it was Lisa. He turned and looked at her. She was smiling and his eyes fixed on her smile.

"Good morning," he said, in an almost airy tone.

"And to you as well," she said, while she continued to walk toward him. "What was it you saw that was so strange?"

"Is it okay if we grab a cup of coffee and then walk-and-talk? I'd like to look into what I just saw to find out what really just happened."

After fixing their coffees, they walked back to the elevator and rode it to the first floor. As they walked toward the corridor that would lead to the adjacent building, he thanked her for the time they shared the evening before, and she thanked him for being such a great listener. Their conversation was polite and superficial, and he felt like kicking himself all the way to the security guard's station because he couldn't think of anything else to say.

When they reached the station and he began to question the guard, it was obvious that something had happened, but the guard couldn't explain any details other than when he got back to his station he saw a woman run by him, throw open the doors, and then ran outside. He tried to follow her, but tripped over several boxes she had knocked down on her way out the door.

"She was fast – really fast. I've called the police to report it, but they're not here yet."

"How come the alarm didn't sound when she threw open the doors?"

"I haven't the foggiest idea. The alarm was properly set at the beginning of my shift because the alarm board showed all green lights. I wrote that down in the log book – right here." He pointed to the entry in the book.

"When you tried to re-enter the building, the alarm went off. Why didn't it go off when she forced open the doors and then ran outside?"

The guard ran his right hand through his hair. "I can't explain that. All I know is that the board clearly showed all the alarms were set properly."

Randy walked over to the doors and stood next to them. He turned to face the guard. "Does your alarm board show all green at the moment?"

"Yes, it does," he replied. Lisa verified it as well.

Without any notice, Randy pushed open the doors. Instantly, the alarms sounded. The guard reacted quickly by taking out his key and resetting the alarm system.

The guard yelled at Randy. "Why'd you do that?"

Lisa responded to that question. "Now he knows that you were telling the truth – that's why."

When he went back to the guard's station, he asked if he could explain why he wasn't at his station when the woman ran by.

"There was an alert sensor that went off in section twelve, and I went to investigate it."

"Did you find any disturbance or problem in section twelve?"

"No sir, I did not. All I saw was a waste basket that had been turned over. I picked it up and set it down where it was supposed to be, and then I started back to my station. That's when I saw the lady running toward the door. Then, she pushed open the doors and ran outside. I thought I might be able to catch her, but she was just too fast for me."

Lisa and Randy saw the police cars pull up near the entrance to the paper. "It's time to leave," he whispered to her.

They thanked the guard for his cooperation and walked back to the break room.

"Wow," he said, as he refreshed his coffee, "and all this before seven o'clock." Out of the corner of his eye, he saw her looking at him. "Why are you here so early?"

"I had a hunch you might be here; and, I wanted to talk with you about last night before our day gets started."

He wasn't sure where this conversation was going. So with coffee in hand, he suggested they sit down and talk. She moved closer to him, instead.

She walked up to him. "This is what I should have done last night as you were leaving." She leaned forward and kissed him on his right cheek. "I really enjoyed our evening together."

He smiled.

Chapter 17
Wednesday, March 27, 2013

After they finished their breakfast, Howard and Carla got into their car and headed for the Reinharts' residence. They drove northeast on Idalou Road for twenty minutes, before spotting the sign for the road that would take them to the Reinharts' house. The road weaved its way through small sets of trees and beautifully manicured landscaping, until they emerged into a large clearing. The house was clearly visible from a mile away as it sat on top of a knoll surrounded by a white picket fence. The gate was fashioned after the western entrances displaying the name of the ranch and the brand used on its cattle. The driveway was a straight dirt road that was also lined the entire distance with white picket fences

As they drove toward the house, Carla saw who she would later come to know as the Reinhart's eight-year-old grandchild, playing near the porch on the side of the house. A windmill, which was not far from a very large barn, was turning slightly in the early morning breeze. The grass hadn't turned completely green, since the spring weather had been unseasonably cooler than usual.

When they drove up to the house and stopped the car, Mrs. Reinhart came out onto the front stoop to welcome them.

"Lydia called and said you might be coming by this morning."

Howard walked around the front of the car to shake hands with her. "Who's Lydia?"

"She was the waitress who took care of you last night. We go back a long way."

He turned to Carla and whispered. "I told you this was a small town."

Mrs. Reinhart invited them inside where she had prepared some cinnamon rolls and coffee for them. After they introduced themselves and had taken a seat in the living room, Carla commented on how beautiful her house was.

"Thank you, but I don't think you drove all this way to compliment me on my home. When Lydia called last night, she told me you showed a great amount of interest in my late husband." She took a sip of her coffee.

Howard and Carla glanced quickly at each other. "Actually, Mrs. Reinhart, we –," he started, but was interrupted by Mrs. Reinhart.

"Please, call me Emily."

"Thank you, Emily. Yes, we would like to speak with you about your late husband."

Emily was a gracious hostess. Despite the recent memories of her late husband's death, she held up well during the discussion. She answered all of their questions – even giving them a little bit of the history of how the television industry had changed so much in the past few years. She hesitated a few times, fighting back tears while responding to questions about the accident, but she didn't back down.

"You know it was the darnedest thing. I still don't know why he was on that road. It didn't make any sense to me at the time, and it still doesn't."

"What road was that?" Howard asked.

"He was traveling west on Highway 41 near a little town called Sundown."

"How far is that from here?"

She paused for a few seconds. "It's about fifty miles or so."

"Did the police investigate the accident?"

"Oh my, yes, they did. Look, I know you are news reporters who are just doing your jobs, but what does any of this have to do with you?"

"We're following leads wherever they take us right now. We lost a good friend several weeks ago under similar circumstances."

"Did you find out what caused the accident?"

"We're working into that." He cleared his throat. "Do you know who the lead investigator was in your husband's case?"

"Yes. His name is Sheriff Buddy McCrae. He and Gerry were friends since they were kids."

"Where's his office located?"

He wrote down the directions and motioned to Carla that it was time for them to leave.

Howard stood up. They started walking toward the front door.

"Emily, could you tell us who replaced your husband at the company?"

"His name is Mack Hayes. He's from somewhere up north – Chicago, I think."

Carla stopped at the front door, took Emily's hands into hers, and expressed her sympathy once more. "As soon as we know the truth, you'll be the second person we tell."

"I'll be second? Who will be first?"

"Our dear friend Eileen Leopold back in Florida."

They hugged each other. Carla started walking toward the car, and Emily stepped out onto the front porch to wave good-bye.

As they drove off, Howard looked at Carla. "Did you notice what she said about her husband being where he was when he died?"

"Yes, I did. She had no earthly idea what he was doing on that road just like Eileen told us about Max."

"Do you believe that is just a coincidence?"

"No, I do not. We have evidence of another suspicious death of someone involved in the news industry. Didn't you always say that nothing is a coincidence when you can see the web spun in the midst of a conspiracy?"

"Imagine knowing that we've connected the dots as far west as Texas. This means, if we are correct, which I think we are, we now know this spans several states in the South. Whatever it is, it's rotten and it's beginning to smell."

The directions Emily gave them to the Sheriff's office were perfect. The drive took them about thirty minutes before they were parked in a visitor's spot in front of his office.

They got out of the car, walked inside, and were met by an off-duty deputy who had come in to take care of a few loose ends with one of his cases he was working. He directed them to the Sheriff's office which was on the second floor.

They used the stairs. "Everyone seems friendly enough," Carla said.

When they reached the second floor, they turned right and looked for the second door on the left. When they got there, it was open, and Sheriff McCrae was sitting behind his desk.

"What can I do for you folks this morning?" He stood up and went to shake hands with them both.

"Mrs. Reinhart called and told me you were coming." That brought a smile to both Howard and Carla.

"Sheriff," Howard began, "we're working on a story and one of our leads brought us to your fair city. What can you tell us about the investigation into Gerald Reinhart's death?"

"There's not much to tell, except he wrapped his car around a telephone pole just outside of Sundown."

"Were there any signs of foul play?"

"The only strange thing about this is no one seems to know why he was on that road when he was."

"Was an autopsy done?"

"Yes, but it was inconclusive. The Coroner indicated he died from the impact of the vehicle hitting that pole. The troopers estimated his speed was excessive. They estimated he was doing eighty in a thirty-five zone and lost control of the vehicle."

"Had he been drinking?"

"Look, I knew Gerry for going on nearly sixty years. We grew up together. Trust me when I tell you that he was not a drinker. He didn't even raise a glass of champagne when he and Emily attended my daughter's wedding. Instead, he raised a glass of lemonade when we went to give her a toast."

Howard shook his head, looked at Carla, and then stood up as if he planned to leave.

"Sheriff, do you have any idea where he was going when he had his accident?"

"It's funny you should mention that. I received a call from a couple who live in Morton which is not far from Sundown. They called a couple of days after Gerry died telling me that somebody saw a television crew near the tower right outside of town. They told me it looked like they were filming surrounding land. It didn't make much sense then, and it doesn't now, but if it helps you –," he said, without finishing his sentence.

Howard thanked him and then nodded for Carla that it was time to leave.

"Sheriff, here's my card. If you can think of anything else, please call me day or night. Right now, we've got to get to the airport to catch our flight to Houston."

Carla stopped at the doorway, turned around, and looked directly at Sheriff McCrae.

"It would mean a great deal to us, if you think of anything else."

They said their good-byes, went back down stairs, and got into the car. "He might be one of the law enforcement types we can use later on as a sounding board," Howard said, as he fastened his seatbelt. "He may be one of the good guys we might be able to count on."

They started for the airport where they had made arrangements the day before to catch an early flight to Houston with connections to Orlando. As they drove, she began making more detailed notes from the information they had learned and created a series of questions about the leads they wanted to discuss with everyone on Friday. One of the concerns they talked about on the flight to Houston was about their growing need to contact someone in law enforcement they thought they could trust. Most of Howard's contacts had retired. He wasn't sure about Randy's, but he thought his best hope might be through Calvin.

Just after they had boarded their plane in Houston, Carla fastened her seat belt and looked out the window as the baggage handlers were putting the luggage into the underbelly of the airplane. She leaned over toward Howard. "If nothing else, right now we've got a story that has legs."

Howard nodded in agreement. "There's only one problem: we've got no ending – only theories – and right now, a bunch of them and they aren't making much sense."

CHAPTER 18
Thursday, March 28, 2013

They were right. The story had begun to grow in size and significance. The circle was widening every time they followed another lead. It had taken on a life which Howard believed was much larger than small time reporting and local politics. It had grown into a full-blown, extensive investigative story where catastrophic consequences for everyone presently involved hinged on secrecy and how well they managed their next moves. The depth of the story wasn't yet known to them – and their footing was not on solid ground. Something about it attracted each one of them, and they could feel it beginning to pull them inward and downward by forces that were all too appealing – much like the proverbial moth to the flame.

Randy had spent most of his previous work day on local assignments, except for the time he spent with Lisa at lunch. One of the other newly hired reporters had been given the story about the apparent burglary attempt at the paper. Howard and Carla's flight had landed on time, and their drive home was uneventful. Calvin and Susan got in late that evening at his apartment, where she slept in the guest room and he catnapped on the sofa in his living room. It was the beginning of what seemed like a typical Thursday morning, with one exception. Waking up at five-thirty wasn't exactly how Calvin had planned to start his day. He woke up on the sofa in his living room with a headache. Her name was Susan.

"Calvin, where's your coffee maker?" she whispered.

Half dazed and wanting to go back to sleep, he rolled over onto his right side. He realized she was sitting on the sofa leaning slightly over him. He could smell the faint aroma of the perfume she had worn the night before. He could feel the warmth her body was generating being next to his. That's when his senses kicked in, and so did his reaction to her being on the sofa with him. He sat up quickly causing her to fall onto the floor.

He reached up and turned on the lamp that was on the end table. She stood up and started to walk away. Although his eyes were adjusting to the sudden brightness in the room, he could see she was wearing one of his navy blue and green plaid flannel shirts as a night shirt that was barely modest. It was just long enough, but it also was sufficiently provocative. He couldn't take his eyes off of her as she walked toward the kitchen.

Still limping slightly from a swollen knee and sore leg, he watched as she made her barefooted way from the living room and into the hallway that led to the kitchen. Her shoulder length, dark brown hair was a tad uneven from her night's sleep, but it only.enhanced her image to him that much more. He sat there, on the sofa, almost mesmerized by her presence when it hit him. As much as he was enjoying the early morning view, he knew she was in big trouble and someone wanted to hurt her – or worse.

He raised his voice slightly and directed it toward the kitchen. "You'll find it in the cabinet to the right of the stove. The coffee's in a canister on the counter."

"Okay. I've found it."

He stood up, put on his slippers, walked over to the doorway to the kitchen, and then leaned against the doorframe.

"You're up awfully early. How's your knee?" Still captivated by her presence in one of his flannel shirts, he walked over to the cabinet where the coffee cups were kept. He retrieved two of them, went over to the refrigerator, took out the carton of cream and placed it on the counter next to the two cups.

"Do you use sugar?"

She turned and faced him. "No, thank you. Cream will do."

"You seem totally at ease being in a stranger's house, wearing one his shirts, and standing in the middle of his kitchen bare feet and all. Aren't you the least bit worried?"

She shook her head and took a step toward him. "I'm not worried because you've been nothing but a gentleman toward me since we first met. I am flattered by the way you've been looking at me, though."

He could feel that he was blushing. "It's been a few years since there's been a woman in my house who is half my age." He paused for a second. "Don't go anywhere. I'll be right back."

He hurriedly went to the closet in the spare bedroom, selected a dark blue-colored, terry cloth robe that was hanging on the back of the closet door, and carried it to the kitchen.

"Here, try this on. If nothing more, it might help me from being attracted to you. My ex-wife used to wear this."

She laughed, took it from him, put it on, wrapped it around her and tightened the belt slightly around her waist.

"How do I look?"

He thought for a few seconds. "You are still very appealing, but also a pleasant reminder of danger in the forecast."

They both laughed.

For the next hour, they sat at the kitchen table talking about the events which occurred the evening before. She was much more open with him than she had been at their two previous meetings. Their conversation, although centered on questions about Peter Theron and what exactly it was that might have gotten him killed, drifted occasionally more into her background and how she and Peter had come to know each other.

"He was a charmer," she said, before taking a sip of coffee. "He had a way with the women. It's not that he and I were sleeping together or anything like that. We only dated a couple of times." She looked directly at him. "It was nice being around him; much like it is with my being here with you. He made me feel good about myself. Do you know what I mean?"

She could see the distant look on his face, even though he appeared to be looking in her direction. He was charmed by her beauty and was taken by her composure. She wasn't sure what to think, except she felt he was thinking about something or someone else.

"Calvin, are you okay? You look like you took a vacation there for a minute or so."

He looked directly at her. While he looked deeply into her eyes trying to understand what it was that caused him to be attracted to her, memories of his first wife, Jacquelyn, walking out on him jolted him back to the reality of the moment.

"I'm sorry. I guess I was lost in thought. I'm sorry. You were saying?"

"I was saying that Peter and I weren't an item, even though the news articles made it sound that way. He trusted me, but not enough to tell me where he hid that CD." She got up from the table, grabbed the coffee pot and refilled her cup; then she refilled his.

"My guess is that it's either at his apartment or a locked box somewhere."

"Where's his apartment?"

"He had a nice little condo on the west side of the city near the causeway."

"That's been seven months ago. Who's in it now?"

"His sister still uses it from time-to-time."

"He had a sister? Where does she live?"

"She's an airline attendant. Mostly, she stays there only a couple of nights each week. Her flight schedules take her between Tampa, Chicago, and New York City."

"Do you think she'd let us look around a bit?"

"She probably would. I'll call her later today."

He stood up, put his coffee cup in the sink, and started toward his bedroom.

"Aren't you going to sit back down with me and talk some more?"

"Susan, I'd love to, but there's someone I'd like for you to meet. After I grab a shower and shave, I'm going to call to see if the Ewing's are home yet from their Texas trip. If they are, we're going to go visit with them. You'll have a better idea of what's going on after that."

She got up from the table, put her cup into the sink as well, and started to follow him through the hallway to his bedroom. "Would you like some company?"

"Your bathroom is there on your left. The towels are already hanging on the rack. I should be ready in about ten minutes."

"What's your hurry?" she said, as she continued toward his bedroom door.

He shook his head.

CHAPTER 19
Thursday, March 28, 2013

Carla had just returned from an early morning trip to the store and had begun putting the items away when Howard came in with the morning newspaper.

"Would you like another cup of coffee?" He started to pour a cup for himself.

"Yes, but I'll get it when I'm done here."

He took both the paper and his coffee with him into the living room. After sitting down in his favorite chair, he took a sip of his coffee and then began reading the paper. Within a couple of minutes, she had joined him with her coffee, picked up the metro section from the coffee table where he had placed the rest of the sections, sat down in her favorite chair and began reading as well. The room was quiet. All you could hear was the whirling sound of the overhead fan and the ticking of the wall clock – that is until his cell phone rang.

It was Calvin.

Howard answered the call, speaking very few words. She sat there and listened to his one-sided conversation, until he disconnected the call and turned to her. "That was Calvin. He and his guest Susan are coming over in about an hour."

"He has a guest? Isn't that the name of the woman he was going to meet in Tampa?"

He grinned. "Apparently, there must be more to this than we know."

Meanwhile, Randy was just arriving at the location for his first assignment of the day. He had been instructed to interview the owner of a store that had been burglarized for the third time in less than two months. He parked his car, got out and started walking toward the outside entrance area of the building. When he reached for the handle of the door, he could see the reflection in the glass door of a vehicle parked across street. He didn't know why it seemed unusual or even why it caught his eye, but after he entered the building, he turned around and casually looked in that direction. He was glad he did.

He stepped back from the door and moved slightly to his right where he would be hidden by one of the shelving units just inside the door. He stood there for a few seconds making sure he saw what he thought he saw when he had glanced in that direction and then directly at the vehicle parked across the street.

There were two men seated in the front of the vehicle. The one behind the steering wheel was holding a camera and taking pictures. The other had slumped down into his seat making it difficult to get a good description of him. He wasn't sure why or how long they had been sitting there, but he quickly wondered if he was being followed.

He took out his cell phone and called Howard.

"I'm telling you there are two guys across the street taking pictures."

"Are you telling me you're being followed?"

"It seems like somebody's put a tail on me."

They talked for another minute, before Randy disconnected the call.

Howard looked at Carla. "Randy thinks he's being tailed by someone. He's not sure who it is, but he's certain he's being photographed."

"Do you think it could be someone from the paper? Maybe he's let something slip and they're checking it out."

"That's not like Randy. I know this: he's going to find out who they are. I just hope he's discreet about it and doesn't fly off the handle if they are following him."

In the meanwhile, Randy had gone about his assignment of interviewing the store owner, got all of the particulars he believed he would need to write the story, and then headed for the front door. He stopped a few feet from the door, peaked over the shelving, and saw that the vehicle was still parked across the street.

When he exited, he made sure not to make direct eye contact with the men in the vehicle. Nonchalantly, almost as if disinterested, he looked up and down the street before he got into his car. He took a few seconds before starting the engine, acting as if he was writing something on his note pad. Before steering the car away from the curb, he made certain he got a good view of the license plate of that other car.

As he drove, he checked his rearview mirror every few seconds to see if he was, in fact, being followed. His suspicions were confirmed within a minute after pulling into traffic. The vehicle that had been parked across the street pulled a perfect U-turn to get in behind him, but kept a reasonable distance. As he drove, he knew he was being followed, but he wondered if the men in the car following him realized they had quickly become the hunted.

The one good thing about the parking lot at the newspaper building is that it is a gated property. As he entered it, he could see the other vehicle that had followed him, for more than a half-hour, pull off to the side of the road and stop near a car wash which was across the street. When he got out of his car, he could see out of the corner of his left eye that whoever was behind the wheel of that vehicle had begun, again, to take pictures of him. Armed with the license plate number and a description of the vehicle, he entered the building and went directly to his work station.

Once seated, he reached over to start his computer. That's when he noticed a handwritten note on a piece of his orange-colored sticky note paper that Lisa had stuck to the bottom portion of his computer screen knowing he wouldn't miss seeing it. She wanted to know if he was free for dinner and had signed it with a smiley face. As he sat there smiling and reading the note, his cell phone buzzed twice. It was Lisa.

"Did you get my note?"

"I did – and yes, dinner sounds great. This time, though, we're going back to that restaurant. How about I pick you up at six-thirty?"

"I don't mind cooking."

"Let's call it a mulligan. Besides, you said it was your favorite restaurant."

She finally agreed, but he wasn't ready to hang up. "What is the name of your contact within the police department who will run plates for you?"

"Her name is Sergeant Wilma Monroe. Why do you ask?"

"I've got a plate that I need to have identified without digging into the data base here at the office."

She paused. There was a short hesitation. "Uh – of course, I can do that. What are you working on? Is there a problem?"

He didn't want to lie. "There's none that I know of. I just want to verify something about a vehicle I saw today. It would be a really big help if you'd do this. How long does it usually take to get an answer?"

"I can call you back in less than ten minutes. Is that okay?"

"That would be great. I'll stay here at the office until I hear from you."

As soon as he was finished with that call, he phoned Jerry Locker. "Have you got a minute?"

"Sure, what's on your mind?"

"I'll be right over."

After hanging up the receiver, he stood up and started for Mr. Locker's office. As he was walking, he went by the window nearest to his work station, and looked outside through the blinds. He wasn't able to see the vehicle that had followed him. *It must have given up and left,* he thought.

As he continued toward Mr. Locker's office, his cell phone buzzed, again. It was Lisa calling back with the information about the license plate. He stopped at one of the vacant desks nearest the elevator, sat down, and wrote down the information.

"The car is registered to someone named Clyde Vicente." She gave him his address and phone number as well. "Does this help?"

"Oh yes, it does very much. Thank you. This calls for dessert as well this evening."

"This meal could be very expensive, if you're not careful."

"It's already paying off and we haven't even eaten one of those fresh yeast rolls yet."

They said their good-byes, while he continued walking to Mr. Locker's office.

When he got there, the secretary greeted him. "He's expecting you."

"Is he in a good mood?"

She grinned. "It's better than usual."

He thanked her, then opened the door and went in.

"Jerry, I've got a proposition for you. When I was much younger, I use to carry a camera with me to help with the details for whatever story I was working on. What's the chance your budget will allow for me to get one of those new digital gizmos?"

He leaned back and to his right and reached into the bottom right hand drawer of his desk. He pulled out a case for what obviously was a camera. Lifting it by the long leather strap that was attached to it, he then handed it to Randy.

"Ask and you shall receive," he said, as he grinned.

Randy opened the case and recognized that it was indeed one of the newer models of digital cameras. His was an older model, but it was nothing compared to the one Mr. Locker was handing to him.

"This thing has a bunch of bells and whistles on it." He inspected it carefully.

"Take good care of it. It set my department back over fourteen hundred dollars." He reached behind him and handed him a larger leather case. "Use this to store it in when you're not on the road." He stood up. "There's an instruction booklet in that case, too. If I were you, I'd read that thoroughly first thing before using it."

He thanked him. "I promise that I will take good care of this. Do you need for me to sign anything for it?"

Before he could finish asking, Mr. Locker had pushed a hand receipt across the desk and requested his signature.

Randy, still smiling, signed the receipt. "I promise. You won't regret this."

"I think I already have. Don't you have something you need to be doing right now?"

He took the hint and left.

While walking back to his work station, being back at work felt right to him. He didn't think he'd ever think it or say it, but he was beginning to feel that old rush he'd get when he and his colleagues were deep into a story that couldn't wait to be written. As he walked, he felt invigorated and with each step he began to feel a sense of purpose. It was more than just him and his colleagues digging into Max's death. It was about being committed and looking forward to something. It was about him remembering how he felt when he realized he first wanted to become a reporter. The juice started to flow, and he felt like he could leap tall buildings in a single bound. He even started whistling. He hadn't done that in long time.

When he got back to his desk, he sat down and immediately did a web search on Clyde Vicente. Nothing of importance popped up, but that didn't stop him. He went into the paper's resource data base and searched his name there. The only result he could find was an article printed in April 2007 about the purchase of a building in downtown Orlando that had been put up for public auction. Clyde Vicente won the bidding frenzy that day with a bid of two million three hundred thousand dollars. What got his attention in the article was the next sentence: He paid for it with cash.

He sat back into his chair just looking at the screen. He began to wonder about the purchase price and method of payment. *How does someone come up with that amount of cash for an auction in downtown Orlando?* He got up from his chair, grabbed his newly acquired camera, and headed for the exit.

As he was nearing the lobby, his cell phone buzzed. Howard was trying to reach him.

"Are you busy?"

"I'm on my way to the records hall in Orlando. What's up?"

"Carla and I got home a day early. Are we still on for lunch at *Harry's?*"

"Yes, as far as I know, but I've got dinner plans tonight. What's Calvin doing?"

"You wouldn't believe me if I told you. He's got a guest named Susan at his house."

"What? Did I hear you correctly that he's got a woman staying with him? Isn't that the name of the reporter he was supposed to meet in Tampa?"

"You got it right. I'm sure you'll get a chance to meet her tonight at my place. Maybe we should skip our usual meeting at lunch and just meet here after dinner. Carla's cooking meatloaf."

Randy, not wanting to give away his recent budding relationship with Lisa, realized he needed to rethink his dinner plans so that he could meet with Calvin and Howard.

"Let me call you back to make sure my work schedule is clear. If there's a problem, I'll let you know."

They both disconnected the call.

Randy stopped in the lobby to call Lisa. Before the call connected, he hung up because he realized that he wasn't sure exactly what he was going to tell her. Plus, he wasn't sure if the other members of his group would appreciate his skipping the meeting or how they would react to his inviting her in on their undertaking. He didn't get much chance to think about it because she returned his call.

"Did you call? Your number flashed on my screen for a second."

He hesitated. "Can I call you right back? I'm kind of in the middle of something that I need to really get done right now. I'll call you back in just a few minutes. Okay?"

She agreed. He immediately called Howard.

"Hey, have you got a minute? There's something I need to talk with you about."

CHAPTER 20
Early Evening, Thursday, March 28, 2013

Randy stood outside Lisa's front door for almost three minutes debating whether or not to go through with the plan that he and Howard had discussed. He knew it would be a gamble, but he believed taking this chance might prove useful because he believed the odds of getting the story right were stacked against them as they moved forward with their investigation. Also, he believed that having one more head, especially as becoming and attractive as Lisa's, to help them work through the myriad of information was worth rolling the dice.

Howard had agreed with him, even though he didn't really know Lisa. He had only heard briefly about her, while he was still with the paper. Randy convinced him that she would be an asset to the team, after he explained her background and contacts she had made over the many years with the paper.

He hadn't realized that those three minutes had slipped by so quickly, until he checked his watch. "Let's do this," he whispered, and then rang the doorbell.

She opened the door and let him in. "I'll be ready in just a minute," she said, as she quickly walked into her hallway that led to the back of the apartment. "Please, make yourself comfortable."

Two minutes later while he was enjoying the view of the sunset through the sliding glass doors, she reappeared. "Okay, I'm ready."

When he turned around, he was struck by her presence. She looked amazingly together. Her outfit was perfect, and she stood close enough to him that the aroma of her cologne filled the air around them both with a hint of excitement.

He didn't say anything at first. The look on his face must have been priceless because she reached out and touched his right arm.

She smiled. "See something you like?"

He was at a loss for words for just a moment, but remembered why he was there.

First, he cleared his throat. "Are you ready for an adventure?"

"What? I thought we were going out to dinner."

"We are, but not where you think."

She picked up her coat and purse, and they went out the door. He followed behind making sure the door was locked. She handed him the key and he locked the deadbolt.

As he drove to the restaurant, she talked about work and other mundane things that seemed to help pass the time. Occasionally, she'd ask him a question about how his work was going, and he'd respond cordially and matter-of-factly. During the ride, she never mentioned his looking into the rear-view mirror to see if they were being followed. *If they're behind me,* he thought, *they must be using a different vehicle.*

After arriving at and entering the restaurant, he whispered something to the maître d'. He then turned to Lisa. "Follow him – and please, don't ask any questions."

She followed him through a set of doors that led to a back-office area. With a quizzical look on her face, she turned and asked Randy what was going on.

"This is part of the adventure," he responded.

Before the maître d' went out the back door, he asked them to wait for just a moment, until he had returned. It seemed that those twenty seconds lasted for an hour, but Randy was relieved when he returned and told him everything was ready. He slipped him some cash that brought a smile and heartfelt 'Thank you' from the man, before they exited.

Just outside that door was a taxi waiting for them. Randy opened the rear driver's side door for her, and she got in. When they were both seated and the cab had pulled out of the parking lot, she turned to Randy and was about to speak, but he preemptively spoke first.

"I apologize for the surreptitious actions, and I truly hope you have not been offended. I just can't be sure right now that we're not being followed."

"Followed? Who would be following us and for what?"

"I'm not exactly sure." He turned to look out the rear window of the cab.

"What have you done?"

"It's not what I've done. What I'm about to tell you is known to very few people. You're about to meet them for dinner and your discretion in all of this is important."

As they rode toward the Ewing's, Randy began to lay out the story he and the others had been working on. He knew he didn't have enough time to tell her all of the particulars, and he knowingly didn't want a cab driver for an audience, but he was able to explain why they were going through all of this.

Before they arrived, she asked some very difficult questions related to the motive for Max's death, and he didn't feel it was the appropriate time to respond. He promised, however, that all of her questions would be answered, before she returned home.

When the cab pulled into the Ewing's driveway, Randy noticed that Calvin had already arrived. He paid the cabbie; they both got out and walked to the front door.

Before he rang the doorbell, he turned toward her. "Last chance," he whispered.

He waited for a few seconds, before pushing the lighted doorbell button. Right after that, he turned toward her again, only this time he didn't say anything. He just looked at her – and she looked at him. Their eyes locked on to each other. It was when she smiled, and gave him a slight squeeze of his left hand, that reassured him he had made the right decision.

When co-workers meet, social gatherings can often reflect the everyday, mini-world cliques that form at the office. Tonight was different. From the outset of their gathering that evening, all of them realized that each one brought something unique to what they were about to undertake. Much to Randy's pleasure, there was a collegial bond that formed between Lisa and Susan. It made the initial greetings seem more than cordial and go that much easier.

As a group, they spent the first fifteen minutes or so just getting to know one another. Calvin kept his distance from Susan, but he was close enough to step into the conversation if he felt it was warranted. He wasn't afraid of what she'd do; he was afraid of what she might say that could mislead the others about her stay at his house.

They all stayed in the living room, until it was time to eat. Carla enlisted Susan's and Lisa's help in the kitchen, while Randy showed off his new camera to Howard and Calvin. They got a big laugh watching him try to figure out what all the buttons meant because he hadn't completely finished reading the booklet of instructions. He managed, however, to take a few candid shots of the group before the evening was over.

Carla's meal was superb. Everyone agreed: the meatloaf was delicious. Lisa raved over the potatoes au gratin. Susan loved everything and ate like it was her last day on earth. Randy and Calvin had an extra helping of the homemade yeast rolls that came piping hot to the table. Afterwards, they all pitched in and helped to clear the dining room table. It only took a few minutes before the kitchen was clean; and then, everyone was invited to join Howard on the porch for coffee.

Once everyone was seated, he stood up and began telling them about their trip to Austin, Texas and their side trip to Lubbock. Then, he turned the floor over to Randy, who spoke for another ten minutes. He spoke about how he picked up on someone who had started following him earlier that day. He then turned the floor over to Calvin who spoke for ten minutes telling them about his and Susan's incident in the parking lot at the restaurant.

When he was done, Lisa pointed to the paneling. "I see you've started your story board."

"Yes, and we've got several things to post tonight," Howard said, as he set down his cup. "Sadly, we have begun to see several pieces of a twisted puzzle begin to fall into place."

Lisa walked over to the board and began reading the articles. Carla retrieved the coffee pot and began refreshing everyone's cup. "Who's ready for dessert?"

Susan, still limping slightly, walked over to Calvin and stood very close to him. "Have you spoken to Carla about my staying here for a few nights?"

He looked at her. "No – I haven't yet."

"I wish you wouldn't. I don't want to be a burden or imposition on you, but I really wish you'd let me stay with you." She paused and then leaned closer and whispered in his ear. "I promise that I will behave myself. Just let me stay with you. It's only going to be for a brief while."

He didn't reply. Instead, he thanked Carla, who had already started to refresh his coffee. He looked at Susan, nodded his head, and went back to where he had been sitting.

Lisa, who had looked through some of the material already posted, got Howard's attention. "I don't think you remember me, but I did attend your retirement party at the paper. I was only there for a moment or two. I used to work directly for Leo Clark, and I know the two of you go way back together."

"I haven't seen Leo in months. He hasn't retired, yet?"

"No, he hasn't. He's working in the political division now; but, he mostly handles copy editing and sometimes handles the scheduling for local events. I still work with him occasionally, but I see him more at the copy bin on the second floor. It seems he's been living there a lot lately."

Carla came into the room right then carrying a three-layered cake. "No, I didn't do this," she announced. "It jumped into my grocery cart this afternoon. I took pity on it and brought it home." After serving everyone a healthy slice of the chocolate-on-chocolate cake, she returned it to the kitchen and then rejoined the others.

Howard got everyone seated and refocused on the paneling. "We've added a few more things to the story. The question now is," he said, before pausing to look at both Susan and Lisa, "who's going to take the next step? Randy's gone back to work, and from the sounds of things I don't think we need to go public about what we're doing – at least not yet."

Lisa joined in. "From what I see on the board, there seems to be a connection in the alleged accidental deaths that cannot and should not be overlooked."

Susan spoke up. "I still can't see why someone would want me dead. I'm telling you I don't know anything. I admit that I knew Peter, but somebody thinks I know where the CD is. Calvin and I can look for it, but our leads are limited."

Carla got out of her seat and walked over to the door to the patio. She turned and pointed to the information on the paneling. "Suppose we ask this question: Since the connection seems to be in the communications business, what is the common link between all of them? We haven't established a theory that links them together."

"We must be missing one or more of the connections that will complete the network," Howard said.

The room went silent. He looked at each of them, before he spoke again. "All of these communication connections are with relatively minor news or television companies. What if the connection is much larger than these little companies we've been looking at?"

They all looked at each other around the room.

"There's one way we can find out," Lisa said boldly. "I know someone who can find that information for us." Then, she walked over to where Susan was seated and sat down next to her.

"You know more than you think you do. Some how you're going to figure out how you're connected – and it might surprise you. Right now, it's hard to find it – let alone see it."

"She's right," Calvin supposed, nodding his head in agreement. "When we were in the back end of that restaurant, you kept looking over your shoulder like you were expecting the Boogie Man. What, or who, were you expecting?"

Susan leaned slightly forward in her chair. "Does anyone here know anything about a guy named Ben Rozier?"

Lisa nodded her head. "Yes, I do. He's a pretty bad guy from somewhere near or around the Orlando area. He's been connected to several cases of assault or battery, but to my knowledge never convicted. He seems to always end up beating the rap. I remember a story I did a while back where he was involved in the disappearance of a young lady who was supposed to testify against one of the kingpins running drugs in the state. She disappeared and ended up being found in a shallow grave near Polk City. The prosecutors said there was insufficient evidence to charge him or arrest him in that case, despite two different witnesses who described him perfectly as the man who strong-armed her into a van. Nothing ever came of it. There were no prints and no DNA evidence that could link him to the crime."

Susan looked at Calvin. "He's the Boogie Man. I was volunteering my time with the local food sharing service centers and that's where I first met him. He was thought to be a homeless person by most of the business men in the area, until he started leaning on them. He'd show up at the center looking for groceries pretty regularly. The director there refused to serve him one day and offered him counseling, instead. The next morning the director was in the hospital with three broken ribs and a very badly bruised and bloodied face. He wouldn't testify against him and no charges were ever brought."

"He's a two-bit thug," Calvin added. "He can't be the one who's behind this. He's the enforcer who's paid do to the dirty work in this area. How do we explain Austin or Atlanta? More importantly Susan, how can you possibly be seriously connected to this guy?"

She shook her head and shrugged her shoulders. "I don't know."

Howard reiterated his notion. "There's got to be a connection much higher up."

Lisa had been on her phone for a few seconds speaking with one of her contacts. "That was Josh. He knows the ins-and-outs of the market and the latest goings-on in the world of corporate dealings. If anyone can find what we think is a corporate connection with these organizations, he can."

"Can he be trusted?" Carla asked.

"I know he can. He's my brother."

Again, the room went silent. The quietness was unnerving.

Lisa looked at Howard. "My brother is a market analyst who used to trade on the floor of the New York Stock Exchange. He'll find out for us, but it might take a little while. My little brother is also known for his discretion."

Howard leaned forward slightly. "That's not what I'm worried about. We seem to be inching our way along with this thing to a point that now we may be dealing with thugs and strong-armed types. We've got very little leverage with them, and frankly I'd like nothing better than to stay clear of them."

Randy stood up and walked over to the paneling. "We need someone who can help us with that. Otherwise, we'll be sitting ducks when the season opens on reporters. Does anyone have any ideas?"

Calvin raised his hand. "I know a private investigator that might be exactly what we're looking for. He can handle himself, plus he carries."

The room went silent, again. Carla stood up and started for the kitchen. "Does anyone want more cake?"

"Yes, I would," Howard said. Then, he stood up and followed her into the kitchen.

Randy returned to his seat, sat down, and looked at Calvin. "So, what's this guy's name?"

"His name is Abraham Zaragova and he's been in the business for over twenty years."

"You're talking a bunch of money to hire one of those guys. We don't have that kind of money."

Howard came back onto the porch with a slice of cake in a napkin and rejoined the conversation. "It won't hurt to ask him will it? Calvin, what do you think?"

"I suppose he'll listen. I've known him a long time and even threw him a bone or two while I was still with the paper. That was a long time ago, however."

'We need to do something," Susan said. "We're no match for guys like Rozier."

Carla, who had just returned from the kitchen, sat down next to Susan. "You're right, but we don't have the kind of money these guys require."

Calvin stood up. "Maybe we just need to frame our request so that he'll see this as an opportunity."

Randy chuckled slightly. "You mean offer him a deal he'll find hard to refuse?"

"Why shouldn't we?" Howard asked. "We need his help and maybe he just might want to be a part of the greater good."

The next hour went by quickly. They discussed at length Susan's predicament. Calvin agreed to allow her to stay at his place for a few days. His immediate concern was her conspicuous absence from work might be a problem for her. So, he recommended that she take a few days of vacation to cover her trail for now – or at least until things had calmed down.

Randy brought up his concern about being followed and that his car may have been followed to Lisa's house. The group understood what that meant, but Lisa was adamant about staying in her apartment. She didn't feel threatened by any of the possibilities. Instead, she believed it was necessary for her to give the appearance that everything was normal at work and that nothing had changed.

Howard was concerned about saving and storing what he called the 'evidence,' making sure that there would be back-up copies of articles and photographs. Randy and Calvin promised to help.

They had met for three hours, and no one wanted to call it an evening – that is until Lisa leaned over to Randy and whispered. "You need to take me home because I've got to get my beauty rest. Besides, we both have to go to work bright and early in the morning."

She and Susan got up, gathered their coats and started walking toward the hallway that led to the front door. Randy and Calvin followed closely behind. They waited for their cab to arrive.

After agreeing to meet on Saturday evening for dinner at six o'clock, they all said their good-byes and got into their respective vehicles. Howard and Carla waved at them as they backed out of the driveway and drove off.

"Do you think we got it right tonight?"

Carla smiled. "Yes, I think we did. I was somewhat amused how Calvin seemed to shy away from Susan during the entire evening, but wasn't the least bit shy about taking her home."

Howard smiled and nodded his head in agreement. "I think there may be something happening between Randy and Lisa. What do you think?"

She laughed. "That woman is in full hunting mode and she's got him in her sights."

CHAPTER 21
Early Friday Morning, March 29, 2013

Progress isn't difficult to define, but it sometimes can be hard to recognize. It can take on different forms or be sporadic. It can creep up on you without you even knowing it or when you least expect it. At other times, it can come at you so quickly it will knock you down as it thunders right by you. Whatever it is, it is measurable. The standards by which some choose to measure it can be cruel, especially when the price is counted in human lives.

Calvin woke up at five-thirty that morning wondering how long it would be before someone would come looking for Susan. Although he hadn't said much the night before, he considered that the bottom line to what they had all agreed to do. He recognized the seriousness of what they had stumbled into, and he saw the ugly possibilities of what their investigation could lead to, especially if they decided to be proactive. He knew that Susan was like a magnet that attracted trouble; and no matter what, it would not ignore her as she approached it. He believed that at some point the bad guys were going to show up. This morning, he began to set about putting his feet to an idea.

When he went to the bedroom door to wake her, it was slightly ajar, and he could hear her snoring. He fought back his desire to laugh, quietly opened the door gradually, walked over to where she was lying, reached down and nudged her shoulder to try to wake her. There was no response. So, he called her name softly – still no response.

At first, he was glad and felt honored that she was able to sleep so soundly, despite all of her problems, but he believed it was time for her to start earning her keep.

He called out her name louder the second time. By the third effort, she finally responded.

"What is it?"

"You've got to get up because we're leaving for Tampa in a little while. There are things that we need to get done before the weekend. So get up, get dressed, and get moving. Breakfast is on the table."

While she was getting dressed, he went back to his bedroom, sat down on his bed, and opened the drawer to his nightstand. There under a few old telephone books was 'Betsy.'

Betsy was his name for the .45 caliber pistol he had purchased the year before he got out of the service. Since then, he made time each month to go to the pistol range to keep his skills sharp. When he was on active duty, he had qualified as Expert in its use. He could still disassemble, reassemble, load it and fire a round in less than forty-five seconds. When he spoke about Betsy, he left you with the impression that there was a special relationship between the two of them. If he spoke to you about Betsy, then you possessed a special relationship with him as well.

After putting Betsy and four clips of ammunition in a padded, leather carrying bag, he went to the garage, opened the vehicle's glove compartment, and placed it inside. After closing and locking it securely, he went back into the house to check on Susan. He found her sitting at the kitchen table.

"Okay, I'm up and ready to go. What were you doing in the garage?"

"I was making preparations for the trip." He poured a cup of coffee and sat down with her at the table. "Did you want something to eat?"

"Can we stop on the way, instead? My stomach hasn't shown up for work yet."

Some people are seriously so not morning people. She wasn't most mornings, but her looks on this morning fooled him. As he studied her, he could tell she was tired, but her posture conveyed that she was trying to make the best of a difficult situation. Her outfit drew attention to her physically fit body, while her make-up was such that it heightened the roundness of her eyes and the upturn of her lips. He thought she might think he was staring at her because to him, she looked gorgeous and he was enjoying the view.

"What's the name of the perfume you have on? It's not the same as the one you were wearing last night."

"Do you like it? It's my favorite. It's called, 'Wild Intimidation.'"

"Seriously — it's called what?"

"Actually, that's my name for it. It sounds more interesting than just 'Aria Fresca.'"

"Do you do that with all of your perfumes? I mean, do you rename them?"

"No, I only rename the ones that seem to do what I want them to do."

He turned slightly to his right. "We better get going. We've got a three-hour trip ahead of us."

He stood up and started for the garage. As he went by her, she reached out and grabbed his left hand. He stopped and looked down at her, as she was looking up at him.

"Thank you," she said.

The look on her face was sincere and revealed her caring for him. The sound of her voice was one of heartfelt thankfulness.

Instinctively, he reached down and touched the top of her left shoulder. She stood up and embraced him. It was so quick that he hardly knew what happened, until he found himself standing in the middle of his kitchen hugging her in return.

After a few seconds, she leaned back and looked up at him. Their eyes met, only this time her look told him she wanted more. He knew that look – and it was inviting. He was aware of her directness and he respected that. But right now, he knew he did not have the time or the luxury for an affair. He hugged her once again, kissed her on the forehead, and started to break the embrace. She resisted slightly, but finally let go.

"We've got to get onto the road, or we'll be late."

"What's so urgent?" she asked, before picking up her purse and following him toward the garage.

"We've got a ten o'clock meeting with an old friend of mine."

He stopped and turned around so he could speak directly to her. "I thought you said you'd behave yourself."

She moved closer so that she could lean in and whisper to him as she walked by. "You can't blame a person for trying."

He watched her as she continued walking, taking in every movement she made, until she turned the corner leading to the garage.

Yes sir, you are trouble with a capital T, he thought as he continued to walk. *My mother told me about women like you, but I'm beginning to think she might have been wrong.*

Later that morning, Randy was sitting at his desk, with his feet propped up on its corner, and his keyboard to his computer in his lap. He was looking over his copy of an article he had written, when Mrs. Rhoden approached him and pointed at the phone on his desk.

"Mr. Tomlin, there's a phone call for you on line two. The gentleman wouldn't say what his name was or what he wanted. And before you ask, he said not to transfer his call but to deliver the message in person."

"Tell him I'm not in."

She looked down at him with her eyes peering over the top rims of her glasses that had fallen slightly onto the bridge of her nose. "Now you know I am not going to do that. It's impolite, and I would rather not lie to someone simply because you don't want to be bothered." She started to walk away, but turned to speak to him. "You'll be a better person for taking his call." She continued on her way back to her desk.

He picked up the receiver. "Who is this?"

"Whatever you're doing, stop and write down the information I'm about to give you. Make sure you check it out. You can thank me later."

Whoever it was calling him rattled off two different addresses. He frantically wrote them down on the back of a folder that had been on his desk for two days. When he finished, he leaned back into his chair.

"What am I supposed to do with these?"

"You're a smart guy. Go check it out." Without saying another word, he was gone. Randy tried to ask him another question, but all he got was the monotonous sound of a dial tone.

He got up from his desk, picked up the folder with those addresses that he had written on it, and walked over to where Mrs. Rhoden was seated. "Tell me something, can we trace where that call came from?"

"Of course we can, Mr. Tomlin. It won't give you an address, but you will be able to know from what phone number he called."

"Who do I contact about that?"

"I'll take care of that for you," she said matter-of-factly. "It should take about ten minutes. I'll bring the information to you as soon as I receive it."

"Do we still have that phone book where I can look up addresses? You know – it provides us with phone numbers and vice-versa."

"You'll find the other area codes right there," she said, while pointing to a group of shelves with several different phone books on them. "The information for the local area codes has been uploaded onto the data base." She wrote down how to access the information from the paper's data base, the pass word needed, and handed it to him. "Just make sure, that if you take any of those books back to your desk, you put them back where you found them."

"Thank you very much," he said. "I'd give you a hug, but I don't want either of us to get into trouble for doing that."

She started to blush, which he realized immediately.

"Mrs. Rhoden, I apologize for embarrassing you like that. I just meant –," he said, before she cut him off.

"I know what you meant." She waved at him as if she were chasing a fly off of her desk. "Go on about your business. I'll bring the phone number information to you shortly."

He thanked her, again, and went over to the shelves and began looking for the phone numbers connected to the addresses he had been given by the caller. He knew that once he had a phone number, he'd not only have their address and phone number, but he'd have their name as well.

He found the book he needed and carried it back to his desk. As he searched the first of the two addresses he had written down, he began thinking about the caller. He hadn't recognized the voice, but there was something familiar about his tone and speaking patterns. Try as he could, he wasn't able to make any connection.

He found the phone number listed for that address. Next he went to the computer data base and looked up the phone number. It seemed like the search engine took forever, but it finally produced the name of the person who lived at that address: Reece Sheppard.

He stared at the name for a few seconds. He bolted out of this chair and ran over to where Mrs. Rhoden was still seated.

"Can you get me an appointment with Mr. Rayner?"

"I can try." She picked up the telephone receiver and selected the extension for his office.

"Hello, Joyce? This is Patricia Rhoden. What's the chance of getting an appointment for Mr. Randy Tomlin in to see Mr. Rayner today?"

He stood quietly watching and waiting for some kind of response from her.

She hung up the phone and smiled. "You're in. Your appointment is set for twelve-thirty today."

He went around to where she was seated and hugged her, and she hugged him back.

She looked up at him. "What's so urgent?"

"You wouldn't believe me if I told you. Let's just say it's important and let it go at that."

He went back to his desk, sat down and began looking up the other address, until he found the phone number located for that address. Then he searched the phone number in the paper's data base and came up with the other name. It was Leland Phillips.

He stood up immediately. "Eureka!" he whispered.

He took out his cell phone and called Howard. "I'll be over in just a little bit. You've got to see what I've discovered."

"We were just leaving to go grocery shopping."

"It can keep. Stay put. I'll be there shortly."

"Okay, but will you at least tell me what this is all about?"

"It's all about control and power. I'll be there shortly."

CHAPTER 22
Later that morning

Political campaigns have seen politicians overcome the damage done when their youthful indiscretions were uncovered and aired by the media. Even after being given the ugly facts from different media outlets about how wayward the candidate may had been, the public has proven amply forgiving, often allowing the candidate to survive the inevitable attack from an opponent, perhaps even surge in public appeal, for however long the news cycle may last.

Many, who have made what some would have considered to be a slam dunk run for public office, have fallen by the wayside in the eyes of the public during those campaigns, not because of the disdain the public developed for the candidate's errant behavior, but because of how poorly the candidate was handled by a cadre of handlers during the media's concentrated effort to expose those headline-grabbing deeds.

The phone call Randy took wasn't from someone spilling his guts about a good person gone bad, it was about how political posturing can be quickly and so easily forgotten – even by the very people and institutions who supposedly are the watchdogs and advocates for the American public in general. He was as shocked as anyone could be when the little bit of research he accomplished led him to the doorsteps of Reece Sheppard and Leland Phillips.

He had forgotten the news headlines that had been generated in 1998 during the mid-term elections. He had forgotten how the major news media and their affiliates would often routinely overlook some stories, after a few days of front-page postings, for more timely or juicy affairs. He had forgotten the heated and harsh words that had been exchanged by those two men, once the Feds had become involved in the accusations made by one about the other. He had forgotten how adamant Reece was about retaliating and how Leland seemed immune to any of those threats. It wasn't that he just failed to remember; it was old news and it didn't seem to matter anymore – that is until now.

Now, all of the pieces to an old story, which had flourished because of the reporting by major news outlets for more than a month over fifteen years earlier, began to resurface and he saw what he thought could be the underpinning for the big picture. He was ecstatic because it reinforced the narrative to what they had been working on for a few short weeks. The story suddenly became better defined and exponentially gave it believable proportion and depth. It was as if a heavy fog had been lifted clearly marking where the stepping stones were.

When Mrs. Rhoden handed him the phone number the mysterious caller had called from, she knew that something was out-of-place. "This number is one of ours," she said, after handing him the slip of paper. "I don't know from which phone or what department, but that call came from within our building."

"Are you sure? There's no possibility of error?"

She responded firmly. "There's no error here. The communications technician confirmed it."

He thanked her, went back to his desk, grabbed his coat and headed for the exit. He stopped in the lobby to call Mr. Locker to inform him about his twelve-thirty appointment with Mr. Rayner and to let him know he was more than welcome to join them.

As he walked to the parking area, he became keenly aware, again, that someone might be watching him. The last thing he wanted was to lead whoever it was to Howard's house. Everyone had promised to make every effort to keep that location private. To throw anyone who might be watching or waiting off guard, he got into his car, drove toward the exit while looking to see if anyone was sitting and waiting across the street at the car wash for him to leave. Without leaving the safety of the gated parking lot, he pulled into one of the last remaining parking spots near the exit, turned off the engine, and took out his newly acquired camera that had come with an exchangeable, multi-functional 70-200mm telephoto zoom lens. Using its zooming capabilities, not only was he able to look for anyone sitting in a nearby car, he could clearly see them and capture their image, making certain that if he was going to be followed he would have proof of it later.

He sat there for a few minutes surveying nearby parked vehicles looking for suspects. Satisfied that he was at least able to get out of the parking lot without being followed, he restarted the engine and drove the vehicle into traffic.

He decided to take the long route making several turns along the way. He constantly checked his rear-view mirror looking to see if any of the vehicles behind him had been tailing him for any lengthy time. Satisfied that he was not being followed, he turned onto a major access road that would take him directly to Howard's house.

As he drove, he thought about what Mrs. Rhoden had told him and that the technician confirmed the caller had made that call from within the building. It troubled him that someone who worked at the paper, other than Lisa and himself, knew about what they were working on. It troubled him because he was concerned for her safety.

Whoever he is, he thought, *at least he was helpful.*

While he was still about ten minutes from Howard's house, Calvin and Susan were making excellent time toward Tampa. The traffic on I-4 was smoother than usual for a Friday morning, and it didn't hurt Calvin's feelings that Susan wasn't full of questions about the trip. She realized that whatever Calvin had up his sleeve, he was looking out for her. Although not knowing the location and purpose of the meeting, she believed he had a plan and that he would let her know more about it as the time approached. She decided, however, to move it along a little faster.

"Who are we going to meet with? Is it anyone I might know?"

"Yes, I'm pretty sure you know her. She's your boss, Mrs. Vivian Alexander."

"Why in the world are you taking me to meet with her? She's the last person who might have anything to say to you about what happened at the parking lot the other night. All she's probably going to do is fuss at me."

"How do you know that? She might know something you don't. After all, she is your boss, and I'm sure she would like a copy of that police report."

"I'd rather not do this, if it's okay with you. I don't see any good coming out of this."

He had expected her to say that. "How many stories have you worked on that started out as nothing stories, but ended up writing themselves?"

She thought about that for a moment. "Um – I've worked on maybe three or four like that over the years. But, they were all stories that had been assigned to me by someone other than her. Plus, they were all human-interest stories with a delicious twist."

"You don't have to sit in on the conversation, but I think we need to know more about the assignments she's been giving you lately. She may not be steering you away from something. She may actually be unwittingly steering you toward something, instead. Did it ever occur to you she just might be able to fill in the blanks – so to speak?"

She turned slightly in her seat so that she could look directly at him. "To what exactly are you referring? Do you have any idea what you are looking for? So far, all you've done is to speak in something just short of riddles. You could be a little more forthcoming, you know."

As he drove, he wasn't sure how much he should tell her about what he and Howard had discussed. He knew she wanted to know, but he wasn't sure of when the timing would be right to tell her. He thought about it, and reasoned now might be better than later.

"Susan, you need to listen and not interrupt as I explain this to you. I know you'll have a thousand questions as I go through this, but I want you to just listen for now. Agreed?"

She nodded her head in agreement.

He looked at her for just a moment, as his hands tightened their grip on the steering wheel. "Do you agree not to interrupt?"

"Yes, I promise. I won't say anything else until you're finished."

"Good. Now we're on level footing"

For the next forty-five minutes, he told her of the conversation he and Howard had, about what they suspected, who might be involved, why they needed to return to Tampa, and what they would be looking for while they were in the Tampa area. He explained that he believed her life was in danger, and that it was possible her boss had no clue as to the significance of what was beginning to unfold. He and Howard believed that the connection her boss had to Peter Theron was more than circumstantial, and that her link to him was something more than just colleagues working on a story. He believed whatever it was that entangled the two of them would not only prove disastrous, but deadly. They both believed, especially Howard, Peter's death was no accident and her boss was quickly becoming a target as well.

As she sat there, trying hard not to interrupt, she was finding it difficult to grasp how she figured into all the incidentals and details. She figured out she was a pawn in all of this, but she failed to see how important her role was and how it was going to play out. He reiterated to her how none of this seemed to be a circumstance of pure chance, but of some elaborate conspiracy that had not been fully understood by anyone other than those who started it. When he mentioned the part of Peter's death connected to the parking lot incident, she couldn't restrain herself from asking a question.

"You're trying to tell me someone wants me dead."

"I thought you promised not to ask any questions."

"That wasn't a question. It was categorically a concluding statement based on what you have explained to me so far. Am I right?"

He looked at her, and then he let out a sigh. "I believe so. That's why you're going to stick close to me today, and I don't want any arguments about that. When we get finished with our meeting, we're going to your apartment, collect a few of your things, and head back to my place. Are you good with that?"

"You mentioned the word conspiracy more than once this morning. You're not going paranoid on me are you?"

"If you don't believe me, ask Peter Theron, Gerald Reinhart, Max Leopard, and about three or four others we're beginning to connect in all of this. I'd understand if it was limited to one location or even one city. We're talking here about crossing beyond state borders and about some pretty powerful people who have extensive connections with a host of resources."

"So what is it you believe all of these powerful people have conspired to do? What is it you believe these people are after?"

He looked at her for just a second, and then turned his attention back to the highway.

"Well, what is it you think they're after?"

"What they're after," he started, "they've already partially achieved. Now, what they plan to do with it is the real question."

She turned and looked out the window. She watched as the world went by her at seventy miles per hour. "What are they planning to do, whoever they are, with whatever they've achieved? I'm not following."

"I told you that you'd have a thousand questions."

She turned and looked at him, again. "How stupid do you think I am?"

"It's isn't about whether or not you're stupid." He glanced at her for just a moment. "I don't believe for a minute that you're stupid. What I do believe is that you have a blind side that's a mile wide and you've been over compensating. I can tell you know something's not right. Why else would you have behaved like you did back at that restaurant?"

"You're going there, again?"

"Yes, I am because it's exactly the kind of thing that I'm talking about. We've stumbled upon something. I'm pretty sure they know about us, but they haven't yet begun to react. Plus, we have no idea who to look out for. I'm sure they don't know how much we've discovered so far because they're not sure where to look or how many they're dealing with."

"Then why are you worried so?"

"Because –," he said, but stopped talking and pointed at a road sign they were fast approaching. "Are you still hungry?"

"Yes, I am."

"Good. I think we'll stop there for a few minutes," he said, and then signaled to move over into the right-hand lane. "I wouldn't mind using the little boys' room."

She turned and looked at him. "I could use some breakfast now – and some very strong coffee"

"I think we can manage that," he said, as he turned off of the highway.

CHAPTER 23
March 29, 2013, Friday morning, 9:30 am

"What do you think?" Randy asked

"You have no idea who it was that called you?" Howard poured both of them a cup of coffee and pointed at the sugar bowl. "But, you are positive it was someone in the building?"

"Yes, Mrs. Rhoden confirmed that for me through the techie people down in the communications division."

Howard walked on to the porch. Randy followed directly behind. "She wasn't able to tell me where exactly inside the building the call came from, but she thought she might be able to track that down later today. She wasn't making any promises, but she said she'd try."

Howard stood next to the pieces of paneling and looked at the leads that had begun to take up a considerable amount of space. "This is huge," he started, then turned to face Randy, "because when Reece Sheppard went to prison, he promised he would get his pound of flesh when he got out. Have you been able to locate Leland?"

"Actually, yes I have his last known address and phone number. I have the same for Reece. Isn't technology amazing?"

They sat down and started sharing their personal memories of the stories that had captured the headlines, and the imagination of the country, for a solid month back then. Howard made the point of how well both of them knew so many of the people who were involved.

"Leland had only been with the paper for a couple of months, when he was assigned to the political desk with Leo. I remember how much Leo hated having to cover for him because Leland kept over-reaching in his daily column. It was tough on him because the story just kept growing on its own. It didn't seem to matter what he did, some other news organization or television group would use Leland's column as gospel and run with it as their lead story on the evening news. Leo hated every moment of it, until the day Reece was sentenced by the judge."

"I remember that," Randy added. "I was at the paper that day when Leo heard about Reece's fifteen-year sentence. He was all smiles, until he saw on television where Reece promised to exact his revenge for what he called his being 'ramrodded by the press.' If I remember correctly, Leo helped with parts of that story, even though he tried to keep his name off the by-line."

"What about Altman? He was Leland's go-to guy for research on the money flow. He's the one who did all that leg work. How did he manage to get himself on the story in the first place?"

"Didn't it have something to do with a connection in Washington, D.C.?"

"That's right. His brother-in-law worked as a liaison between the Justice Department and the Office of Management and Budget. He kept pushing the case in front of people until someone at the department showed a greater interest, especially once it made the headlines."

Randy sat down in the chair nearest him. "I remember that story. One or two of the attorneys within the department somehow got tangled up in the money part of it, but I don't remember how exactly. Plus, it seems to me that Altman ended up being transferred somewhere else, after all of the flap died down. What I can't remember is what happened to those attorneys. There was something about how the two of them were connected to the money, but I can't remember how."

Howard grinned. "Altman's work behind the scenes wasn't so behind-the-scenes then was it? I wonder what he's doing right now."

"Right now, he's probably sipping margaritas and sitting on a beach somewhere in South America. He retired early, remember?"

"It's hard to believe that we're still talking about this story. Do you remember the day Biederman called all us into the conference room and told all of us that his paper wasn't going to print anything else about this story because he was tired of reading about it?"

"I not only remember that, but I remember the look on his face. He wasn't kidding."

"There were so many parts of the story that seemed to be left hanging. Do you think Altman decided finally to back off and only now jump back in with both feet? You don't suppose, do you, that he might have been the one to have called you?"

"How did he manage to get inside to make the phone call?" Randy asked, and then sat down as well.

"Wait a minute," Howard said, and then took out his cell phone.

"Who are you calling?"

"I've got a friend who knows about these kinds of things." He connected his call and waited. "I've got an idea."

While Howard was on the phone, Randy picked up the note pad he had looked at the last time he had been there. As he looked through it, he was struck by what seemed to be random remarks that Max had made in the margins of several pages. He especially was interested in the comments he found in at least three different locations about references to flights or flight numbers. Then he recalled the comment about JAX several days earlier.

He went over to the paneling and found where he had seen that reference. It was something about a flight that Peter Theron had taken to Jacksonville. At least, that's what Carla thought at the time.

Howard spoke up. "According to my source, that phone call could have been made by someone outside the system and make it look like it was coming from inside the building."

"That puts a new wrinkle on things," Randy said.

"Suppose we're looking here at Altman trying to help us out and his trying to stay out of the picture like he did once before. Maybe we should try to locate him and talk to him. He'd be a great ally and one helluva resource."

While they searched for contact information on Altman, Calvin and Susan had reached her office building, entered through the side door, and processed through the security desk located near the elevators.

"Miss Leeds, it's nice to see you back at work. Are you all right?"

"I'm fine Mr. Evans." She reached for the pen and then signed in. "We need a visitor's pass for my friend here."

Once processed through security, they got onto the elevator and went to the third floor.

After getting off the elevator, they turned left and headed for her boss's office. "So, what do you think about this place?"

Calvin had to admit that it was bigger than he had imagined, but he had seen corporate sized headquarters facilities before. "All I've seen, so far, are glass-enclosed conference rooms and miles of low-level, dark maroon colored pile carpeting. Where is your cubicle?"

"I work on the second floor." She stopped, reached to her right and pulled open one of the large glass doors. "Here we are." She held the door open for him. "After you," she said.

The receptionist, sitting behind a very large dark brown, granite-covered, curved shaped counter area recognized them and asked them to be seated until Mrs. Alexander was ready for them.

"Don't worry; we won't be seated very long. She's usually prompt and hates to be late."

He sat there taking in the luxurious surroundings. Also, he was impressed with how quiet the facility was and how everyone and everything was in its place. He smiled.

She noticed it. "What are you smiling about?"

"I couldn't help but to think about how in my day, the news room was noisy. There were no cubicles. We had a desk, a typewriter, and a phone – and sometimes we had to share that with two or three colleagues."

"When we're through here, I'll take you to the second floor. You'll probably feel more at home there."

They waited for fifteen minutes, before Susan asked the secretary how much longer it would be. She leaned over to Calvin and whispered. "It's not like her to be late. She's usually quite punctual. I guess it's something anal or something like that."

"We're not in any hurry, are we?"

"I'm not, but I'm telling you it's not like her."

They noticed that even the receptionist started looking at the clock on the wall behind her work space. Ten o'clock came and went. Susan decided to wait five more minutes, before pursuing the matter. She didn't have to wait that long.

The receptionist, instead, decided to check in on Mrs. Alexander. Two seconds after she opened the door and disappeared into the room, they heard her scream. Then, they saw her run back to her desk and pick up the phone. She was visibly shaking, as she tried to speak as calmly as she could, but there was urgency in her voice. "We need an ambulance and the police at the Sullivan building."

Calvin bolted from his chair and moved quickly into Mrs. Alexander's office where he saw her lying on the floor, face down, in front of her desk. To him, it looked like she tried to make it to the door for help, but collapsed during her effort. Susan was right behind him.

He turned to her. "Go back and question the receptionist. We need to know who was in this office before us, what time they came in, and how they got out of here without anyone seeing them."

After she left the room, he went over to her desk and checked to see what was on the desk top. Other than the usual office supplies, his eyes went right to an envelope sticking out of her day planner.

He took his handkerchief from his left rear pants pocket and used it to move the envelope just enough so he could see the writing on it. It was addressed to her, but it had no return address on the front of it. He flipped it over. On the back were the initials M.C.

He wouldn't tamper with what he knew would be evidence, so he didn't open it, but he did take a picture of it with his cell phone. Susan came back into the room at that point.

"Her last appointment was at nine-thirty. It was scheduled to last for twenty minutes with someone named Brent Goodson. She wasn't sure what it was about, but she did tell me that this is not the first time he's met with her. He's been here several times over the last couple of months."

"How did he get out of here without us seeing him?"

"She doesn't know."

They both exited the room and went back to the receptionist's area.

Calvin, trying not to upset her any more than she already was, grabbed a tissue from the container on her desk as he walked by it and handed it to her.

"Did their meeting start on time?"

"Yes, it did. She met him in the hallway outside her office, shook hands, and then she asked me to make sure that there were no interruptions."

"And, were there?"

"No, there weren't. There was a phone call that I took a few minutes before you arrived, but it was nothing."

Calvin looked at Susan, then back at the receptionist. "Who called you and what did they want?"

"It was someone from receiving telling me that I had a package to pick up."

"And, did you? I mean, did you leave and go pick it up?"

"Yes, but I met them at the elevator – right over there." She pointed to a landing within viewing distance of her desk.

"You didn't see this Mr. Goodson leave?"

"No, I didn't"

Just as she had finished answering that question, two security officers arrived.

The receptionist pointed at Mrs. Alexander's office and they quickly moved in that direction.

"Where are the back stairs, in case of fire?"

She pointed to the other end of the hallway. "The exit sign is right there," she said, while wiping her eyes.

"Is that the only other way off of this floor, besides the elevator?"

Susan tugged on his left sleeve. "Can I speak with you for a minute?" She led him a few feet away from the receptionist and back to where they had been sitting. "I see where you're going with this, but she's not the one who can give you the answers. We need to go back down and speak with Mr. Evans."

"The security guy I met at the front desk?"

"Yes because he's not only been here since the building first opened in 1993, he can tell us if this Mr. Goodson logged out on his way out of the building."

They could hear the police sirens as the cruisers pulled into the circular driveway at the front entrance.

"We'll need to stay and give our statement to them, before we go back down," Calvin instructed.

"I thought you'd say that," she said as she plopped herself onto the sofa. She patted the cushion next her. "Care to join me?"

He grinned. "Remember, you're supposed to be on your best behavior."

She smiled at him. "I'm sorry. Do I have to go to time out?"

"No, but I might ask one of those police officers who just got off the elevator if he would let me borrow his handcuffs."

"Oh," she said, "now who's misbehaving?"

It took them an hour, before the police let them leave. Like them, the police immediately homed in on the idea that whoever killed Mrs. Alexander left the building by some means other than the elevator.

While they were sitting there, waiting to be interviewed by the police, Calvin made a phone call to Howard.

Almost whispering into his cell phone, he tried to let him know he would be sending him a text message with the picture he had taken of the envelope. The initials M.C. were now linked to their investigation, but he knew they needed to be put into perspective. He was hoping to have an answer for that by the time they got home.

Before leaving the building, they stopped at the security desk on the first floor where Mr. Evans was speaking with a police officer. They waited until the policeman left, before Calvin began questioning him.

"Mr. Evans, we're checking on something that you might help us with. Did a man named Brent Goodson sign out through here this morning?"

"No, he didn't because he didn't sign in this morning."

Calvin had a perplexed look on his face, and Mr. Evans recognized it. "I've not seen him since last Wednesday when he came in that afternoon. He had an appointment with Mrs. Alexander, but he left kind of in a hurry."

"Did he sign out that day?"

"Yes; yes, he did."

"Mr. Evans," Calvin began, "is there another way out of this building besides the stairs or the elevator?"

"There is a way, but it's known only to three people: Mrs. Alexander, Mr. Lucas, and myself."

He looked at Susan. "Who's Mr. Lucas?"

"He's the one who designed and built this building."

Looking right at Calvin, Mr. Evans added, "Mr. Lucas died last year."

"Do you know when and how he died?"

"He was the victim of a hit-and-run accident last August near his home. They never did find the person who hit him."

They thanked him, and then exited the building through the door they had entered, and walked directly to his car.

"Where to now?" she asked.

"We're going to stop by your apartment so you can pick up a few things." He opened the car door for her. "As soon as we're done there, we're headed home."

The trip took less than fifteen minutes. When they entered her apartment, it looked as if a tornado had landed on it. Everything in her apartment had been turned over or torn apart.

"They were looking for something. What were they looking for?"

"I haven't the foggiest idea."

"Could it be that CD?"

"It could be, but I don't have it."

"Whoever did this is not going to stop at just this. Get your things together. We need to get out of here right now because they may come back. I'll wait for you in the car."

When he got into his car, he leaned over, unlocked and opened the glove compartment. He took out 'Betsy' and put it under his seat.

She came out through the downstairs corridor carrying a suitcase in her right hand and an overnight bag slung over her left shoulder.

"I'm ready," she said. "There's one more place we need to go to before we leave."

"Where is that?"

"My safety deposit box at the bank."

Meanwhile, Randy had returned from his visit with Howard and spent the rest of the morning sitting at his work station charting the foundations of the story. It was a practice that had served him well throughout his career. He would establish a catalog of what he thought were the important fundamentals of the story and then set about to connect each one with supporting details and facts. A substantial part of the method was making sure the flow chart that would emerge as a by-product of the cataloging process was sequential and unambiguous. It was a technique he had been taught by Hal Eddings, a former professor, a long-time friend and mentor as well as an award-winning novelist.

While others were using a more traditional approach with index cards and scribbling pieces of information on them, Professor Eddings instructed him how to use the story board and connect the pieces of the article before ever writing one word of it. Randy and Howard thought alike in that respect. It mattered to both of them what the story told its readers. They just approached it differently. To Howard, the news industry was the arm of public opinion and was designed to help inform and occasionally mold public opinion – but never at the expense of the truth. To Randy, it mattered more that when a person read the news story he had written, first and foremost, the truth of the news story was the object – opinions came later.

"Connect the facts and the story will tell itself," Professor Eddings would say. "And the way to connect the facts is to make sure you detach fact from opinion. Once you've identified all of the facts to the story, what's left is opinion, rumor, or guessing – and guessing will stomp all over you. Reporting something to someone doesn't mean you have to understand it, but it doesn't mean you ignore it either. If what you have to say is important enough to tell others, then read what you're writing and heed what it's telling you."

He hadn't forgotten about his twelve-thirty appointment with Mr. Rayner, but he wasn't in any hurry to sit in his outer office for any lengthy time either. He tried to reach Lisa on her cell phone about dinner plans, but his calls were going to her voice mailbox.

He had just turned off his computer, got up from his desk, and headed for Mr. Rayner's office, when he noticed two men getting off of the elevator. Each one of them was carrying a tool chest, wore baseball caps and beige-colored overalls with patches that indicated they were with the heating and air conditioning maintenance crews. It wasn't unusual for him to see people coming and going for repairs in a large building, but it was unusual to see them on this floor and in that area.

While pointing upwards, he yelled out at them. "Hey, the maintenance room is two floors up."

It appeared as though neither one had heard what he said. Instead of yelling at them again, he picked up the nearest telephone and called for security.

By the time security responded, the two men had turned and left through the door that led to the northeast set of stairs.

He followed them all the way to the exits, while trying to keep a discreet distance. He was able to jot down the license plate number for the vehicle just before he saw them speeding out of the parking lot, turning left after leaving the gate, and heading west.

Realizing he needed to get to Mr. Rayner office, he put the paper, on which he had jotted down the license plate number, into his shirt pocket and started walking toward the elevator.

With three minutes to spare, he sat down in one of the love seats in the boss's outer office. Two minutes later, he was walking into his office and shaking hands with him.

"What's so urgent that couldn't wait until after lunch?"

"What would you think if I said the names Sheppard and Phillips?"

"I'd think I was having a nightmare and ask you to wake me up from it."

"No, what would you seriously think if I told you these guys are at it again?"

"I'd say it was old news gone wild. What makes you think these guys are, as you put it, 'at it again?'"

Randy leaned forward in his seat. "I know you don't have a lot of time to give me right now, so let me just say that the evidence gathered so far is conclusive and damning. I know that Sheppard has repeatedly spoken of his intent and Phillips is the object of his intentions. Also, I know Sheppard has moved back to Florida, since being released from prison." He paused for just a second. "Oh yes, there's this thing that indicates he's connected to at least three, possibly more, deaths of journalists. That means Phillips, maybe even Altman, may be targeted."

"How do you know all of this? You just started back with us."

Randy stood, pointed to the doors that led to the balcony, and motioned for him to follow him. When they were both outside, standing on the balcony, he closed the doors behind them.

He stood close so he wouldn't have to raise his voice. "I've been working on this story since Max Leopard's death. It's bigger than you want to believe, at first, until you begin to see what it is these people are doing and what they have managed to accomplish so far. We believe it's politically motivated, but revenge is clearly a part of it."

Mr. Rayner stood silent, before he turned and looked out over the landscape beneath him, and then focused his attention on the horizon.

He turned his head slightly toward Randy. "If what you're telling me is accurate, just what are you proposing to do about it?"

He responded quickly. "Expose them – all of them, and see to it that they rot in jail."

"You sound a little bitter for someone who's supposed to be objectively unbiased. After all, you have a responsibility to the truth – to the people who read our newspaper."

"I suppose I am a little bitter. They killed Max, and who knows how many more, because they're corrupt and could care less about the truth. They made it personal – not me."

Mr. Rayner turned and started for the doors. He stopped and faced Randy.

"I've got to get to another meeting in about twenty minutes and a full schedule tomorrow. I want you back in my office first thing Monday morning. We've got a lot a work to do."

"No sir, I don't think that would be a good idea. I'd rather pick you up here and take you to where we're putting all of this together."

"That sounds a little paranoid. Call me at this number on Sunday evening and we'll make arrangements." He handed him one of his business cards.

"Yes sir, I'll call. And by the way, it's not paranoid – just precautionary."

CHAPTER 24
Late Friday Afternoon, March 29, 2013

The drive back home took considerably longer than their trip to Tampa that morning because the traffic on I-4 at three-thirty that afternoon made it seem more like a parking lot than a major interstate highway. What usually took thirty minutes to travel through Orlando took an hour-and-a-half, before they made their way to Maitland and eventually over the bridge at the St. John's River.

During their ride, conversation mostly was focused on Mrs. Alexander's death – that is until Susan decided to spice it up a bit.

She turned and looked at him. "Calvin, I haven't been completely honest with you."

"Okay – what have you not told me?"

At first, she didn't say anything. Instead, she reached over the front seat and into one of the side pockets of the overnight bag she had placed on the back seat. She found what she was searching for and showed it to him.

He looked at it and then at her. "Is that the CD they were looking for? I thought you said you had no idea where it was."

"I lied. In case you haven't noticed, my life has been threatened lately because of it. I wasn't going to talk about it, until I knew we were safely away from that place."

He shook his head. "What else is there that you haven't been honest about?"

"Nothing – I swear on my mother's grave."

"You told me yesterday that your mother was still living." He shook his head. "You really are a piece of work; do you know that? What's on that CD?"

"I don't know because I haven't looked at it."

"Am I supposed to believe that, too?"

"It's the truth." She reached over and touched his shoulder. He glanced in her direction. "It's the truth. Please believe me."

He thought about what she said. Her voice sounded real for the first time since he had met her. When he glanced at her, the expression on her face showed hurt and sadness. "You missed your calling. There's an Oscar in Hollywood with your name written all over it."

"You've got to believe me." She turned her face downward, as if being rejected.

As he drove, all he could hear for a brief moment were the muffled sounds of the motor and the road passing under the tires. When he glanced over at her, he saw that she was crying. She hadn't made a sound, but the tears had started and were falling under both of her eyes.

She tried to smile at him, but that only made things worse.

He reached into his coat pocket, pulled out a handkerchief, and handed it to her. "If that's the case, then we need to find out what was so important that's on that thing. After all, he died trying to protect whatever's there."

For a few moments, she sat there wiping her eyes, while she wept quietly.

"If you blow your nose on that thing, you can keep it. I don't want it back."

She laughed. Then she really did need to blow her nose.

When she finished, she sat there, clutching the handkerchief in her left hand, looking out the window to her right. He saw her staring and recognized that look. Her posture and the awkward silence made it seem as if she had lost her last friend.

"My face must be a mess." She reached for the visor in front of her to look into the lighted mirror.

He felt he needed to say something, but didn't.

Several seconds went by, before he spoke. "There's a gas station just up the road where I usually stop to fill up after a long trip. I think it'll be good for us to stretch our legs and maybe get a cup of coffee. There are restrooms inside."

Back at the Ewing house, Howard was sitting in his favorite chair on the porch looking at the facts that had been placed on the panels. The different colored strings that had been used to connect particulars of different news stories now created a pattern similar to what you would see as if you were taking an aerial photograph of a major highway exchange. As he sat there studying the pattern, he noticed where several strings intersected each other. Immediately, he called for Carla to join him on the porch.

"Look at this," he said, as he walked over to where she was standing, and then pointed to a place on the paneling. "What do you see?"

"I see a whole lot of string going everywhere."

"Exactly," he said. He pointed again at that specific place. "This is the focal point. From here, we can go almost anywhere else and still be connected to the main part of the story. Do you know what that means?"

She thought for a moment. "I see at least six different strings converging at this point," she said as she put her finger where they crossed on the paneling.

"It means we may have found the center – the hub on which we can focus most of our attention. There are six strings coming and going. It's as simple as playing the old match game. Remember?"

"You've lost me."

Again, he pointed to the same six strings, only this time he started at one end and ran his finger along one of the strings. "What is it about this one string between these two different news stories that cause them to intersect with these others?" He pointed to where the strings began to overlap the others.

"That's easy – somebody died," she said. She took a step toward the center panel. "And, they were all connected to newspaper companies in some fashion – except for the two television companies that are affiliates and are part of a conglomerate."

Howard's face lit up. "They are part of a larger media corporation as in parent company."

"That's right. That means they have a big boss calling the shots." She pointed to one of the articles on the paneling. "Maybe," she said, and then pointed at two separate articles on the paneling, "these big bosses are talking to each other and no one knows about it."

Howard took a step backward and then looked at her. "Maybe the big bosses are talking to each other because they have to."

Carla was puzzled. "What does that mean? Why would anyone who's in charge of multi-million-dollar corporations have to do anything like that?"

Howard smiled. "Because – it means they're not the ones calling the shots. They're being played by someone or something else. Don't you see it?"

She shook her head. "You've lost me."

"Take a seat and let me run this by you one more time."

It took about twenty minutes for him to go through the process from beginning to end, but when he was done she realized what he meant by big bosses having to talk to each other.

She stood up and went back to the center panel. "If that's the case, we're looking at something worse than a conspiracy. We're looking at such enormous political maneuvering that there's got to be an inner ring driving this. Where's it coming from?"

"Where else would anything of this size that is political be managed? It's got to come from Washington. The real question is who is capable of doing this? Someone has got to be in charge to keep everybody in line or everyone would be acting on his own – and that doesn't make sense. Politics is about power and political power is all about moving belief systems and pushing a way of life forward. To do that, politicians need a very large bank account or someone willing to underwrite the effort."

She turned and looked at him. "Multi-million-dollar corporations certainly have the means, but they're run by duly elected boards and CEO's. They just can't move money around as if it's pocket change."

"They can if those who currently hold key political positions make allowances or look the other way. If those who are supposed to be watching turn their heads for just a moment, or if they ignore or refuse to implement certain checks and balances designed to guard the integrity of the process, then lots of things slip under the radar. By the time enough of that happens, it's too late. The ball game is over. It's one of two things: Either there's one person who has a bunch of henchmen working for him, or a very small group of very important people have managed to cover their tracks so far. This whole thing seems so outlandish, but that's why it stays off the radar at the national level. We've caught wind of it because of Max's untimely and unlikely death. Somebody screwed up and overplayed their hand before they were ready."

"Before they were ready?"

"Yes, before they were ready to launch or implement whatever they think must be done. Max's death caught our attention before they really wanted anyone to know what they're up to."

"That might explain a few things, but what you've said so far is all conjecture. Where's the proof?"

He pointed to the documents on the table and then to those on the panels.

"When people die, there are funerals where people say nice things about the dead. Afterwards, those whose lives have been celebrated are placed in the ground and a hired hand comes along and covers them up with dirt. No longer does their story grace the front pages of the papers or lead the six o'clock news. When several people die, who are inexplicably yet significantly linked by their deaths, and they happen to be news reporters or media people, it's anything but conjecture. Their story hasn't been told because the ones who can are telling you something entirely different, while doing whatever they want covered up. I just don't know why yet, but I'm willing to bet you all the tea in China that it's politically motivated."

She went back to her chair and sat down. "Honey, you do realize that we're in the news business – right?"

"I know. That's why it's important not to grow this too quickly. We've only got bits and pieces of the puzzle. When Randy and Calvin get here, I think it's time for us to look at stepping up our game and design a more in-depth plan – one that will keep us off the radar as well. The first rule in dealing with unraveling a conspiracy is to remember that the element of surprise is crucial. It's what levels the playing field – at least before the bodies start dropping."

"If this is political, then what are the issues? What are they pushing for or reacting to? What is it they want to change?"

"That's the sixty-four-thousand-dollar question."

Forty-five minutes later, Calvin and Susan arrived. Randy had called just after they arrived and told Howard he was on his way to pick up Lisa. He said he would be there within the hour.

XXXXX

When they finished with dinner and the dishes were done, they all went out to the porch with coffee cups in hand.

Randy had borrowed an LCD projector from work, and brought it with him knowing it would help everyone to see things a little easier, took it out of the carrying case and handed it to Calvin. After he got all of the technology working, Susan gave him the CD which he placed in the drive. "It's show time. Everyone, quiet on the set, please."

At first, no one was surprised by the documents Peter had gathered and saved in different folders. When Calvin clicked on and opened a file that was marked, "H&M," Lisa leaned forward in her chair. "Well, I'll be. He's up to his old tricks, again."

Howard saw it and clapped his hands. "Son-of-gun if this doesn't beat all."

Calvin shook his head. "The more things change, the more they stay the same."

Susan looked at Carla and she shrugged her shoulders. Carla leaned toward Howard. "What's so important about this?"

Susan looked at Calvin with a quizzical look on her face. "Well?"

Calvin spoke first. "See this document right here?" Using the mouse, he pointed to a copy of a news article Peter had downloaded. The article, one written only three weeks earlier, was about how Senator Trevor Haskell had several contracts issued to certain news outlets around the nation. Those contracts came about because of the work he had done though the Congressional committees on which he sat.

Carla, still mystified about what she was looking at, spoke up. "I've heard of Senator Haskell, but who's Herman Mittick and how does he figure into this?"

Susan chimed in. "Herman Mittick just got out of prison. His name was all over the front page about eight years ago. How does he connect with Haskell?"

Howard turned to Carla. "Mittick was all about money and corruption. If Haskell and Mittick are connected, and it appears that Peter was working to prove that, then we have the political link we've been looking for."

Susan looked directly at Calvin. "When Mittick went to prison, no one knew where the money went. They couldn't find it, and no one knew who had it. Now that he's out and free as a bird, it probably won't be too long before that money will show up somewhere. Apparently,

Peter thought that Haskell was going to be the recipient of a windfall of cash."

"Even so," Randy said, "that doesn't prove that Haskell's the head honcho. All we know is that Peter found a connection. I think we need to drive that wedge as hard as we can and see what shakes out of the trees."

"Calvin, are there any other articles or documents we haven't seen?" Lisa asked.

He searched through the document list and found two others. He opened the first of them. It contained an article about a near miss between two airliners. One of passengers on the plane that was headed for Washington, D.C. died from an apparent heart attack. The other, which was headed for Philadelphia, had a passenger die from an apparent heart attack as well.

"That's unusual. But, what does that have to do with any of this?"

"Peter thought there was something to this or he wouldn't have included it on this disk," Susan said. "I think we need to dig into both of these – like now."

Calvin stood up and walked over to where she was seated and stood next to her. "Guys, I have reason to believe that Susan's life is in danger. That being said, I think we need to play defense at the moment – at least until we know she's safe and we can protect her."

Howard agreed. "We need to stay off the radar for a while."

Carla smiled. "I have an idea."

CHAPTER 25
Sunday, March 31, 2013, 11:00 a.m.

"What do think?" Carla asked.

Susan, who had just walked in through the front door, set her suitcase and carry bag down. "This is adorable." She pointed to the living room area. "It's so comfy looking."

"That's the idea. We decided that's exactly what we wanted. There are two bedrooms in the back, two full bathrooms, and a very large storage area in the basement. We've added a few conveniences including our telescopic, rotary mounted television antenna. It's not cable, but you can get several channels of free TV. It also serves as our CB radio antenna. Howard put in a wood burning stove as a backup last winter that will heat the entire house. We use propane for cooking. Everything else runs off solar and batteries."

Howard came in carrying several plastic bags of groceries and placed them on the kitchen counter. "I'll go downstairs and hit the switches."

"Carla, are you sure this is what you want to do? We have no idea how long we're going to be here. Plus, it's forever off of the main road."

"Honey, that's the only way we would have it. I think you'll be safe here. Your cellphone is useless because there is no signal here. The only connection we have to the outside world is that CB over there," she said, while pointing to it, "and that stays off, unless there's an emergency. If we need groceries, it's a four-mile drive on a dirt road to the nearest hole-in-the-wall where canned goods rule the day. The gas tanks are full, the batteries fully charged, and we have a three-hundred-gallon storage tank full of potable water. I'm talking paradise here."

Susan smiled. "And, a year's supply of pretzels. What more could anyone else want?"

Carla came up with the plan. Calvin and Randy liked it. Lisa was jealous because of it, and Howard decided it was the best of all of the ideas they had talked about. They wanted safety for Susan, and they all knew it would become increasingly more difficult to keep her whereabouts unknown. The cabin would give them the ideal set-up and location.

Howard went back out to the car, grabbed the remaining bags of groceries and carried them into the cabin. Carla, who had shown Susan to her room, went into the kitchen and started to make coffee.

"Are you sure this will be enough for the two of you for the week?"

"We'll be fine," Carla said as she plugged in the coffee maker. "There are still plenty of canned goods in the basement, if we need any more."

When Susan walked into the living room area, Howard asked her to join them. "I want you to know about these two items." He pointed to the shotguns that he had taken out of the closet near the hallway. "They're loaded. All you've got to do is to release the safety like this," he said, showing her how to do it, "and you're ready to roll."

Carla stood next to her. "We'll take them outside later and practice a little with them. You'll get the hang of it."

Then, he unzipped a carry bag, reached in, and pulled out a .38 caliber revolver. "Keep this near you at all times. Carla's got one just like it."

"We'll practice with that, too," she added.

He went over a list of things he felt he needed to reiterate. He reminded them how to set and turn off the alarm system they had installed a few months earlier. If they wanted fresh air in the house, he advised them against opening any windows, except for the one over the sink. He reminded Carla about making sure the motion-sensing lights were on, before they went to bed each night. He showed Susan where they kept the extra ammunition, spare batteries, and the flashlights as well as the candles. The last thing he did was to go over radio procedure with both of them.

He turned to Carla. "I better start back. I'd like to get in before dark." They hugged and kissed each other, before he started walking toward the door. "Please be sure you check in like we agreed. If I need to get a message to you, the only person who will bring it to you will be Mr. Patterson."

He kissed her one last time and then went out the front door.

XXXXX

Just about the time Howard started for home, Lisa and Randy were walking through the side door entrance to the newspaper. After signing in, they got on the elevator and got off on the fourth floor, checked in with the security guard at the main desk, and headed for the research and files division.

"What is it again you think you're going to find?" she asked.

"I'm not exactly sure, but when I do we'll both know it. Who was that contact at the police department you called?"

"Her name is Sergeant Wilma Monroe."

"How well do you know her? Can you trust her?"

"We've been friends since seventh grade, and I'd trust her with my life."

"That's good to know because if I'm right about what I'm looking for, we'll need her help for sure."

They walked over to one of the cubicles next to the window, sat down, and he turned on the computer.

"While this thing is loading, would you like for me to get you a coffee? There's a machine right over there," she said, pointing to the opposite wall.

"Sure, that would be nice."

As he sat there watching her walking toward the coffee machine, he noticed a message had popped up on the computer screen.

It read: *I think it is a good thing you're doing.*

He was stunned. "Lisa you need to come here – like right now."

He stood up and looked around the room to see if someone else was in the room with them. He saw no one. He peered out the window, checking to see if anyone might have been watching from a safe distance. The only people he saw were driving cars on the adjacent street.

He pointed at the screen. "What do you make of that?"

"Obviously, someone else is aware of what we're doing. They would have to be in the building and not far from us."

She reached over his shoulder and typed in a response: *Just what is it you think we're doing?*

Their eyes were glued to the monitor waiting for a response. They weren't disappointed.

There's a lot more than meets the eye, but you'll see that too. Although important, the story is not just about the deaths. It's about the people who came in behind them and replaced them. Get to know who they are and what they stand for. Don't just connect the dots – connect the dashes as well.

They watched as each word appeared on the screen. Lisa sat down next to him – shoulder-to-shoulder. Her perfume caught his attention, and so did the body heat she generated being seated next to him.

He cleared his throat. "Other than us, who could know we're looking into the deaths?" he asked.

"That's not what bothers me at the moment." She stood up and started to walk away.

"Where are you going?"

"I think we're going to need that coffee, before this day is over. We've got work to do and there's no better time than the present to get started."

"Started on what?"

"You and I have been given the back story all to ourselves. We need to come up with the names of the persons who filled those positions. Whoever this is," she said, and then pointed to the screen, "understands what we're trying to do and thinks we're missing the mark. If we can figure out this part of the story, who knows where that might lead us?"

"Suppose it's a wild goose chase meant to throw us off our game?"

"And, what if it is?"

"We'll have wasted a lot of time and effort for nothing."

She didn't respond at first. Instead, she finished getting the machine to fill two cups of hot coffee, and then returned to where she had been sitting. She handed him one of the cups.

After taking a sip of her coffee, she leaned closer to him. "I don't consider this a waste of time. After all, we've learned something about ourselves today."

He took a sip of his coffee. "And, what would that be?"

"We may be old dogs, but we can still hunt." She smiled at him.

He laughed. "Who are you calling old?"

Just then another message popped up on the screen: *I suggest you start with Michael Carlon.*

Randy rubbed his chin. "Does that name ring any bells?"

"It does not."

She reached over, commandeered the key board, and started typing. She asked how to get in touch with this mysterious person.

They sat there, again, watching for a reply. It took a little longer, but they got one: *I'll find you. Don't rush this – please be careful.*

They sat there for a few seconds without saying anything. Lisa reached over with her left hand and placed it on top of his right hand. "I'd say we have some work ahead of us today."

He took another sip of his coffee. "I think we need to know more about this Michael Carlon person, before this day gets away from us. You stay at this station. I'll take this one," he said, as he got up to move to the station immediately to their right.

"You'll do no such thing." She grabbed his right hand as if to tell him to sit back down. "Four eyes on this screen will be better."

"We can cover a lot more ground the other way."

"Think about this for just a minute. If this person has been watching us through this monitor, whoever it is certainly seems technology literate and probably will know what we're looking at on this screen. They may not be leaving messages for us right now, but they could still be watching over our shoulder – so to speak."

He smiled. "You win." He sat down and pushed the keyboard toward her. "I'm all eyes and ears. Let's do this."

While they started searching the newspaper's data base for information on Michael Carlon, Calvin was seated in his kitchen just getting ready to leave for the store, when the wall phone in the kitchen rang.

"Hello?"

"Is this Calvin Rolle?"

"Who's calling?"

The phone went dead. He knew they just didn't hang up. It sounded more like the phone line had been cut.

He got up from his seat, went into the bedroom, and picked up Betsy from the nightstand. He opened the drawer and gathered two additional clips of ammunition which he put in his left pants pocket. He went into the living room area and drew the curtains. Then, he went over to the window that overlooked the parking lot. He saw three men getting out of a black SUV. Each of them appeared to have a firearm of some kind.

He picked up his cell phone and called 911. When he explained what was happening, the operator instructed him to not hang up. She informed him that the police had been notified and that help was on the way. He put his cell phone down on the coffee table in the living room. He moved to the hallway and positioned himself between the door in the living room and his bedroom. Then he waited.

First, a minute went by without hearing anything. Then, two minutes went by.

They should be here by now, he thought. He was right.

The door exploded into splinters, and the first man through the door was carrying an automatic rifle. Calvin dropped him before he managed to take two steps into the apartment. The second man ran in behind him, spraying the room with rounds from his automatic rifle. Calvin ducked out of the hallway and into the opening to his kitchen. The loud popping noises made by the weapons pounded his eardrums.

The third man entered, walking methodically and fearlessly, firing each handgun he held in both hands. Calvin reached around the corner and squeezed off two rounds. The third round found its target and the third man went flying backwards into the wall.

He waited for a few seconds. He heard the second man running down the hallway toward the stairwell at the south end of the building. A few seconds later, he heard the squealing of tires from the parking lot below and the faint sound of police car sirens farther off. He quickly walked over to the window and looked through the drawn curtains at the parking lot. He saw the black SUV hurriedly leaving the south exit then turning right and driving out of sight. The passenger was trying to close the door as the van sped away.

He walked over to the first man near the door and picked up his weapon. Then he picked up the third man's weapon.

Knowing the police would be there any minute; he put the weapons on the coffee table, sat down, and then picked up his cell phone.

The operator sounded upset. "Are you okay? Have the police arrived?"

"They're just getting here. I can hear them in the parking lot. Please tell them that they need to be looking for a black, late model SUV, and the license plate starts with the numbers three, six, and five – I think. It's from out-of-state – maybe a Tennessee plate. I didn't get that great of a look at it as they drove off. They were headed west at a high rate of speed"

He disconnected the call, went over to his easy chair, sat down, and put Betsy on the coffee table. Then, he located Howard's cell number and connected to it.

"Hey, do you want to hear about the kind of day I'm having?"

Just then, a county deputy walked through what was left of his apartment door with his handgun pointed directly at him.

He waved at him. "I've got to call you back. I'm sort of in the middle of something."

CHAPTER 26
Sunday, March 31, 2013, 4:00 p.m.

Calvin was interviewed by three different deputies, while sitting in his living room. They confiscated Betsy for ballistic purposes and took several pictures of his now disheveled apartment. There were several small, bright yellow numbered markers on the floor near shell casings, and the medical examiner had come and gone. He had spent the last twenty minutes trying to collect some of his belongings, when the lead investigator, Captain Edward Connors, walked in and began to interrogate him.

"Mr. Rolle, I know you've already given these other officers your side of the story, but I'd like for you to tell me what happened."

Calvin indulged him and explained, again in methodical fashion, exactly what he remembered from the time his wall phone went dead to when the police had arrived.

"Why do you suppose these men wanted to kill you?"

He knew that question was coming, but he hadn't really come up with a good answer. He didn't want to lie to him, but he didn't know if he could be trusted. He decided to strike a deal with him, instead.

"Captain, would you mind if we answer that question somewhere else?"

"Did you have someplace particular in mind?"

"Yes, I do."

He recognized the proverbial rock-and-a-hard-place in which he found himself. He had been there several times before. This time, it was different. He was willing to gamble at this point. The story depended on it – and maybe even his life. The last thing he wanted was to be hauled off to jail where he figured whoever had tried to kill him would have easier access to him.

"Okay, Mr. Rolle, we're in my cruiser driving around the neighborhood as you requested, and you have my undivided attention. Now would you mind telling me what's really going on?"

"This may take a while."

As Captain Connors drove, Calvin explained what he and the others had been doing. The more he talked, the more Captain Connors became interested. When they stopped at a traffic light, several blocks from his apartment, Calvin turned to him and decided to explain what he and the others believed was the motive behind all of this.

"Do you think the government is being upfront with the citizens in this country?"

"What do you mean by upfront?"

"Do you think those who are in power in this country are being honest and plainspoken with us, the citizens in this country?"

"Okay, I think I see where this is going. You want me to believe that there is some kind of government conspiracy and you're caught up to your eyebrows in it."

"Captain, it's a simple question that deserves a yes or no answer. There is no hidden agenda here. I'm asking you if you believe that our government has been truthful – that it is not playing us."

The traffic light turned green. Instead of accelerating and moving with traffic, he pulled the vehicle over to the curb and turned off the ignition. He turned slightly to his right so he could look directly at him.

"Look, I don't know you, and you don't know me. What I think about the government is none of your business. What I think about you at the moment, on the other hand, should be a real concern for you. Right now, I think you're crazier than a bed bug. You're a suspect involved in a shooting resulting in the death of two individuals. For all I know, you could be trying to dupe me into thinking you're innocent. My job is finding the bad guy. Are you the bad guy in this Mr. Rolle?"

Calvin smiled. "If you choose to believe that those in power are truthful, you have not only been duped, you have been cheated as well. They have morphed the truth into a mind-numbing narrative that sounds smooth and logical, while advancing their own agenda. That's what they want you to hear.

I'm not the bad guy here. Everything I've told you is the truth. Everything I've told you can be verified with documents, pictures, statements, and whatever else you detectives would like which would stand up in a court of law. I'm asking you again, do you believe that those who are sitting in Washington D.C are being truthful with you?"

They sat there for a few seconds staring at each other. Captain Connors reached into his coat pocket, pulled out a package of gum, and offered him some. "Okay, suppose I think that I've been lied to. What do you expect me to do about it?"

He waved off his offer of gum. "That's the point. They expect you to feel helpless and powerless. You have been deceived."

He thought about it for a few seconds. "If that's the case, please tell me then why if they thought you were helpless, why would they have to come after you?"

"Dead guys don't talk."

"So, you want me to believe that you killed them in self-defense and their attempt on your life was some kind of plot to eliminate you from exposing them?"

"See? You already understand it. You're just not willing to believe it. The problem is that they have to move fast right now because they know that we're on to them, and the connection seems to be through this woman I told you about – Susan Leeds. She's got herself wrapped up into this somehow –hook, line, and sinker."

"Where is she? I'd like to talk with her."

"Well, let's just say she's somewhere safe for the moment."

Captain Connors heard the lieutenant come over the radio indicating the deputies had located the black van and that a suspect was in custody. He responded telling them he was in route to their location and to wait there until he arrived.

"Before we get there, is there anything else you want me to know about what happened back there at your apartment? You said something about a second shooter."

"He took off down the stairwell and got into the van. Maybe your guys caught him."

"Can you describe him?"

"He's white, about five feet ten, and goes about one-sixty. He was wearing a grey shirt and what looked like dark brown pants."

"Did you get a look at his face? Any tattoos?"

"No, but I saw his shoes as he went out the door. They were black sports shoes with black laces."

He picked up the mic and radioed the team about the description he was just given.

The officer at the scene responded. "Sorry Captain, that's not the guy we've got in custody. Your guy must have fled the scene or got out somewhere before we pulled over the van."

Calvin was disappointed. "I was certain he got into the van. I could have sworn I saw him on the front passenger side trying to close the door as the van was leaving."

Immediately, the Captain put out an APB using the description Calvin had provided.

As all of that was happening, Randy and Lisa were diligently working their way through a myriad of websites and internet records trying to locate as much information as they could about Michael Carlon. They found a few details, but neither of them was able to locate a current address or phone number.

Lisa leaned back in her chair. "I'm beginning to wonder if this guy is still alive. There are some pictures and old articles, but nothing current. Do you have any other ideas? I'm just about at my wit's end."

For the last fifteen minutes, Randy had been sitting at the computer station to their right. At first, he started searching and tracking background information from a story he had discovered from a previous search. "Actually, I think I do. Let me try something."

He pulled the keyboard closer toward him and typed in the name Michael C. Trout. His search discovered a connection between a series of articles about a person living in Miami, Florida.

"Who's Michael Trout?"

He pointed at the screen. "He's Michael Carlon. He's got a list as long as your arm of other aliases he's used over the last eight years."

She moved her chair closer to his and leaned forward slightly for a better view of the screen.

"Where did you find this?"

He grinned. "If we had searched the arrest records first, we would have saved ourselves a bunch of time. Thank heavens for aliases. Those took me right to him."

He brought up an arrest record he had found so she could read it for herself.

She pointed at the screen as she read. "The arresting officer on this event indicated he was charged with burglary, breaking and entering, and a bunch of other low-level crimes. This doesn't sound like the same guy we learned about through Max's notes."

He scrolled down the screen until he was able to point to the date the arrest record was made. "This was six years before he ended up rolling into the big time. I'm interested in knowing who his connections were during that time period. He had to have help along the way."

"What do you suppose interested Max about this guy?"

He shrugged his shoulders. "I'm hoping that will come out when we get back to the note books tonight. Let's finish up here, grab some dinner, and then head over to the house. Howard should be back in a little while, and we can pick it up at that point."

They printed all of their findings, shut down the computers, and headed for the elevator.

After getting off on the first floor and saying good-bye to the security guard, he held the door open for her as they exited the building.

She smiled at him and brushed his shoulder as she walked by him. The perfume she was wearing was like a breath of fresh air to him. He watched the wind take her hair and blow it away from her neck making it look as if it was dancing in the early evening breeze. The angle of the fading sunlight gave her hair a look as if it was glistening. She noticed his looking at her and smiled at him. She stopped and turned toward him.

"I know a nice little restaurant that some might call a hole-in-the-wall, but they've got a really great omelet. How about letting me treat you tonight?"

He was looking forward to spending more time with her and dinner was high on his list. "That sounds like a plan to me."

CHAPTER 27

At the Ewing's House, Sunday evening, March 31, 2013

Howard had managed to get back to his house by four-thirty. He grabbed a bottle of water from the fridge and made his way to his easy chair. His intention was to catch a quick nap before the others showed up.

Just as he leaned back and put his feet up, the phone rang. It was their son, William.

"I wanted to let you know that I'm on my way over. I've got something you might want to see."

"Like what?"

"I found some other pictures that I took for Max. They were on the end of another roll I had forgotten to develop. I should be there in about thirty minutes."

"Okay, but come in through the back porch, and park your car on the side."

They said their good-byes, and Howard stretched out once more to try to finish the nap he wanted. This time his cell phone buzzed. He picked it up and noticed that it was Calvin.

"Hey, do you mind if I come over a little early? I'm bringing someone with me, too."

"Who are you bringing home this time?"

"No, it's nothing like that. I've been talking with Captain Edward Connors about this, and he's interested in seeing the details we've put together."

"Are you sure we can trust him?"

Yes, I believe we can. Before we get there, we'll swing by the sub place and pick up a few sandwiches for dinner."

"Be sure to get one for William, too. He'll be here in a little while.

"What about Randy and Lisa?"

"They're on their own for dinner but should be here before too long."

"Okay, we'll see you in about thirty minutes."

He glanced at the clock, after disconnecting, and decided a nap wasn't in the cards this afternoon. Instead, he picked up one of the note pads that was on the top of box number four and sat down on the sofa where he started searching for information that might help advance the story. The next thing he knew, William was pounding on the sliding glass doors to be let in.

"I'm coming," he yelled, "hold your horses." He unlatched the lock.

"Are you okay, Dad? I was beginning to get worried."

"I guess at my age if your body wants to take a nap, it does so. I guess I just dozed off."

William came in and walked over to the table. He opened a large envelope, removed several pictures that he had taken for Max, and put them on the table. Howard began pushing them around looking quickly at most of them.

"What am I looking at here, son?"

"Mostly, these are shots I took at the same two locations the other pictures were taken." He searched for one particular picture which happened to be near the bottom of the stack. "This is the one you might find interesting." He handed it to him.

It was a photo of a group of people standing near a street corner. It seemed nondescript at first glance. "Again, what am I looking at here? It looks like a bunch of people with nowhere to go."

William picked up the magnifying glass from the table. "Check the dude near the center of those people. He's the one with the newspaper under his left arm. Tell me, who does that look like?" He handed the magnifying glass to him.

He studied the photo for a few seconds, before chuckling softly.

"Hello, Phillip Seaver. It's funny that you should be seen amongst such an esteemed group of individuals. Senator Haskell must be involved somehow." He turned toward William. "Where was this picture taken and tell me about the time frame in relationship to the others."

"It was taken almost a block south of the State Attorney's office, but less than an hour before I shot the others."

Howard located the first group of pictures William brought, which had been placed under a stack of documents, and started searching to see if any of those who had come out of the building in the first group of pictures had met with the senator prior to entering.

William searched through the stack he had just brought and pulled three photos to hand to him. "These are the other shots of that same group. It appears that Phillip Seaver is talking with several of them in each of these."

"I still have no idea who some of these guys are. Somehow, we've got to identify them and figure out what in tarnation they were all doing at that corner."

He went back to the sofa and sat down. "You know, there's something we haven't considered here. Suppose that the State Attorney's office was the intended meeting place and the State Attorney is involved in this. What do you think of that idea?"

"That's a lot of supposing. If he is involved, then what is the connection between Senator Haskell and that office? And, why is Phillip Seaver there instead of the Senator?"

"To find out, I think a trip to Orlando is on tomorrow's agenda."

Just then, the doorbell rang. It was Calvin and Captain Connors.

Howard let them in. Calvin introduced him to Howard and William, while they were at the door. Then, they all headed for the porch.

Captain Connors saw the paneling and wasn't sure what it was he was looking at or what it represented. He turned to Calvin. "Is this the proof you were talking about?"

"Yes, but it's only part of it." He motioned for Howard to jump into the conversation at that point.

Captain Connors had not expected to hear the amount of detail or see the amount of evidence they had accumulated in a relatively short period of time. Howard was agonizingly thorough as he unfolded the story and the evidence that supported it. He didn't mince words or play word games. His language was clear. His voice never wavered.

"Captain, our friend and colleague was murdered because he knew about this – apparently from the beginning. He never said anything to us about it or anything about what he did researching it. However, he documented a lot of this. That's pretty much what you're looking at here. In a little while, there will be two others here with more details. We believe there is more to this than what we know so far. We're not sure how far up the chain it goes or who's involved. What we know is that Max died a senseless death and that one of these persons we've uncovered is probably responsible for his death. It's not just about a story anymore. It's about bringing Max's killer to justice. We could be going up against some serious manpower."

Captain Connors shook his head, and then looked directly at Calvin. "What is it you want from me?"

"It's like Howard said. We're a little short in the area of leverage or muscle. We know that news reporters in several areas have become targets. Those who took their place were hand-picked and conform immediately to directions. We need protection while we continue to investigate this."

"You've indicated that there have been incidents in several states. That's a little out of my jurisdiction."

Calvin put down the pictures he was holding and faced the captain. "We know we don't have a lot of contacts outside of Florida. I was hoping you might."

"I've got a couple of buddies who work at the FBI out of the Jacksonville office. How do you feel about my contacting them?"

Howard spoke up. "You do realize, of course, that if any of this gets out, before we know who's behind all of this, we'll never get to the bottom of it. They'll manage to cover it all up like they have so far."

"They probably will, except these buddies of mine know how to work behind the scenes. Would you be willing to meet with them and discuss this in greater detail?"

Howard thought about it and nodded in agreement. Calvin did so as well.

Back in Georgia, Carla and Susan had just returned from taking an extended walk through the wooded area north of the cabin.

Susan went over to the sink to wash her hands. "I could get used to living in a place like this."

Carla, who was stirring the crock pot meal she had started earlier, agreed. "That is the intention that Howard and I have. We're just not ready to leave the city – so to speak. It is quiet up here."

"It's kind of nice to be able to hear yourself think. Tampa traffic can be so loud at times. I've actually had to check my apartment windows to make sure they were all closed. It is refreshing, however, to walk among such a beautiful setting. I could hear myself breathing as I walked."

"Howard and I love that about the woods." She put the lid back on the crock pot. "Supper should be ready in about thirty minutes. Would you like some corn bread with the soup?" She reached into the cabinet where she was standing and got a bowl from the bottom shelf.

"Sure – that sounds really good." She sat down at the kitchen table. "What do you know about Calvin? I know he lives by himself."

Carla smiled. "He's had a pretty rough go of it lately. He was dating some gal from St. Augustine – not too long ago. I'm not sure exactly what happened with that relationship, but I don't think he's seeing anyone at the moment. Why do you ask?"

Susan leaned forward and put her elbows on the table. "He just seems like a lonely sort who needs someone to take care of him. I know he's modest and is quite the gentleman. I can attest to that."

"He's always been a gentleman. He's a good man whose luck with women hasn't been the best. He was married a long time ago to a woman who divorced him and ran off with another man – I think to Memphis. They only had been married for a few years when she decided that she didn't want to have any of his children or to live in a small town. She wanted the life of a big city girl and wanted to move back north. So, she latched on to the first thing that came along that showed any promise of her not having to settle down. She's somewhere in the Chicago vicinity now, I think. It about broke his heart, but he seems to have recovered from it."

"You mean he doesn't have any children?"

"No, he doesn't, but he treats our William, however, as good as any father could treat his own son."

"He's kept himself in pretty good shape – for someone his age, I mean."

"He runs a lot, and I think he goes to the gym two-or-three times a week." She paused for a few seconds, stopped what she was doing at the kitchen counter, and turned around. "If I didn't know any better, I'd say someone your age might be a little confused here about him. He's in his early sixties."

Susan smiled. "I've read somewhere that's like being in your forties nowadays."

Carla grinned and went back to making the cornbread.

Susan walked over to the refrigerator, opened the door, and grabbed the rest of her bottled water she had brought with her. "How long do you think it's going to take before it'll be safe enough for us to go home?"

Carla stopped beating the cornbread batter, turned, and looked at her. "I wish I knew, but it won't be until they've figured out who killed Max. Honestly, I have no real idea. I just know that Howard is not going to let this rest, until Max's killer is brought to justice."

"Were they good friends – I mean Howard and Max?"

"Yes, they were. They worked on several stories at the paper over the years. When Max and Eileen moved to Charlotte, they kept in contact with each other. Things changed a little when they moved back, but their friendship was solid. They hung out a lot together during the work week, but the weekends belonged to the families. Our son, William, is named after Max's father."

Susan got up from her chair, went over to where she was standing, and leaned against the kitchen counter. Carla stopped; put down the spatula she had been using, turned, and looked directly at her.

"One of the reasons you and I are at this cabin is because Howard thinks this story doesn't have a happy ending. Max's death came as a shock to him – and to me, as far as that goes. He hasn't been able to let go of this for almost two months. All of what we've learned so far points to something that is pretty big – and very ugly. You're a reporter. You know what that means."

"It means that the truth must come out – no matter who's impacted."

"It means that these three guys are not going to let up until somebody's going to jail." She paused for a few seconds. "Plus, while you're here and if you should think of anything that might be helpful, you need to let me know so I can contact Howard."

"I thought we were supposed to lay low and stay off the grid."

"We are, but we still have appointed times to make contact. Howard wanted me to let you know that."

"He's thought of just about everything."

"He usually does."

Chapter 28

*Two miles east of Washington, D.C. 6:30 p.m., Sunday evening
March 31, 2013*

A telephone rings at an upscale townhouse two miles east of Washington, D.C.

"They didn't get him."

"You assured me they would. What happened?"

"They went in with guns blazing, and that's not what I told them to do. The deputies were all over the place by the time we found out about it."

"What are your plans now? You've been paid handsomely for this, and I expect you to finish it."

"Don't worry. We've got it covered. We should be able to deal with this in the morning. I'm moving assets to the location as I speak, and I expect results by noon tomorrow."

"Don't make such a mess of it this time."

That quickly, the telephone call ended.

XXXXX

Randy and Lisa were just finishing dinner, when his cell phone buzzed.

He connected the call. He listened for a few seconds and then responded. "Howard, we should be there in about thirty minutes. We're just finishing right now."

"That's not why I'm calling. There was an attempt on Calvin's life earlier today. I recommend you and Lisa take every precaution before driving here. I expect him and a local sheriff's deputy to arrive in about ten minutes. We've got a lot to go over."

"Yeah, he called me a little while ago. I guess you know the deputies took Betsy away from him and took it down to headquarters for ballistics."

"There's no doubt that he shot and killed two of them, but the third guy apparently got away. They managed to commandeer the vehicle and to arrest the driver, but the other suspect fled the scene, and no one has seen or heard of him since."

"Just make sure that you and Lisa are not followed. I suggest you implement what we talked about at our last meeting."

Randy understood. "It will take a little longer, but we'll be there shortly." He disconnected the call.

Lisa, who sat quietly and watching him as he spoke, leaned forward slightly. "Obviously, that was Howard. What is it that might take a little longer?"

Randy waved for the waiter and asked for their bill. Once he paid it, he called for a cab. She wasn't thrilled about what he told her she had to do, but she agreed. Once he was certain she understood his directions and the reasons why, he gave her cab fare, and waited until it arrived.

As soon as the cab drove up to the curb, Lisa stood up to leave. He reached out and grabbed her hand. She smiled at him. He squeezed her hand slightly as if to say, 'be careful,' before she exited the restaurant and got into the back seat. He waited until the cab was out of sight before leaving and getting into his vehicle. He drove around for about twenty minutes checking to see if he was being followed. That's when Lisa called him.

"How much longer do we need to keep doing this?"

"You're certain I'm not being followed?"

"There has been no car or cars that have tailed you for the past twenty minutes. I think we're safe."

"Have the cabbie drop you off at the gas station just ahead up here on the right, and I'll pick you up."

After getting into the car with him, he told her about what had happened to Calvin.

"What have we gotten ourselves into?"

"Apparently, something that someone wants to keep off the radar."

"How can you make such a callous remark like that? Your friend might have been killed and you speak as if nothing happened. What about us? Are we next?"

He didn't want to answer that question because he knew the truth might upset her even more. His silence was damning.

"Obviously, you're being way too cavalier about this. Maybe, you should be just a little more concerned about our safety. I'm in this too, you know."

His grip tightened on the steering wheel trying not to react too quickly. Her safety was all he could think about. "Once we finish at Howard's tonight, you and I are going off the grid for a few days. It's the only way I know to keep from being an easy target."

"What does that mean? I'm not in this like you are. Maybe you should consider staying at my place, instead."

"Once they connect me to this, they will connect you to it as well. You'll be safer out of sight for a few days until we are able to counter all of this."

"Randy, we both need to go to work tomorrow. I've got a job to do – and so do you."

"I know, but there are some things we need to do to make sure that we at least try to cover our tracks."

"That settles it. You're staying at my place, and that's final."

The last three minutes of the car ride to Howard's home was quiet. Neither one of them said one word – that is until Lisa decided to break the silence.

"Just wait and see. There are a few surprises I've got in store for you."

Once all of them were seated on the porch and introductions were completed, Calvin explained why he had asked Captain Connors to join them. Lisa sat quietly through all of it, even managing a smile every so often. She asked a question or two, but let Randy do most of the talking. William didn't budge during any of it, except to fill his coffee cup on two separate occasions. He was zoned in on everyone's comments and all of the details that were flying around the room.

Randy explained about who he had named 'the anonymous computer friend,' and the information that lead him to the background on Michael Conlon, AKA Michael C. Trout. The contact with Phillip Seaver connection was made for the others to understand that he believed this was a political overreach that had splinter groups making mistakes.

Captain Connors' interest grew the more they were able to connect a criminal element to a known political figure. He started asking pointed questions that pushed Randy's and Howard's findings. Lisa saw what was happening.

"Captain, what are we to do about the threats that have been made so far? We know that several news reporters and communications people have been either killed or ended up missing. We've got no one to watch our backs, except for the ones you see in this room."

"Miss Jacobs, I might be able to rectify that over the short term. For long term effects, I'll need to make a few phone calls and visit with an old friend of mine."

Howard stood up and looked at Randy. "You might want to take a look at this picture that William gave me tonight." He handed it and the magnifying glass to him.

"Look carefully at the guy in the picture holding the newspaper under his arm."

Randy's face lit up. "That is Phillip Seaver – Senator Haskell's aide. What was he doing down here that day? And, why was he meeting with these folks?"

Calvin sat straight up. "Do we know who those folks are?"

Howard walked over to the paneling and pointed to one of the articles posted. It had several strings attached to it, and it was connected to several other articles. "Take a look at their faces one more time. We know one of them is Peter Theron – and he's dead now. We also found Gerald Reinhart – and he's dead now as well. I suspect that Mr. Seaver was making a list, checking it twice, and he marked those who hadn't been nice. The real question is: who are those other guys in that picture?"

Captain Connors walked over to the paneling. "Tell me, again, what these strings represent."

Howard began his spiel but was interrupted by Calvin. "Captain, we've giving you as much as we have. We feel that someone or some group is coming after us before too long. Frankly, I don't think any of us are safe."

He had seen and heard enough. "I agree, but it's going to take time to get things set up." He walked over and stood next to Howard. "I'd like to use your house as a command post, for the time being, because we can piggy-back off of your paneling to save a lot of time getting people up-to-speed. Until I'm able to provide you protection, I am suggesting that you not leave here tonight."

Lisa reacted. "I've got to go to work in the morning, and everything I need is at my apartment."

Randy spoke up as well. "I'm supposed to pick up Mr. Rayner and bring him here in the morning, too."

Calvin chuckled. "Howard, I told you a while back that your guest room would be just right for me."

While the three of them continued their conversations, Captain Connors called his FBI contact in Jacksonville. He and Earl Walker had known each other since their days in the United States Army. They met while serving for three years in the U.S. Army with the Military Police. They both had been assigned to Fort Gordon, Georgia at the same time for training and they both ended up being assigned to Fort Jackson, South Carolina.

Once he was discharged, Earl took advantage of the GI Bill benefits he had earned, attended the University of Florida, and graduated with a degree in Criminology in June 1978. He applied for a position with the Federal Bureau of Investigation that fall, was accepted, took his initial training at Quantico, Virginia, and upon graduating was immediately assigned as a field agent working through the Laboratory Division. After six years of intense field work, he was reassigned to the Records Management Division where he spent most of those thirteen years honing his skills and establishing a strong intra-agency network of colleagues and friends. In 1998, he resumed his field work, until 2006, working with the Critical Incident Response Group as one of its team leaders in Atlanta, Georgia.

In the spring that year, he was assigned to the headquarters office in Jacksonville, Florida where he became the lead investigator for the State, reporting only to the Criminal Investigative Division in Washington, D.C. It was during the early part of his assignment at the Jacksonville office that he and Captain Connors renewed their friendship and established a strong working alliance.

"Before I let you hang up, I need to ask you a couple of questions about your sources."

Captain Connors excused himself and stepped out onto the patio, closing the sliding glass doors behind him. "Earl, these folks are on to something that smells really bad. I'm strapped on jurisdiction issues because they've proven that what apparently is happening is taking place across state lines. These guys are credible and thorough. Right now, one in particular is being pursued with prejudice. What I haven't told them is that the three guys we're aware of, that tried to take him out this afternoon, are three thugs we've linked as possible suspects in two other homicides and a kidnapping."

"What exactly is it that they have managed to get themselves into?"

"It appears to have something to do with the takeover of the news business. Don't ask me who it is because I don't know – and neither do they. They've stirred up a hornet's nest for sure."

"Aside from crossing state lines, what else is there?"

"They've allegedly connected one of Senator Haskell's aides into it somehow. I'm not too clear on all of this yet. I think it would be a good idea for you to come down here tomorrow and listen to what they have to say. Let them tell you what they've got and what they think. Tonight, I plan to secure this house and the evidence they've accumulated."

"I won't be able to get there until a little after ten. I'll call you before I leave headquarters to let you know I'm on the way."

After they said their good-byes, Captain Connors went back into the house. Everyone stopped talking and directed their attention at him.

"I just got off the phone with my contact at the FBI in Jacksonville. He'll be here in the morning a little after ten o'clock. In the meanwhile, we need to put a collective plan together about securing these premises for the evening." He turned to Lisa. "If you decide to go back to your apartment for the evening, it would be wise to let me have a deputy camp outside your place for the evening – just in case."

Randy chimed in. "In that case Lisa, I'll take you up on your offer."

On the way to pick up a few things at his place, Randy and Lisa had a heart-to-heart discussion about the addition of the FBI becoming involved. They both agreed that it was probably best for everyone's safety at this point, but Lisa still wasn't convinced that she was a target like he was.

"I haven't had anyone following me around like you have."

He chuckled slightly. "At least you don't think you have. Like it or not – you need to remember that you and I are connected in this thing. Even our anonymous computer person knows we are joined at the hip."

She smiled at him. "Now that's a picture I'd like to erase from my mind's eye."

When they reached his place, it only took him five minutes to gather some clothes and toiletries, put them in an overnight bag, and secure the windows and the door to the back stairway. He made sure that his cat, Calli, had plenty of water and food and that her potty box was clean. On his way out the door, he flipped the security light switch that set up the motion sensor he had installed last fall. "Okay, I'm done here."

They went downstairs and walked toward his car. "Before we head for your place, I just want to make sure the officer in the patrol car following us has your address and my cell phone number."

Lisa agreed. "Make sure he has my cell phone number, too."

When he got back into the car, he turned to Lisa. "I hope you're right about this."

"You're forgetting about that surprise I told you about."

"Oh – you're right. I did forget."

"When we get there, I guarantee you that you'll never forget this evening – ever."

CHAPTER 29
Sunday Evening, 9:30 p.m., March 31, 2013

"You can sleep in the spare bedroom," Lisa said, while pointing to the room across from hers. "The bathroom is the first door on your left."

She went into the kitchen. "Would you like something to drink?"

"That sounds great."

When he opened the door to the spare bedroom, he turned on the light and then put his overnight bag on a chair that was in front of a small desk. He glanced around and realized the spare room had been decorated in a more masculine fashion. The featured colors were dark blue and a dark tan. The walls were light beige and the bedspread was a shade darker that blended well with the plush, light brown carpet. The pictures hanging on the wall were of forest settings, wildlife, and hunting scenes from what appeared to be the New England area.

"This is unexpected," he whispered. When he finished unpacking a few of his things, he joined her at the kitchen table.

"I see what you meant about being surprised. I hardly expected to find your spare bedroom decorated so nicely in those colors."

She smiled and made eye contact with him. "I wonder how Susan and Carla are getting along."

"I imagine just fine – but I haven't heard anything."

She stood up, picked up a bag of chips, and offered him some. "Are you hungry? I guess I didn't eat enough dinner tonight because I could really eat something right now."

"No, thank you. I'm okay, but these chips will do just fine." He smiled. "I see what you meant about being surprised. I didn't expect a spare bedroom to feel right at home for me," he said. "Really? But that's not my big surprise for you. Let me show you. Follow me," she said, as she headed for her bedroom.

When she walked into her room, she flipped on the light switch and asked him to come in. She then walked over to her closet, pushed one of the sliding doors to the right, and then pushed several of her hanging clothes to her right as well. He watched as she pulled some kind of lever that caused the back wall of the closet to pop open. There, behind all of those clothes was a secret compartment where several weapons had been hung on the wall. His eyes gravitated to the Browning 12-gauge, pump action shot gun and the .357 magnum pistol below it. She turned around and smiled at him.

"I think we have enough to handle whatever may come our way this evening. Are you surprised?"

He was speechless. He sat down on the edge of her bed staring at six different weapons that looked as if they were brand new. Ammunition for all of them was neatly stacked at the base of the compartment – enough to start a war.

His expression must have been priceless because she couldn't help but to laugh at him.

"Well – are you going to say anything or not?"

He cleared his throat. "Where did you get all of these?"

She was still laughing. "It's a hobby of mine." She pointed at the .357 magnum. "My father gave this to me when I first moved here." Then, she pointed at the 9mm Ruger SR9 pistol. "My husband gave this one to me the year before he died."

"What's this," he asked, pointing at a rifle.

"It's a Marlin 60SS, 22 long rifle. I bought that as a gift to me two years ago."

He was still speechless. He had no clue that she knew anything about weapons. He listened as she told him about the others, making sure he knew the story behind each one. When she finished talking about them, she handed him the 9mm Ruger and told him to keep it with him during the night. She preferred the shotgun and told him that it would be by her bedside during the entire time they were here.

"Who else knows about this?"

"At the moment, only you do – and I'd like to keep it that way. These are for protection."

She reached in and picked up the shotgun, a box of shells, and sat down on the bed next to him. She loaded it and then leaned it against the wall between her nightstand and the bed. Then she handed him a box of 9mm rounds for the Ruger. "Now, it's your turn."

He managed to figure it out, completed the loading of two magazines of seven rounds each, and engaged the safety,

"Nicely done – you've done this before, haven't you?"

"Nope – tonight's the first time for this one."

She reached over and put her right hand on his left thigh. "I think the coffee's ready."

He placed his left hand on top of hers. "I certainly am surprised. And, I'm likely to never forget this evening – ever."

She leaned toward him, shoulder-to-shoulder, and smiled at him. "The night is early, and we've got a full pot of coffee." Before she stood, she leaned over and kissed his left cheek. "Come on, we've got a lot to talk about and plans to make for tomorrow."

Back at the Ewing's, Captain Connors had welcomed two additional officers who carried in large, black leather briefcases containing communication devices. There were two other officers who were stationed outside, but they remained in their vehicle.

Howard showed the officers, who had set up their equipment on the table in the porch, where they could sleep for the night.

"Captain, what exactly are we going to do here tonight?"

"You're going to tell me, again, about these incidents and show me all of the data you have collected. I want to be able to explain to Earl, when he gets here in the morning, a lot more detail than I have at the moment."

Calvin, who had been watching and listening to everything, sat down on the sofa. "When am I going to get my weapon back? I'm kind of feeling a little naked here without it."

"You needn't worry about that. We've got enough manpower to do the job for the evening. Like Mr. Ewing, I need for you to make sure I'm up-to-speed on the details of your investigation." He paused for a second. "I really wish Mr. Tomlin and his girlfriend had stayed here for the evening."

"She's not his girlfriend," Howard said. "They're working on this story together with us."

Captain Connors chuckled slightly. "You could have fooled me. She's got a thing for him – or am I off base here?"

Calvin looked at Howard. They both shrugged their shoulders.

William, who had hardly said a word all evening, walked over to where his dad was standing and whispered to him. "Is all this necessary?"

He smiled at him and put his right hand on his left shoulder. "It may not be, but I sure feel better knowing they're here. We won't have to call them later tonight should we need them."

By eleven o'clock, Howard, Calvin and William decided to call it an evening. Captain Connors checked the doors and windows one more time, before he stretched out on the sofa. Five minutes later, the lights at the Ewing household had been turned off, everyone was accounted for, and it was quiet. It was the kind of quiet where you can hear yourself breathing, while the clock hanging on the kitchen wall announced the passing of each second, almost daring someone or something to break the silence.

Back at Lisa's apartment, Randy and Lisa were sitting on the sofa talking about how the story was taking on new meaning. For more than thirty minutes, they had been discussing whether or not it was a good move to take Susan to the cabin and away from the area. Randy tried to explain why Howard felt much better about it, especially since the attempt on Calvin's life.

Lisa, sitting on one end of the sofa with her feet curled up under her, reached over and put down her coffee cup on the end table. "I think I'd like to take my shower now and get into my night clothes. We can continue this when I'm done. If you'd like to shower, there are towels and a wash cloth on the vanity in your bathroom."

She got up and walked toward her room. He got up, retrieved a set of pajamas he had brought with him, went into the bathroom and closed the door. He reached into the shower stall and turned on the water, and periodically checked the water flow to adjust its temperature. When it was to his liking, he got undressed and then stepped into the shower. That's when he realized he had forgotten to check for a bar of soap. Finding none, he stepped back out, wrapped one of the towels around his waist and checked under the sink. Then, there was a knock on the door.

"I forgot to put some soap in there for you."

He opened the door just enough and found her standing provocatively close to the open door in a very sheer nightgown with a bar of soap in her left hand. "Will this do?" She smiled at him.

"That's very nice – thank you."

He opened the door wider to take the soap from her. When he did so, she leaned forward putting both hands on the door frame and looked directly at him.

"It's the last bar of soap I have. Would you like to share it?"

CHAPTER 30
Monday morning, 0300 hours, April 1, 2013

Things that go 'bump in the night' usually are not just coincidental. Generally, there's a reason and it isn't always bad. But at three o'clock in the morning at the Ewing's place, there was more than mischief afoot. There were four armed men quietly approaching the east side of the house. The security light, which Howard had installed ten feet up on a tree on the east side of the house, came on. One of the officers in the unmarked patrol car across the street saw it.

"Hey, Justin, wake up. I think we've got visitors."

Deputy Justin Sekel sat up and tried to focus on the field area at the east end of the house. Deputy Sergeant Stuart "Stu" Biers got on the radio and alerted Captain Connors.

He picked up the mic and responded. "Just sit tight and wait. We'll check on it from here." He directed one of the deputies, who was sitting at the table and reading the newspaper, to take up a position in the room where Howard was sleeping. "When you go in there, make sure the lights stay off and he gets out of there pronto. Tell him to go into the bathroom down the hallway – and to stay there." He ordered the other to go into the kitchen and to position himself where he could see the foyer and the hallway.

Deputy Sekel, using binoculars, was watching the area east of the house, when the movement-sensing security light, which only had been on for a minute, turned off.

"They're moving again. I see three. Where'd the other one go?" The light came back on revealing three of the four heavily armed would-be attackers approaching quickly.

"Captain, we see three of the four hostiles carrying MP10's. We don't know where the fourth guy went. He must be in the back heading for the patio and the porch."

No sooner had he said that than the sliding glass doors were shattered into thousands of pieces from automatic weapon's fire.

Captain Connors dove behind the sofa and got as low on the floor as he could. He drew his weapon and waited for the intruder to stop firing.

The gun fire woke Howard from a sound sleep, and he sat straight up in bed. Instinctively, he went into the master bathroom and locked the door behind him. The deputy didn't have time to tell him to get into the other bathroom because one of the intruders had started spraying the room with several rounds. He had just walked into the room, was hit by one of the bullets, and went down near the doorway.

Calvin recognized the sounds of the weapons and knew they were outgunned. As he ran into the hallway, he could see the officer lying on the floor. The intruder sent several more rounds pounding into the wall on the other side of the room – destroying everything in their way.

In between bursts, he ran into Howard's room, and saw that the deputy had been hit and was lying face down on the floor. He wasn't moving. He quickly checked for a pulse but heard the three intruders outside the window directing each other's movements. He picked up the officer's 9mm Glock handgun, and the officer's radio, and moved toward the wall immediately to the left of the window. While he was standing there, he could hear the two deputies, who were now moving cautiously toward the patio, talking to Captain Connors on the radio.

"We're moving to the west side of the house and approaching from the back. We've called for backup and they're on their way. They're two minutes out. Is anyone hit?"

"I don't know." Captain Connors rose up to look over the sofa.

He heard three shots that came from the backyard. The intruder, who had shot up the porch, fell to his knees, and then fell head-first through what was left of the sliding glass doors. Deputy Sekel entered right behind him. He leaned down and felt the neck of the intruder for a pulse. "Captain – where are you?"

Three more shots were heard. This time Deputy Sergeant Biers yelled out. "They are fleeing on foot to the east. I'm in pursuit."

Captain Connors stood up, directed Deputy Sekel to secure both the scene and the body and then went to check on Calvin and Howard. When he discovered the injured deputy, he immediately called for an ambulance. Calvin leaned down and offered his assistance. At the same time, he raised his voice. "Howard, where are you?"

There was no response.

He yelled a second time. Then, he heard Howard's voice coming from the bathroom.

Calvin smiled. "You can come out now. They're gone."

William, who had stretched out on the sofa in Howard's office, heard Calvin's voice, came out from behind the filing cabinet he had managed to hide behind, and walked into Howard's room.

"Where's my dad?"

Howard opened the door and hobbled out of the bathroom.

Calvin noticed the limp. "Are you okay?"

"I think so. I must have twisted my ankle when I dove into the tub." That's when he noticed the deputy on the floor. "Is he dead?"

Captain Connors looked up at him. "He's been injured, but help's on the way. I need for all of you to stay here with him until the paramedics get here. Keep pressure on his wound and don't move him."

He stood up and moved quickly toward the front part of the house. He could hear the sirens of several patrol cars blaring that were headed in their direction. He listened to the radio chatter of the deputies tracking the fleeing intruders. Deputy Sergeant Biers had captured one of them, but the other two had made it to a vehicle that had been waiting for them at a predetermined location. It was now speeding south on an access road trying to avoid three deputies who were in pursuit. Shots were reported being fired from the fleeing vehicle.

When Captain Connors reentered the house, he instructed Deputy Sekel to take up a position at the southeast corner of the house. He walked onto the porch and checked his communications equipment. It had been damaged, but it was still working.

Pressing a series of buttons and quickly typing in entry codes and passwords, he was able to connect with headquarters.

"Patch me through to this number." He was calling Lisa's home phone. It rang several times before she answered the call.

His voice wasn't initially recognized by her. "Are you two okay?"

She mumbled that she was, before realizing who it was that was calling. "Why – what's happened?"

"There's been an incident here. I'm sending two officers to assist both of you to vacate those premises and to be taken to headquarters. Put together a few things that will last you for a few days and be ready to go in about ten minutes. Keep this line open – just in case."

She nodded her head, as she walked toward Randy's room

Randy, who had been awakened by the call, met her at his door and took the phone from her hand.

"What's happened?"

"I'll fill you both in later. Right now, you two need to vacate those premises and go with the deputies who should be arriving there in ten minutes or less. "

"Are the others okay? They're not hurt, are they?"

"Everyone's fine. One of my deputies, however, was hit, but he's going to be okay."

"Can I speak to Howard?"

"He's a little a busy at the moment. You'll see him a little later this morning. Right now, you two need to get yourselves together and get ready to leave. Make sure this line is left open, until the deputies arrive, and you exit that building. Is that clear?"

"Yes, sir, it is."

He set the telephone receiver on the kitchen table and returned to her bedroom. Lisa already had begun packing a small suitcase. She called out to him.

"When you've finished, I could use a hand with my things."

He knew what she was talking about. She had grabbed the .357 revolver, two other pistols, boxes of ammunition, and put them into a leather carrying case that also had room for her shotgun. "We're not leaving here without these."

He marveled at how cool she had remained throughout all of this.

He had started to change clothes, when she stepped into the room. She was still wearing that extremely sheer nightgown that showed off her amazing figure. His eyes met hers and she walked over to him, hugged him, and then leaned back slightly while still in his arms.

"I told you this would be an evening you would never forget. I just wish I would have been able to fix you breakfast later this morning."

She turned and walked to the door, paused, and then turned around. "You can't say I'm not fun." She smiled at him and then went back to her room to get dressed and finish packing.

CHAPTER 31
Monday morning, 0630 hours, April 1, 2013 at a safe house

When the proverbial "cat is out of the bag," all of the mice, that had something to do with trying to do in the cat, should feel threatened – especially when the mice just can't wait to rat on their buddies.

One of the intruders, who had been captured during his attempt to flee the scene, started talking and didn't quit. Captain Connors, after reading the suspect his rights, detained him at the house until he was transported to headquarters. During those forty-five minutes, he answered every question thrown at him without flinching or batting an eye lid. Howard, Calvin, and William witnessed the questioning and took copious notes during the entire process.

What they learned was that they had only scratched the surface of a conspiracy that involved several groups in several States. Everything had to do with connections to newspapers, television stations, and several of them ran websites as well. It was pure luck, as Calvin called it, that they had been able to put together enough information early in their investigation to find the involvement of political figures. The suspect confirmed their suspicions about Senator Haskell, but called him the "point man," not the person-in-charge. He didn't know the name of that person, but he knew that he was from the Washington, D.C. area. When they examined the suspect's cell phone, several of the calls he had received came from the D.C. area code.

Howard, who was sitting on the sofa on the porch trying to figure out how he was going to repair the damages to his house, heard his cell phone buzz. It was Randy calling.

Randy's voice sounded as if he was out of breath. "We're on our way to a safe house, and I've been told to make this short. The lieutenant told us that arrangements were in the works for you three to be picked up within the hour and transported to the same location. You may want to ask Captain Connors about what they're going to do with the note pads and other materials you've put in the utility room."

"He's indicated they're planning on bringing them to the safe house as well. I get the distinct impression we're going to be holed-up like hamsters – possibly until this thing blows over."

"That's pretty much what the lieutenant told me, too. Look, I've got to get off of the phone. He's about to go ballistic on me because he thinks I already have been on this thing too long."

"I understand. I guess we'll catch up with each other a little later today."

Howard heard Randy disconnect the call. He put his cell phone in his front, right pants pocket, stood up and walked over to where Captain Connors was standing.

"If we're going to be penned up somewhere, could you at least let me inform my wife?"

"You'll have time enough for that later. Right now, you three are to get your things and load that van that just pulled up."

"What about the repairs to my house? I've got windows and doors that need to be boarded up and there's glass everywhere."

"I've got a team coming later this morning to secure all of this for you. Just get yourself and your things and get in that van. Time is of the utmost importance at the moment."

It took them another couple of minutes before they could load the van. Howard insisted on taking the boxes of note pads they had been working on. Once they were on the van and everyone was seated, Captain Connors leaned in and gave them instructions.

"The three of you have upset some very influential and important people. I just got a call from Special Agent Earl Walker. He's on his way here right now, after being rudely awakened by the United States Attorney General wanting to know more about what is going on than we know at the moment. My boss is about to have a hissy fit because nobody's going to get any sleep until we have those answers. The sooner we can get you isolated and protected, the sooner you'll be able to continue your investigation. Whatever you do, you must make sure that Agent Walker is aware of it – before you wander off and try to do something stupid by yourself. Is that clear?"

They all nodded in agreement, except Calvin got out of his seat and stood next to the van. He cleared his throat and then pointed at the captain.

"It's going to be tough to follow up on leads without being able to do that in person. I'd like my car and my cell phone back, if you don't mind."

Captain Connors smiled and shook his head. "All in due time – but not until we get you tucked away nice and safe like. That will happen after you get in the van and we get you out of here."

Howard leaned forward. "Come on Calvin, let's get this thing done. We need to get to work." He looked at the captain. "Will we get a chance to interview the suspects you have in custody?"

"You guys just don't get it. Your lives are in serious danger right now. For all I know, there could be another team headed this way – and they're probably a little annoyed about having their buddies shot up and captured. In case you've forgotten, they were heavily armed. Those were not the common, everyday bad-guy-kind-of-weapons."

Calvin got back into the van. Then Captain Connors closed the door behind him and pounded on the door twice.

Once the van was on the road, two unmarked deputy vehicles provided an escort. What they didn't know was that they had a helicopter following them at a discreet distance – and it didn't belong to the County Sheriff's office.

Captain Connors went over to his command vehicle and radioed headquarters.

"I need to speak to Major Cummings. Patch me through to him."

There were ten seconds of dead air, but Major Hugh Cummings' voice could be heard over the radio.

"Ed, what's going on? I've got the U.S. Attorney General's Office breathing down my neck. They didn't stop at the Governor. He climbed straight down the ladder and personally jumped right on my back. He's advised us to stop whatever we're doing, before he sends the Feds down here to clean this thing up."

"I can't Hugh. I don't have all the answers, but Earl will be here in a little while."

"Good grief, man – you called the Feds already?"

"You don't understand. This is more than just us, and it's bigger than we know. I'm just now trying to figure out who the good guys are. I'm not sure who to trust. For some reason, these guys tried to take out a bunch of low level, retired reporters this morning and came at them with an assault team loaded for bear. They outgunned us and their moves were well planned. We got lucky."

"Where are these reporters now? Talk to me."

"They're safe, but I'm going to need more manpower to protect them. We need to go ten-six in two seconds."

Four seconds later, Captain Connors came back on the radio. "Do you copy?"

Major Cummings responded. "Ten four – I copy loud and clear."

He understood. Captain Connors switched channels to an alternate frequency as part of the protocol established to prevent typical scanners from listening to their discussion.

Major Cummings responded. "Eleven-ninety-eight," he ordered, followed by, "Cupid's place."

Captain Connors responded. "Ten four can be in forty-five minutes."

Major Cummings clicked the mic once. Their conversation was over. They went silent because he realized that Captain Connors preferred a face-to-face meeting and Cupid's place was known to very few people. It was a remote location with limited access and would provide greater security from prying eyes and big ears.

XXXXX

Back at the cabin, Carla was just waking up. She slept soundly during the night but was ready for an eye-opening cup of coffee. She sat up on the side of the bed, put on her slippers, and started for the kitchen. She could smell the aroma of the coffee, while it was brewing. That's when she noticed Susan sitting in the rocking chair in her robe.

"You're up early." She walked over to where she was and sat down in the love seat near her. "The coffee should be ready in a few minutes. Did you sleep well last night?"

"Actually, I did. It was so quiet in my room; I woke up the way I went to sleep last night. I could hear myself breathing."

Carla smiled. "You'll get used to it." She pulled her feet up under her and leaned toward Susan. "After breakfast, I think a nice walk around outside for a while will help get the day started. How does that sound?"

She chuckled slightly. "It sounds boring, but I'm looking forward to it." She paused for a few seconds and then looked at her. "When can we talk to the guys?"

"We don't for now. If they contact us, it will happen this afternoon at two o'clock. We'll turn the radio on for a couple of minutes without transmitting and just listen. If they call, we can answer. If they don't, then we turn off the radio and try again at eight o'clock tonight."

"That sounds so cloak-and-dagger like. It seems kind of unnecessary."

"I know what you mean, but it keeps others from getting a good fix on us." She leaned back into the cushions. "Remember, the idea is to not have a bunch of unwanted visitors. I promised Howard to be really careful about the schedule. We do have other means to communicate, but only in an emergency."

Susan could hear the urgency in her voice. "I appreciate what you and Howard are doing for me, but I had no idea it would come to this. I was just doing what Peter asked of me. I knew he was desperate, but it never occurred to me that someone might try to kill me." She pulled her robe more tightly around her. "The story didn't seem all that important at first – until Peter's co-worker, Colleen, called to tell me she thought Peter was in trouble."

"Who's Colleen?"

"She's Peter's friend from work. When she called, she told me about how Peter had a huge argument with his editor. She was worried about him, but she didn't know who to talk to. He had given her my card and told her if anything should happen to him to call me. She called, but she never talked to him again. He died a few days later while jogging."

Carla got up and headed for the kitchen. "Do you want a cup of coffee? I think it's ready."

She followed her into the kitchen. "You know what really seems strange, now that I think about it, is Peter was a health nut. Doesn't that just beat all? I mean – a heart attack at his age. Who would have thought it?"

"How well did you know him?"

"We had dinner a couple of times, when I went to Atlanta. We worked on a story for a few weeks about the demise of several companies in and around the Atlanta Metro area. It wasn't until he called me a month after we finished working on that story when I learned about all of this mess. He didn't really say a whole lot, but you could tell he was worried."

She stopped talking and looked directly at Carla. She saw her standing there looking at her and turned to face her. "What is it? Did you remember something?"

She nodded her head. "He told me that we shouldn't talk over the phone anymore because he thought somebody might have been listening to his phone calls."

Carla put down the coffee pot and leaned on the counter. "Did you meet with him after that?"

"Once – that's when he gave me the CD and told me to keep it in a safe place. He said it was his get-out-of-jail-free card."

"We went over what was on that CD. There didn't seem to be anything there that pointed to the likes of what we've come up against."

"He told me that what was on that CD connected the dots."

She thought for a second. "There must be something we missed. We've got to look at that CD again."

XXXXX

As Calvin, Howard, and William were being taken to the safe house, their ride wasn't exactly quiet. Calvin jump started the conversation by making an observation.

He looked at Howard. "That was some serious firepower back there. Those guys were equipped with MP10's which are not easy to get your hands on." He paused, and then turned to face the other two. "Did you hear what Captain Connors said just before we pulled away from the house this morning?"

William spoke up. "He said his boss was all over him because his boss wasn't aware of what was going on and what to tell his boss."

Calvin nodded. He then looked at Howard. "He said the United States Attorney General called his boss this morning." He paused and waited for a response. There was none.

He looked at Howard and made a gesture with his hands as if to say, "Think about it." Then he repeated his last sentence. "He said the United States Attorney General called his boss this morning." He paused one more time, waiting for a response. That's when Howard understood what he was trying to tell him.

Howard smiled, leaned forward in his seat, and looked at Calvin. "How did the United States Attorney General know to call Captain Connor's boss about what happened?" He paused a few seconds. "Even more important, when did he know what occurred at the house this morning?"

William's expression showed he understood what he was trying to tell them.

Calvin got the attention of the deputy who was sitting in the front passenger seat. "We've got to contact Captain Connors. It's very important."

"We are to maintain radio silence, until we arrive at our destination."

Howard spoke up. "This is really important, and the Captain is going to be mighty annoyed with you because we didn't get this information to him sooner."

The deputy turned around and looked at him. "Whatever it is, it is going to have to wait until we get you, and all this stuff, to the safe house. Just sit back and relax. I'll see to it that you get in touch with the Captain as soon as we get there – and when everything is secure."

CHAPTER 32
Monday morning, April 1, 2014

Randy and Lisa were in the back seat of a deputy's car on their way to join the others at the safe house. She sat quietly looking out the window on her side of the car. He sat quietly watching her. They could hear the calls coming in over the radio. One of them got the attention of the deputy sitting in the passenger seat up front.

"This is Mobile Sixteen, over."

The message was short and to the point. "Mobile Sixteen, this is Captain Connors. Take every precaution on your approach. Make certain you are not followed prior to commitment. Do you copy?"

The deputy confirmed receipt and that the message was understood.

Randy turned around to look out the rear window. There did not appear to be any vehicles behind them. "Deputy, it looks clear from where I'm sitting."

"Mr. Tomlin, we're about five minutes before we commit. Just keep your eyes open and let me know if you see anything suspicious."

He turned to Lisa and smiled. "You're not the only one who knows how to have fun."

Meanwhile, on the third floor of a condominium three minutes from downtown Bowie, Maryland, a phone call was about to end.

"He just gave us our marching orders. Contact your man in Florida. Tell him he's to finish the job tomorrow, and the assets have been relocated to Point B. He'll know where to pick them up."

"Yes, sir, I will take care of it."

"See that you do. The first group has been neutralized. Your team must finish this tomorrow. Is that clear?"

"Yes, sir, I understand." They both disconnected the call and hung up.

The three men in the room all looked at each other. The one who had just finished taking the call stood, walked over to the door that opened onto the porch, and lit a cigarette. He turned around and looked at the other two.

"We can't mess this up. Everything is riding on this. I know what the man will do if we don't get this done by tomorrow afternoon."

The second man, who was sitting nearest him, leaned forward and put his elbows on the table in front of him. "I'd like to contact another cleaner to work with us, if you don't mind. That way we can make sure there's no mess and there'll be nothing left behind."

The third man smiled. "If you're thinking about Woolsey, he's not available."

The first man walked back to the table and sat down next to the second man. "Then it's settled. It is our team that has the assignment, and our team needs to finish it. I'm going down there to supervise it personally."

The second man shook his head in disagreement. "I don't think that's a very good idea. You need to stay here to manage the team. It might get a little dicey."

"I want to make sure there are no screw-ups this time – and I can't do that sitting on my butt in this building."

At the other end of that phone call, a person was calmly pouring a drink for himself. He turned and offered one to his guest. "Would you care for some thirty-year-old Scotch?"

He smiled. "Yes, I would. Make it about two fingers worth."

When he finished pouring it, he handed his guest the glass and offered a toast. He raised it and said, "Here's to us. May we prosper by noon tomorrow – and to those about to die, we salute you."

His guest downed the drink in one gulp. Nodding his head, he proudly pronounced agreement. "Amen to that, brother."

He put his glass down on the table because his cell phone was buzzing. He answered it but didn't sound very happy to do so.

"What is it you want now?"

He listened for several seconds before speaking. When he did, all he said was, "That sounds reasonable," and then he hung up. He turned and looked at the other man.

"There's been a slight change of plans. It seems as though the man wants us to locate and eliminate Mr. Rolle and Mr. Tomlin. They're going to be together at a safe house in short order. He wants us to take them out at first light tomorrow."

"I don't think that's prudent. At the moment, we've got them pinned down and out of circulation. We need to be focused on Miss Leeds and that CD."

"That was considered, but that has been determined to be of less importance for now. He wants Mr. Rolle and Mr. Tomlin neutralized."

"It'll take more than just one team."

"He has sanctioned a squad out of Baltimore, and they will be arriving in less than four hours. When they get here, we're to make sure they receive all of the intelligence we have on those two. He said this strike must be surgical and swift. Whoever it is coming from Baltimore, they'll have their hands full."

"The AG doesn't care. Why do you think he's sending this team? He just wants it settled so he can get back to dealing with what's on his plate."

XXXXX

Meanwhile, Major Cummings had arrived at the rendezvous point. After Captain Connors pulled alongside him three minutes later, they both got out of their vehicles and walked toward a large oak tree near a small pond. The water glistened in the fading sunlight and reflected a parade of colors revealing what the oncoming evening sky predicted. The rustling of the leaves from the tree indicated a slight breeze from the southwest.

"Eddie," Major Cummings started, "we've got one helluva mess on our hands. If your boys are right, this thing is going to get messy before too long."

Captain Connors leaned against the tree. "There's evidence that someone in D.C. is pulling the strings on this thing. Earl hasn't said much so far, but he's about to meet up with those news guys. He's been here most of the day looking at what they've put together so far, and what they have is significant. He's indicated that it's leading to one inescapable conclusion."

"And, what would that be?"

"Somebody is about to get really ugly because they have been found out. It rings of politics gone haywire. The team that showed up at the Ewing's place, they were well trained and weren't amateurs. We got lucky and caught one of them, and he clearly pointed the finger to someone in D.C. He said it wasn't a local thing. It was much bigger than we knew, and even worse he indicated there are probably others coming in behind them."

Major Cummings walked toward the pond, stopping about four feet from its edge. "You know when we used to come here as kids, I always thought that this part of our little world would be safe from the bad guys. And yet, here we are talking about bad guys. If D.C. is involved in this, it's way over our heads."

He paused for a few seconds before continuing. "When the big man himself called me this morning, I knew something was wrong. Usually, my boss takes those calls, but he was conveniently out sick. All I did was listen to him go on-and-on about the shooting. He wants a report on his desk before dark tonight. I guess I better get busy."

"Doesn't it seem strange that he called you before others in the district, and for that matter the State, knew about this?"

Major Cummings walked back toward Captain Connors. "Don't tell me they've got you hooked. What are you thinking? You don't think this is really some massive cover up do you?"

He walked over to where he was standing. "I think when you took that call this morning you knew there was more to this than just something from D.C. I'm telling you, it's big and it scares the fool out of me. What these people have uncovered is nothing short of a covert operation that is intended to put the news industry into the pockets of a handful of politicians and who knows what they plan to do with it."

"So, you're a right-wing nut job now? You've got to be kidding me. That's impossible."

"No, it isn't. Without so much as firing one shot, the news industry just rolled over and became the political arm of a bunch of radicals. They couldn't get enough of it back in the sixties. They were nurtured by it in the seventies and were bedazzled by it in the eighties. Then the radicals began pushing an agenda of tolerance and promoted redefining the family and family values. We ran amuck in the nineties with the boom and then the bust. It wasn't hard for them to place who they wanted and where they wanted them to skew the news – or worse to conveniently not print the truth. Here we are fifteen years later, and those babies born fifty years ago are now taking control. Look at the mess we're in. Honestly, you don't see it? For God's sake Hugh, even the President of the United States has been caught lying."

"All I see is we've got a bunch of bodies piling up in our district – and I'm not happy about that." He paused for a few seconds. "Okay, let's play your game. Let's just say for argument's sake that you're right. Let's say that someone in D.C. is pulling all the strings. That's a mighty big set of strings. Maybe we need to spend a little time with Earl this evening and play dumb. If what you say is true, there's got to be muscle controlling this and it's got to be controlled by somebody who has easy access to the weapons we've seen so far."

"Doesn't the U.S. Attorney General's office have such resources?"

Major Cummings' expression told him he had struck a nerve.

"You're accusing the Attorney General of these United States of corruption, treason, and a bunch of other things I don't even want to think about?"

"You said you'd play my game. Let's start there and see where it takes us."

"So, what's our next move?"

Captain Connors put his hands on his hips. "We need a game plan for sure. When we get back to the office, we need to figure out how we're going to approach the Department of Justice in D.C. with what we know."

"From what you've been saying that may be easier said than done. Who do we know in DOJ that is trustworthy?"

"What do you think about Andrew Schenk out of Atlanta? He was in Florida for a number of years before being kicked upstairs. He's always impressed me as his own man."

"I went through Quantico with him. He's as straight-laced as there is, in my book."

"Then it's settled. I'll call for a meeting."

CHAPTER 33
At the Safe House, Monday, April 1, 2013, 7:00 p.m.

Dinner at the safe house wasn't anything to write home about, but there was plenty of it. Calvin, Howard, and William were on one side of the table, and Randy and Lisa were on the other. At one point During the meal, they all stared at each other, which brought a smile to each of their faces. Nobody said anything, but they were all thinking the same thing: They had only been there for a few hours and already they were bored. Calvin motioned for Randy to join him in the kitchen.

When they were certain they were out of earshot of one of the agents stationed in the living room, Randy whispered to Calvin.

"Whose idea was this? We're not going to get anything done sitting around in this place. My cell phone signal is none existent and there's no Wi-Fi signal here either. For all I know they've bugged this place. Did you see all the cameras outside?"

Calvin, opening the refrigerator door to retrieve a bottle of water, whispered his agreement. "The control room is the spare bedroom in the back, and it has no windows. These guys probably have our phones and computers wired and under surveillance. Why do I feel like I'm a prisoner, instead of the object of their concern?"

"That's easy – because they want us out of their way. I trust Captain Connors, but he's not been forthcoming with us about everything. I'd like to know what's happening at the moment."

Howard came into the kitchen and joined in the conversation. "We need to get back to work," he whispered. "We're not likely to have any interruptions here. One of my concerns is that we're not able to communicate with Carla and Susan as long as they have us cooped up here. We've got to get a radio system set up so we can keep our appointed time slots. We missed the two o'clock one this afternoon."

Randy walked over to one of the deputies and explained the situation about the radio. He got on a cell phone and texted the information to Captain Connors. His reply was short and curt. "It will have to wait. I will be by there in about an hour."

At the same time Calvin was finishing his bottle of water, Susan was just sitting down on the sofa at the cabin about to work on a series of crossword puzzles.

"You don't suppose the guys are in any kind of trouble do you?"

Carla, who had just finished cleaning the kitchen after supper, smiled at her. "What makes you ask that question?"

"They missed the hook up time this afternoon."

"I wouldn't read too much into that. They may not have had anything to say that was either new or important. Just be patient, they'll make contact with us." She sat down in the love seat opposite her and put her work basket of knitting next to her right foot.

"What's your take on Calvin?" She paused. "Do you think he's too old for me?"

Carla laughed. "What's that supposed to mean? What do you mean by too old?"

"You know – he's in his sixties and I'm in my late thirties." Again, she paused for a few seconds. "That's not too old for someone in their late thirties is it?"

Carla continued to smile, and Susan continued to speak. "He's such a gentleman. I know he wouldn't want me to tell you this, but when we were in that hotel the other night, he was either not interested or embarrassed. I was sitting up in bed in my bra and panties and he told me to get dressed, tossed my clothes at me, and then turned around so he couldn't see me. I find that amusing and also quite extraordinary. He's not gay, is he?"

Carla laughed out loud. "Heavens no girl, he's not gay. He's old school and you should feel flattered that he's taken an interest in you. I've seen the way he looks at you. Believe me, he's interested, but he's reserved to a fault. I'm also sure the fact that someone is trying to kill you might have something to do with it."

After hearing that, Susan smiled. She put down the crossword puzzle booklet, got up, and headed for the kitchen. As she reached the end of the counter, she noticed a painting that hung on the wall to her left. She stopped and admired it.

"This is nice. Do you know who did this? The colors are exquisite."

Carla chuckled. "Your boyfriend did that for us three years ago."

It hit Susan what she meant by that. "Calvin did this?"

"He asked us if we would like one of his works. So, Howard and I hung it at the house for a while. After we set up this place, it just seemed like the right thing to do was to bring it up here and that wall seemed like the perfect place."

She inspected the painting even closer. "Where is this place?"

"It's near an old farm house in Savannah. Howard and I just fell in love with that little town several years ago. We showed him a picture of it that we took a few years back, and he did that from his memory of that picture."

"His initials aren't here. Doesn't he sign his work?"

"Look closer at the farm house – near the roof line. Do you see anything?"

Susan put on her glasses and leaned closer to the painting. "Oh yes, I see them now. That's unusual."

"Susan, so he is as well. He's not too old for you, but he might just seem a little unreal."

"Was he ever married?"

"Yes, but that was years ago – and she just up and left him one day. She wanted the big city and the bright lights. He just wanted to settle down and raise a family."

"Does he have any children?" She retrieved a pencil sharpener from one of the drawers and went back to the sofa.

"No, they never had any children. It's a shame because he'd make a great dad. I wouldn't go getting any ideas in that department. I'm pretty sure he's set enough in his ways that the pitter-patter of little feet is not in his plans."

"Maybe that's because he hasn't met the right woman," she mumbled.

The rest of their evening was spent working quietly on knitting and crossword puzzles.

Back at the safe house, Lisa had been talking with Randy about sleeping accommodations. They spoke of her having a bedroom by herself, but she nixed that idea. She insisted that Randy sleep in her room on the extra bed. He wasn't too keen about it, but finally gave in to the idea. Howard and William took the second bedroom and Calvin the last one. The agents had set up sleeping arrangements in the garage and on the east side of the living room. There were two agents on patrol outside the house and two others that would remain awake on the inside. The other three would serve as relief during the night. It seemed well organized enough and things got really quiet a little after ten o'clock.

Randy waited on Lisa to change into her night clothes, before he took his shower. Her choice of pajamas was much less revealing and certainly more casual. He was relieved that he wouldn't have to deal with the issues from the previous night. He needed his rest.

As he crawled into his bed, he reached over and turned off the light.

"Randy, I hope you sleep well."

"You, too," he said, as he closed his eyes and sighed.

In Howard's room, William had laid down on the bed without changing his clothes.

"Son, are you going to sleep in your clothes like that?"

"If something happens tonight like it did last night, the last thing I want to be in is my pajamas. Thank you, but I'll manage until morning in these."

Howard pulled the covers up to his shoulders and rolled onto his right side. "Nothing is going to happen tonight. They seem pretty well prepared."

"I hope the other guys feel the same way." He paused for a few seconds. "Dad – we need to follow-up a lead that I've been wondering about. If Senator Haskell is involved in this, wouldn't it be prudent to watch what he's doing and see who he's contacting?"

"It would, but how are you proposing to do that? They're not going to just let us waltz out of here. We're under federal protection and they're the ones in charge."

"Suppose we talk to Captain Connors and convince him of what we've got to do. Do you think he'd listen?"

"He might, but it'll have to keep until the morning. Goodnight son."

He reached over to the lamp on his end table and turned it off.

Calvin was in his bedroom lying wide awake and staring at the ceiling. All he could think about was Susan and hoping she was all right. It bothered him that they had missed their contact time that evening. He smiled slightly, while thinking about her. She had gotten to him, and he realized it. It concerned him that he and the others were all in one place – under one roof. Sleep was something he wanted and needed, but the thought of their being in one place would not let him find any peace. He rolled over, turned off the lamp, and closed his eyes.

"Tomorrow's another day," he whispered, "and things are going to have to change."

Chapter 34
Tuesday Morning, April 2, 2013

Few people are gifted with the ability to see into the future. If we all possessed that trait, then it wouldn't be a big deal. It would simply be a list of upcoming attractions not unlike what you see at the movie theater before the feature presentation. Having such a gift is rare. Even rarer is not just being able to see into the future but being able to act decisively to protect yourself and others from its perils – or preparing for its rewards.

When Calvin woke up, he looked around his room. Everything seemed to be in its place, but something felt wrong to him. He sat up on the side of his bed, checked his watch to see what time it was, stood up and walked over to look out the window. It was still dark outside, but he could see one of the guards moving slowly around the perimeter of the backyard. He checked the horizon and could see the dawn breaking in the distance.

He returned to his bed, reached down and picked up his pants that he had placed there the night before, put them on, and then sat down to put on his socks and shoes. That's when he could hear a couple of the agents talking outside his door. It was difficult to make out exactly what they were saying. When he had finished putting on his socks and shoes, he moved closer to the door, put his left ear on it, stood still and listened carefully. He was certain he heard one of the guards say that they expected company in about two hours. To him, that didn't mean his Aunt Sally was coming for breakfast.

He quickly finished getting dressed and quietly opened his door, went across the hall, and sneaked into Randy's room.

It was darker than he thought it would be, so he turned on his cell phone for the light source. No sooner had he done that than Randy had grabbed his arm.

"Easy," he whispered, "I just came over to make sure you guys know what I heard just a few moments ago. One of the agents indicated that they were expecting company in about two hours. Personally, I don't believe he's talking about breakfast guests."

Randy let go of his arm and sat back down on his bed. Lisa was still asleep.

"I'm not sure what we can do but staying here does not sound like one of our better options. We need to get in touch with Captain Connors."

Randy grabbed his clothes he had put on the back of the chair near the door, took off his pajamas, got dressed, and reached for his shoes. "You go wake up Howard and William. They need to be ready at a moment's notice."

Calvin sneaked back across the hall and walked toward Howard's room. As he walked, he looked over his shoulder every other step to make sure he wasn't being observed. When he reached their bedroom door, he opened it just wide enough for him to slip through, and then closed the door. Howard was already awake.

"Randy, what's up?"

"You and William have to get up and get dressed. I think we're in for another round with whoever is trying to get at us. I overheard one of the agents talking about their expecting company in about two hours."

Howard reached over and shook William. "William, wake up. We've got to get dressed."

He didn't respond right off. Howard shook him again – harder this time. That got his attention.

"What is it? What time is it?"

Calvin answered both questions with one answer. "It's time for you to get up and get dressed. We may need to leave here pretty quickly and very soon."

Back in Randy's room, he sat down on the bed next to Lisa and nudged her shoulder. "Lisa, you've got to get up and get dressed. Calvin told me that we may not be safe here too much longer."

She rolled over and faced him. "What time is it?"

"It's four-forty-five."

"The birds aren't up yet."

"You're right, but the bad guys appear to be. We've got to get a hold of Captain Connors and get out of this place. When they come for us this time, they won't make the same mistake they made last time."

She sat up and ran her fingers through her hair. "I must look a mess."

He smiled. "It's too dark in here to tell. Just get up and get dressed. Wear something comfortable and warm."

Out in the living room, the agent who had been manning the communications devices received a call from headquarters to tell the others to be on the alert for intruders. They had received credible information that a reinforced team was moving toward their location. It was expected to arrive there in less than two hours. A helicopter with reinforcements would be there in less than an hour.

He acknowledged the call, put down his headset and went to stand up. When he started to get up to go tell his supervisor, someone hit him from behind and knocked him out. He was placed back in his chair with his headset on. If you had not seen what just had happened, you would think that he simply was asleep.

Randy entered the hallway followed closely by Lisa. Right behind them was Calvin. As they went by Howard's room, William opened the door. Calvin put his right forefinger to his lips motioning for quiet. Howard, standing right behind William, moved into the hallway behind Calvin. William entered as well.

All five of them were walking toward the living room when a helicopter could be heard flying low and going through its rotation sequence for landing. Calvin saw the agent sitting at the communication devices and pointed at him. He motioned to the others to head toward the foyer, while he provided a rear guard. They walked quickly and quietly. They made it to the front door before one of the agents saw them.

"Where do you think you're going?"

Calvin answered. "We thought we'd take our morning walk. Would you like to join us?"

The agent moved toward them but brushed by the one who was sitting at the table with the headset on causing him to fall out of his seat. The others saw what had happened and returned to the living room.

"What just happened?" Lisa asked.

The other agent, kneeling down and checking the man for a pulse, indicated that it looked as if he had been knocked out. She excused herself and returned to the bedroom to retrieve her leather bag. Randy said he'd help. Howard and William went over to watch the helicopter land, while Calvin tried to awaken the injured agent. While doing so, he could hear someone on the headset trying to reach them. He took the headset off of the injured agent and put in on to listen. The message, although only partial, warned of an assault team approaching from the west.

"Hey guys, we've got incoming."

Just then, gunshots rang out in the back yard as men departed the helicopter with automatic weapons blazing. Glass was shattering and flying everywhere in the living room. William and Howard ducked back into the hallway, while Calvin grabbed the fallen agent's pistol and started firing. Lisa opened the door to her bedroom and handed Howard and William each a pistol. She emerged waving her pump-action shotgun. Randy reentered the hallway with the 9mm Ruger in his right hand and the .357 magnum revolver in his left hand.

Calvin was pinned down behind a wall that led to the foyer. Lisa fired off two rounds and ducked back into the hallway. While Randy provided covering fire, Calvin made it quickly to the safety of the hallway.

William, crouched in the doorway to his bedroom, shouted to Howard. "Who are these guys and why are they trying to kill us?"

He shouted back. "I don't know, and I don't know."

There was a brief second or two of silence, before they all heard the helicopter revving up its engines to depart. By that time, Randy had reloaded the Ruger. He peeked around the corner and could see the last of three men get on board the helicopter just before it lifted off. He took aim and unloaded the Ruger and the .357 into its fuselage. A hail of bullets rained down from gunner who was sitting on the left side of the helicopter. One of them caught Randy in his left thigh knocking him backwards and down.

"I'm hit! I'm hit," he yelled. Calvin immediately went to his assistance.

Howard ran to the communications devices and began trying to get someone's attention. It took a couple of seconds, but he managed to raise the base operator and explain what had just happened.

"You are to stay at that location. Reinforcements are two minutes from you. Do you need an ambulance?"

"Yes, we have at least two agents down and one other injured."

"Keep this line open, until help arrives."

"How will I know if they're on our side?"

"They won't be shooting at you."

He had heard enough and threw the headset against the wall. It made a fairly good-sized dent before falling to the floor.

Calvin had begun applying pressure to Randy's wound. "You're lucky. It didn't hit a vein or an artery. You might limp for a few days, but I think you're going to make it."

Howard explained that help would be there shortly and that everyone needed to make sure not to shoot first and ask questions later when they showed up.

It took more than two minutes for help to arrive, but when Captain Connors got out of the SUV, he saw the carnage. As he walked toward the house, he shook his head.

Calvin was the first to see him. "Captain, you're a little late, but welcome to the party."

"You guys just seem to attract all kinds of fun people." He saw Randy lying on the floor near what used to be an exit to the backyard. "Is he okay?"

"Mostly a flesh wound, but he's lost some blood. When's the ambulance supposed to get here?"

"It was right behind us."

"There's something we need to tell you." He motioned for him to join the others in the hallway. "We tried to leave before all of this started. What we saw was that agent there," he pointed to the one who had been knocked unconscious, "had been knocked out, but made to look like he was sitting there on duty at the radio."

"What do you mean knocked out?"

"He was unconscious but positioned to look like he was still on duty. Someone on this team almost got us all killed."

"Whoa, that's a pretty serious charge you just made."

"You need to listen to us because we all saw it."

Captain Connors pointed at the other agent. "What's his story?"

"He stood his ground and tried to fight back."

"Where were the other guys? Were they outside?"

"I have no clue. We haven't gone outside to check. We figured we'd leave that up to you."

That's when he noticed Lisa carrying the shotgun. "Where did you get these weapons?"

She spoke up. "These have been provided with the compliments of the Jacobs' family."

He walked around the living room for a few more seconds. "Obviously, we need to find someplace else for you guys."

Lisa grinned. "Whatever you do, don't even think about taking our weapons from us."

Just then the ambulance arrived at the front driveway. It took the paramedics less than fifteen minutes to prepare Randy for transport to the hospital, but not before he got Captain Connors' attention.

"I'm pretty sure I put a few rounds into the pilot and maybe someone else in the front seat next to him. And by the way, the chopper had no tail numbers, but it did have a decal on the left rear panel. I've never seen it before, but I'm pretty sure I put a round through it."

Fortunately for Randy, his wound didn't require surgery, but he did end up needing a few stitches. They wanted him to stay at the hospital for a day for observation, but he would have nothing to do with that idea. Instead, he hobbled out to the squad car on the crutches they had given him. He had the deputies drive him back to his place where he gathered several of his things, put them into another suitcase, and then had them drive him to the office. He wanted to speak with Jerry Locker for a few minutes.

He spent about twenty minutes with him going over the events of the last few days. Mr. Locker sat spellbound as he listened to what had happened to all of them. Randy left out the part about Carla and Susan relocating, but gave him every other detail he could remember.

"I want you to run this story tomorrow morning."

"It'll have to be approved by the boys upstairs."

"No, you can't take it upstairs because they'll stop it. You're going to have to run it locally and without notification. Your source is clean and there are multiple sources to substantiate the story. You'll be on solid ground." He handed a flash drive to him. "This is everything I've told you and more. Don't make a copy of it – just keep it in a safe place."

"What are you going to do? Where are you going? How am I going to be able to reach you?"

"Don't worry about any of that. I will reach you. For now, they're going to try to keep us off the radar. Once this story goes national, things will be out in the open and we'll be able to stick our heads up out of the hole. Until that happens, you're going to be my contact. I will reach you by landline with any updates and photos as the story develops. Speaking of which –," he took the thumb drive out of the camera and handed it to him. "You might want to keep this in a safe place, too."

"Why are you doing this? I mean, why are you giving me this story?"

"I know you. I know you want this on the front page, and you have the credentials to make it stick. Don't worry about the by-line issues – just tell the story right now."

He sat there as if he had been stunned. Then he looked directly at Randy and smiled. "Is there someone you want me to contact for you?"

"Yes, I would like for you to call or visit with Eileen Leopard and tell her everything I've told you. She deserves to know what's going on."

One of the deputies who accompanied Randy came into the room and told him they had been given orders to start transporting him. They were to leave immediately.

As he stood and grabbed for his crutches, he leaned on Mr. Locker's desk. "Be sure to mention that this story would not have been possible without the work of Max Leopard."

After he and the two officers exited his office, Mr. Locker picked up the telephone receiver and dialed several numbers.

"I want the front page above the fold reset for tomorrow. I will send the story to you by three o'clock today. There will be several additional columns for page two and three. I want a production meeting this morning at eleven in my office."

Another pair of deputies accompanied Calvin back to his place, where he put several of his things into a duffle bag and then had the deputies take him to Howard's place. There, he met Howard and

William and would wait with them until Lisa returned. The three of them watched for the breaking news on television, only to learn that their incident was not covered by any of the local morning news programs. When Lisa arrived, she was carrying another leather carrier.

She walked into the living room, put her suitcase down, and handed Calvin the leather carrier. "Take care of this. I've got to use the little girls' room."

He opened the carrying case and saw one automatic assault rifle and three hand guns.

"She must be expecting company," he said, and then he zipped up the case.

Howard got up and went over to the coffee pot. While he was pouring a cup of coffee, he was grinning from ear-to-ear. William noticed it.

"What's so funny, Dad?"

"Who would have thought that Lisa knew anything about weaponry – let alone own an arsenal?"

Calvin thought it was funny as well. "I wish I could have seen Randy's expression when she started loading all of this stuff. It had to be priceless.

Ten minutes later, Randy had arrived. They were all together, again.

Everybody was thinking it, but nobody said anything until William made the observation.

"It seems that every time we get together, a war erupts."

Captain Connors, who had just walked into the room, commented. "I heard that, and you're right. I've been talking to a couple of friends of mine in Seminole County, and they've agreed to keep you for a few days."

Randy spoke up. "We've got work to do and it's not in Seminole County. How about you guys just let us do our work and we'll try not to cause you any trouble."

Lisa and Calvin concurred. Howard spoke up. "I think we can still operate pretty well from here. We're close enough to wrapping up this story that maybe staying here a couple days wouldn't be too bad."

Captain Connors started to respond but was cut off by Lisa. "Captain, we've gotten really close to something that needs our full attention. Please listen to what we're telling you."

Howard got up and approached him. "We may need a little help, but right now you know who's behind all of this. We've got to get this out to our readers. They need to know that our government, especially some of our elected officials, has a problem with the truth. This isn't the first time that we have been pushed around by politicians. The American public doesn't seem to know about any of this because the news outlets have slowly and methodically been put into the back pockets of certain political figures. I believe once we tell this story, most Americans will be outraged. The bad guys will start scrambling for cover and you'll be right there to nab them. Let us do what we do well. We'll tell the American public the story that needs to be told, and you can catch the bad guys."

Captain Connors sat down at the table. "Okay, I've heard enough." He took a sip of his coffee and then put the cup down. "Have any of you considered how high up the chain this thing might go? Have you really thought this thing through?"

They all looked at each. Randy leaned forward. "Captain, that's the main point. We've got to follow our leads and know that answer. The only way that's going to happen is for people like you to allow us to get our jobs done quickly."

Lisa, nodding her head the entire time he was speaking, stood up and approached him. "Suppose it does go all the way to the White House? Wouldn't you want to know that? I know I would and so would all of my readers."

"Suppose you guys run into more trouble? What happens if we're not around?"

Howard raised his hand and pointed at each of the others. "We know we're vulnerable. We also know that we're good at our jobs. We're not about to do something foolish or stupid. We just want to get to the bottom of this story. To do that, we're going to need a great more freedom than we've had these last few days."

"Do you have a plan?"

When somebody asks a question like that, they're looking for someone to make sense of everything they've heard. Nobody had a plan, but everybody wanted one.

For the next hour, Captain Connors sat listening to them develop their ideas, make suggestions, fine tune them, and put them in a workable sequence that even made sense to him. He was impressed with their logic. He was more impressed with their passion.

By the time they had sequenced their plan, assigned responsibilities, and finished pooling their resources, Captain Connors was about to contact Major Cummings to inform him.

Randy spoke up. "You can't do that. We're going to operate through your office and with your knowledge. If we don't, we won't be far enough off the radar and covert enough to accomplish what we need to do. We don't need anyone outside this room to know what's on the agenda. We need these next three days to put everything into action. Even then, we're relying on a presupposed reaction by Senator Haskell's staff."

Captain Connors got up from the table and walked into the kitchen. "I don't think you'll have any problems with them. I'm worried about some of the low-life he's been affiliated with over the last few years. There's no telling from under what rock they might crawl. Your idea about the set is perfect – just be careful."

"Then you're agreed to this?"

"Yes, but with one stipulation: No one shoots anybody unless I tell them to."

They all nodded, except for Lisa. "I'll try not to," she said while grinning.

CHAPTER 35
Tuesday, April 2, 2013, 2 p.m.

Carla and Susan had just finished eating lunch. Carla got up from the table and went over to the radio. She turned it on and set the frequency to listen for contact from Howard. She went back to the table, picked up her plate, and started for the kitchen. That's when she heard Howard's voice over the radio.

"This is Greyhound. Do you copy Rabbit – over?"

Carla ran to the receiver base to broadcast. "This is Rabbit. Go ahead Greyhound."

"Please write this down. We are proceeding as planned. I will return at next scheduled time for update. Keep a low profile and stay at home – over."

"This is Rabbit. Jill wants to know how Jack is doing."

"Jack is fine. Peter has a hurt leg but is expected to be fine. Little Greyhound says to say, "Hello." Big Greyhound says he loves you – over."

"That's good news. We miss you and will do as you say. We will check with you in about six hours – over."

"Roger – we're out."

It probably didn't fool anybody, but they each understood what had happened, what is happening, and when they plan to talk again.

Carla turned to Susan. "Randy got hurt, but he's apparently going to be okay."

Susan felt better knowing everyone was doing okay, but she wished she had gotten a chance to speak with Calvin. Carla could see it in her eyes.

"Don't worry; you'll get another chance tonight."

"I'm not worried. I'm just wondering how things were going with the story."

"Howard said things were going along as planned. That means that they have positioned themselves to start getting the interviews they need and to break a headline. I'll bet they all start going in different directions by tomorrow morning."

The rest of the afternoon was a great time for everyone to take a deep breath and relax. Everyone except for Lisa was able to catch a good long nap. She only managed about thirty minutes, but she felt rested and alert when she got up from the sofa. The protection team showed up and spent the afternoon cleaning their weapons and checking their gear. Howard wanted to get to know more about the automatic assault rifle that Lisa brought, but she wasn't letting loose of it. She handed him her shotgun, instead. "You can manage this," she said sharply.

At the paper, Mr. Locker was working quickly and with great purpose putting the finishing touches on the story. He was well within the time frame for meeting the deadline issues, but he wanted to make sure he got it right. He had rewritten the lead-in sentence several times thinking to make the story read more like a novel. He double-checked his quotes and the figures he used in the article to be sure they were correct. He was certain that he had gotten everything right. Now, all he had to do was to get this through the production staff meeting. He knew that it would not be an easy task – especially if corporate was represented at the meeting.

Before he committed the story, there was one more thing he wanted to do. He picked up the phone, dialed a series of numbers, and waited for the call to connect.

"Senator Haskell's office," the woman said who answered the phone.

"May I speak with Senator Haskell? I'm a resident of Florida and my name is Jerry Locker."

"I'm sorry Mr. Locker, but he is not in Washington today. He flew home this morning for several meetings."

"Thank you. I'll contact his local office for his itinerary."

He hung up, waited for another dial tone, and dialed another set of numbers.

"You've reached Senator Haskell's office – thank you for calling." For the next two minutes, he worked his way through the automated call directory. He finally reached one of the workers in the office who knew what his schedule would be for the next twenty-four hours.

He had a pleasant conversation with the person, while learning that the senator had a nine o'clock meeting in St. Augustine with the Chamber of Commerce officials. He thanked her, hung up, and waited for another dial tone, before dialing another set of numbers.

"Randy, this is Jerry. I just thought you'd like to know that Senator Haskell is back in town and he's got an early morning meeting in St. Augustine. That means he'll probably spend the night at his house. I just thought there might be more than one meeting happening, while he's in town."

"How's the story going?"

"I think it's ready, but we haven't had our production meeting yet. I'll call you as soon as it's over."

They spoke for a few more minutes about the story then said their good-byes and hung up.

Randy turned to Howard who was sitting with him on the porch at the house. "That was Jerry Locker. We need to talk."

They got up and went outside to make sure they were out of earshot of the others.

"Jerry just told me that Senator Haskell is going to be at his house tonight, and he has an early morning meeting. I think it would be a great idea to sit on him just to see who shows up – unannounced."

"Somebody is going to have to babysit that place tonight."

An hour later, they all gathered on the porch, along with Captain Connors, to discuss what their next move was going to be. When it was all over, Calvin gathered his things, picked up a mug of coffee, two peanut butter and jelly sandwiches, and a listening device he had been given by Captain Connors.

Calvin stopped at the kitchen table. "Where's Betsy? I'm not going out there without her. You said I could have her back."

Captain Connors reached into a satchel he had put on the table, pulled out Calvin's .45 caliber pistol, and handed it to him. "It would be best if you keep this in the glove compartment the entire evening."

"I understand, but she's going to sit next to me on the ready."

"What is it with you guys and your weapons? I thought you were supposed to be reporters."

Calvin thanked him and started for his car that was parked in the driveway. He stopped and looked at Howard. "I'll see you guys at three o'clock. Please try not to be late."

Later that evening after dinner, while they were all watching television, the phone rang. Howard answered it, realized it was Calvin, and put the call on the speaker for everyone to hear.

He had called to tell them he had overheard one of the individuals, who had just exited Senator Haskell's house, talking with another about a planned meeting for seven o'clock in the morning. He wasn't sure who the meeting was to be with, but he was certain he heard the person say something about a payoff for services rendered. He also overheard that same person talk about a meeting across town at Judge Franklin Brooks' house, which was to be an hour before that one. He was certain that it was Judge Franklin Brooks who was mentioned in the conversation. That caught Captain Connors' attention and he jumped on the line with them.

"Are you certain he said Judge Brooks?"

"Yes, I am certain. In fact, I taped the conversation."

"Calvin, there's no need for you stay there any longer tonight. We can take this information and run with it. Come on back and get a good night's sleep. You may need it tomorrow."

"What about the others?"

"What others are you talking about?"

"I've counted six people who went into that house so far tonight and only two have come out."

"Stay there until you can account for the other four. Call me once they leave. If you haven't called by midnight, go ahead and leave. They're probably planning on spending the night."

He understood and disconnected the call.

Captain Connors looked at Howard. "We need to have that place covered tonight. There's something going on and we need to know about it when it happens. Are you up to doing a little stake out?"

Howard grinned. "A little stake out can mean finding out a lot of nothing – or maybe a lot of something." He thought for a second. "I think William and I could probably handle this. What do you think, Captain?"

"Pictures would be nice as part of the package. I'd stay put until you hear from Calvin. You might want to make sure you put a few things together just to make sure you've got everything you need – just in case."

William jumped up and clapped his hands. "This could be fun, Dad. It'll be almost like old times when I was a kid and you were working on that story about the trucking company that was pushing its weight around. Do you remember that?"

"I do. Going on stakeout with you wasn't too bad, except it seemed like you had to go to the bathroom every five minutes."

"This time, I won't bring any hot chocolate."

Their plan was simple: stay awake and make sure they took pictures of anyone coming or going from the house. The camera William had with him was more than adequate for the job – even during the dark of night. The biggest problem they faced was getting into a location to be able to get the shots they could use and not being easily spotted in the process. Driving to the location in the middle of the night gave them all the cover they needed, but when the sun came up that would be another story.

They managed to position themselves near a corner that provided sufficient cover from a direct line-of-sight from the house, but it did give William more than enough visual clearance, with the use of his telescopic lens, so that the pictures he got would be useful for identification purposes. They were on a mission to learn about the contacts, identify them, and get the pictures back to Captain Connors. Their wait and work produced more excitement that they had anticipated.

XXXXX

From the very beginning, they hadn't planned on being used for target practice. In the last three days, there had been two separate attempts to kill them and their friends. After sitting on stakeout for four hours, they thought that kind of extreme activity was behind them. There were rounds in the rear trunk lid, left rear quarter panel, and the passenger side rearview mirror had been demolished. "That was too close," William said, after letting out a long sigh.

Howard was looking into his rearview mirror and then checking the surrounding streets for signs of any traffic that might be less than friendly. They had left the senator's house in a hurry, but it wasn't without its rewards.

William, still somewhat nervous, reviewed the pictures he had taken which clearly showed certain individuals, who would later be identified as hired muscle, coming and going from the house. Then, he played back the recordings from the device he had placed on the dashboard. There wasn't much on it, except for one noticeable comment by one of the unknown visitors before he entered the house: "The man wants you to slow things down a little. We can't afford any more exposure right now because the FBI is sniffing around. The team that came from Baltimore ran into problems at the house yesterday."

When Howard and William returned, Captain Connors was waiting for them.

"From the looks of things, the two of you had an interesting wake-up call this morning."

William pointed to the camera. "I think we've got what you're looking for. There's a recording that ties Senator Haskell to the shooting yesterday at the safe house. I'd say we had a fairly productive meeting this morning."

Calvin noticed the bullet holes in the car. "From the looks of things, you two got out of there in just the nick-of-time."

Randy smiled. "Better the car than either one of you."

CHAPTER 36
Wednesday Morning, April 3, 2013, 9:30 am

Randy and Lisa, accompanied by two deputies, entered their office building, went through the sign-in procedure, and started walking toward the elevator. The security guard behind the desk, who was on the phone when they checked in, called at them to get their attention.

"Hey, that was nice work you two!"

Lisa turned and looked back at him. "Thanks," she said, and then patted Randy on the back. "He already must have seen the early edition of the story."

When they got off the elevator, they first headed for Mr. Locker's office. When they got to his office door, he was on the phone explaining something about the article to someone who obviously wasn't too happy about the headlines.

"That's exactly what they did," he screamed, and then he slammed the receiver down. That's when he saw the two of them standing in his doorway.

"That was corporate. They're not happy with me, but I told him to get in line." He got up and moved a chair for Randy who had leaned his crutches against the wall behind him. "The phone has been ringing off the hook this morning." He sat down in the chair next to Randy.

"I've taken calls from all over this country from editors and managing editors, even one publisher, about how they've had to deal with similar problems. There were three separate callers from St. Louis, Chattanooga, and Birmingham who told me about their situations and how they've had people placed over them that had no experience in the business at all. The calls began stacking up," he continued, as he pointed to the piles of pink slips on his desk. "I need to return these calls."

Randy looked at him and grinned. "Don't throw any of those away because they're all evidence at this point."

Once they started talking about the next part of the story, time went by quickly. Lisa was excited to learn that a follow-up story was already in the works. Mr. Locker had called in two younger reporters whom he believed could handle the pressures being brought to bear upon the paper. She offered to help, as did Randy, but he had other ideas for both of them.

"I've always wanted to write a book, but I'm not sure I could pull it off. You two, on the other hand, seem like such a fit." He got up from his chair, walked over to the window, and looked at the scenery below. "You will have the full resources of the paper behind you, provided you're interested."

Randy could barely stay in his seat. "What about corporate's response to all of this? Who's going to handle them?"

"Don't worry about corporate. After today's headlines, and the number of columns that will be written over the next several weeks, they will love the exposure. Our website crashed this morning because of the number of visitors trying to access it. Circulation has run an extra edition this morning just to meet demands. They were upset about not being told about the story. They're not upset about what the story is doing."

Randy leaned toward Lisa. "What do you say to this?"

She didn't respond immediately. She leaned forward and looked directly at Mr. Locker.

"If we agree to write the book, will you personally see that the book is published? Will our completed manuscript be published without outside influence or rewrites?"

"I personally will see to it that not one word is changed."

She looked at Randy, who was smiling at her, and nodded her head. "I'm all in."

Just then, the phone rang. Mr. Locker picked up the receiver and listened for a few seconds. He picked up the remote control, turned on the television that was in the corner of the room, hung up the phone, and then leaned back into his chair. "That was John Altman. He said to watch the news on Channel 17."

The three of them sat there stunned, while listening to one of the attorneys in the Department of Justice conduct a news conference on the steps of the Capitol building.

"The United States Attorney General has resigned," he announced amid a flurry of reporters squeezing closer and closer toward him. *"He offered his resignation to the President less than an hour ago."*

Mr. Locker put down the remote, stood up, and danced. "Man, this is sweet. Nobody else in the nation carried this story this morning." The phone rang again. It was Altman.

"John, I'm putting you on speaker phone so that Randy and Lisa can hear you." He connected the receiver to the call.

"I just took a call from the AG's office. The FBI is on its way to talk to us about the story. If Randy and Lisa can stay, it might help us with all the particulars."

Mr. Locker looked at them both, grinned, and nodded his head. "They'll stay, but I imagine the FBI will want to keep them here a while."

Randy clasped Lisa's left hand into his. "Are you up for this? It could be a great start for our book."

She smiled. "Yes. We can do this."

Mr. Locker clapped his hands once. "It's done."

At the cabin, Carla and Susan were sitting in the kitchen eating breakfast. Susan decided to turn on the television. She started channel surfing until she came upon the news story that had broken earlier.

"Carla, you're going to want to watch this."

As they watched the story being reported, each of them leaned forward in their chairs almost as if they were suspended in mid-air. Carla covered her mouth with the palm of her right hand, grinning and fighting back tears at the same time. All Susan could say was, "They did it. They did it. They did it."

Carla glanced at the clock above the television. They had less than five hours before they would be able to contact the others. That wasn't good enough for her.

"We've got to go home – and it's got to be now."

She reached over and turned on the radio. She tuned it to another channel and began broadcasting. "Breaker, this is Little Thunder, over." All they could hear was the static noise in the background. She waited for another few seconds, and then tried again. "Breaker, this is Little Thunder. Does anyone copy – over?"

She waited for a few more seconds and then heard a response. "Little Thunder – you've got Red Rider on this end. What can I do for you?"

"Red Rider, I need for you to contact someone for me by landline."

She gave the telephone number where Howard could be reached at any time. Once she was sure that her request and her instructions were understood, she turned off the radio.

"It might take an hour or so, but we should be hearing from Howard by eleven o'clock this morning. I'll turn the radio on at that time and listen."

Susan brought her up-to-speed on the news conference that had been televised. "The U.S. Attorney General has resigned, and the President accepted his resignation. According to the reporter, four other high-ranking Department of Justice attorneys have been placed under arrest by the FBI." She took a deep breath. "The State Attorneys for Missouri and Texas also held press conferences this morning. They announced the beginning of investigations into several disappearances or unusual deaths of journalists over the past two years."

Carla sat down and looked at her. "I'm sure the other states that are even curious will begin theirs soon. I'll bet you a dollar to your dime that Howard has already talked with the State Attorney for Florida about Max's death."

She was right about that. While she and Susan were talking, he was speaking with the State Attorney from Orlando about the very same topic. The problem was that Howard suspected him to be involved somehow in Max's untimely accident. While he was speaking with him, Howard was wearing a wire that Captain Connors had placed on him earlier. The conversation proved fruitful. As soon as he finished and walked out of the room, four FBI agents entered, handcuffed the State Attorney, and led him outside to a row of SUV's that were headed to the jail.

Calvin, who had been sitting on the sofa on the porch, shook his head. "There's something still not right about all of this."

One of the deputies, who had been providing security for the house, responded. "You know what's not right about this?" He paused. "What's not right is that this couldn't have been controlled by just one man. When the dominos begin to fall, I just wonder who is going to be fingered before all of this comes to an end."

Calvin nodded his head. "You're right about that. There has to be someone outside of Washington, but who is close enough to Washington to be able to call the shots."

The deputy looked at him and grinned. "You know the old saying, 'Follow the money.'"

Calvin took out his cell phone, looked through his directory, and selected Randy's number. It took a few seconds, but they connected.

Calvin stood up and began pacing as he spoke. "Who's following the money? That's where we're going to find the brains of this operation. Politicians don't do anything unless they receive some kind of compensation – cash or otherwise."

Randy, still sitting in Mr. Locker's office, smiled. "I'll call you back in a little while." He put his cell phone in his coat pocket and then looked at Mr. Tucker. "Is Mrs. Rhoden in today?"

"I believe she is. Did you want to speak to her?"

"Ask her if she would not mind meeting with us for a few minutes."

Lisa had a puzzled look on her face. "What's with calling in Mrs. Rhoden?"

"I think she can help us do a little tracking."

While they waited for Mrs. Rhoden to make her way to Mr. Locker's office, William was diligently working on the evidence from their time spent at Senator Haskell's house. William expertly handled the printing of the pictures, despite the crude set-up he had to work with. Then, he started documenting much of the events that had occurred over the last two days. He wanted to make sure that he got those things down, while the memories were fresh and vivid.

When Howard returned, he and William finished with the journal entries.

"William let's try to reach your mother and Susan. I'm hoping they've been following these events and might just be listening this morning."

The two of them sat down and Howard turned on the radio base unit, allowing it to warm up for a few seconds. Then, Howard flipped the switch and began transmitting.

"This is Greyhound calling."

There was no answer. He repeated it twice. They both sat perfectly still even leaning forward slightly, each of them turning their head slightly to the left, as if to concentrate all of their hearing capacity at the speaker in front of them.

Still, there was no answer.

"William, they may not have been watching the news and don't know about what's going on. I think we'll just sit here and wait four-or-five minutes – just in case."

Three minutes later, Carla was transmitting. "This is Rabbit. Are your there, Greyhound?"

They gave each other a high-five, before Howard responded.

"This is Greyhound. Have you been watching the news this morning?"

"Yes, we have. We think there's more to this and we've been discussing the possibilities."

"What say you, Rabbit?"

Susan's voice could be heard next. "Howard, the CD that Peter gave me might have used a backdoor access program designed to store other information. I'm not sure how to do that stuff, but I think I know the passcode for it – that is if it's there."

Before Howard responded, he pointed to William to take notes.

"Okay, I understand. What's the passcode?"

"He told me something unusual two days before he died. He said, *'The best movie I ever saw was Of Human Bondage.'* It seemed strange at the time because that part of the conversation came out of the blue and had nothing to do with what we were talking about."

"That's it? That's the passcode?"

"No, it was the character played by Kim Novak whose name was Mildred. I think that is the passcode – Mildred."

William acknowledged he had written the information.

Carla inquired about how much longer she and Susan needed to stay at the cabin. Howard shrugged his shoulders, before answering. He told her he expected things to start heating up considerably, now that the story had broken.

"I will contact you at the usual time. I need to speak with Captain Connors first."

They spoke for another minute or two before disconnecting.

Howard turned to William. "I think your mother is ready to come home."

William smiled. "Listen, I know somebody who can help with this CD business. Who has the CD right now?"

"We put it in the safe. I'll go get it. By the way, who is this somebody you know who might be able to help us with the CD?"

"Do you remember Jesse? It's his little brother, Nathan. He's turned out to be a real computer geek."

"I remember Jesse. He's the one who used to spend the night here – once-in-a-while. I don't remember Nathan."

"He's the one who fixed that old computer we had a few years ago."

"I'll have you know that old computer works just fine."

CHAPTER 37
Wednesday Afternoon, April 3, 2013

William was right. Nathan managed to access a backdoor in the programming on the CD. The bulk of the information pointed directly to Senator Haskell and his staff. There were documents that had been scanned connecting the U.S. Attorney General's office with involvement in covering up fraudulent behavior by a major contributor. More importantly, the banking information showed huge deposits from a benefactor named Gregory Holland. Captain Connors recognized the name.

"Greg Holland was a big name in the importing business on the west coast in the 90's. He came east about fifteen years ago and bought up land in Miami, Jacksonville, Savannah, Charleston, and several other entry ports on the east coast. He was tied to some really shady deals near Baltimore and New York but was never convicted."

Howard pressed him. "How do you know so much about this guy?"

"When he came to Daytona to party several years ago, I stopped him for erratic driving, which ended up with a DUI charge. His lawyers had him out on the streets before I could sneeze. He skipped town before his court date, and no one has seen or heard from him since. I have tried to track him down a couple of times, but each time it's like he's vanished into thin air."

Howard continued. "Do you have any pictures of him?"

"I'm only aware of the ones in his file at headquarters."

Howard put his coffee cup on the table and sat down in front of the computer. "Let's do a search on this guy and see what pops up."

Meanwhile, Randy and Lisa had stopped to get some lunch at a diner on the beach.

The two deputies, who were shadowing their every move, stayed in their vehicle and watched from across the street. Lisa, who had wanted to sit outside on the veranda in front of the diner, waved at them.

"I just love this place. They've got the best pesto in the world – and their pizza isn't half-bad either."

Randy got the attention of one of the waiters and asked for two cups of coffee. "Pizza sounds good to me."

While they were enjoying their coffee and waiting on their pizza, they talked about all of the things that had happened over the last few days. While they were talking, she reached over with her right hand and placed it on top of his left hand and smiled at him. He smiled back at her.

"What happens now that the story has broken?"

He cleared his throat. "I hope it gathers momentum and the news agencies don't bury it."

"We can't let that happen. People died because of what a few people decided to do. The story is more than just a story. It's about a bunch of ideologues and political bullies who pushed their way into the arena and tried to shut down opposing points of view. That's exactly what occurred in Europe before World War II. We cannot let the bullies win this thing."

He heard the urgency in her voice and the intensity she displayed was evident. He knew what she was saying, but he didn't want to promise her something he couldn't bring about.

"Right now, we've got to keep the pieces of the story from being scattered. It's our job to make sure that no matter what, the story stays focused on the truth. Then, we need to make sure that the truth doesn't get buried or passed over because it isn't sexy or it's unpleasant. We've got to stay focused on telling the truth every day.

It's got to be kept in front of the American people, until they understand how important it is for them to be aware of the kinds of behaviors politicians are capable of. So far, everything we've learned about the pieces of this story is that nobody was forcing the politicians to do the things they've done. To them, it's just a way of life – and they believe that they know best for everyone. I'm positive that when the entire story unfolds, there will be one man left standing who will have to answer for all of this. However, along the way, several will be swept away by the floods of outrage and disappointment. Until that day, you and I have to keep pushing this forward."

Just then, his cell phone buzzed. "Excuse me, but I think I need to take this. Howard is calling."

"Randy, you're not going to believe what we just found out."

"Don't make me guess, Howard. I hate playing that game."

"Remember those pictures that William took for Max? One of them was of a guy named Gregory Holland. We've also learned that he's the money behind much of the shenanigans we've uncovered so far. That picture puts him in Orlando at the State Attorney's office along with several other guys we can now identify. Thanks to Max's diligence, Captain Connors has contacted his boss who then contacted his boss – well, you get the picture. As we speak, there are teams searching for Mr. Holland and his cronies. They're wanted for several felony counts.

During the preliminary work up for the search, they questioned someone from the Justice Department and learned there's an enemies list that included several names of reporters and journalists. Mr. Rayner is on that list. The story has blown up big time."

After they hung up, Randy leaned toward Lisa and whispered to her. "Howard just told me that links have been established connecting the money guy to the State Attorney in Orlando. Plus, the DOJ has been holding an enemies list with names of reporters and journalists on it. Mr. Rayner is on the list. It won't be long before somebody rolls on somebody else for a deal." He rubbed the palms of his hands together excitedly. "The only thing left to do is to start writing the book."

Lisa was not amused. "How far up the ladder does this thing go? Who developed the enemies list? Are we ever going to find out?"

"We know the Attorney General has resigned – and he's one of the President's main guys."

"But what we have so far does not put any of this into the White House."

Randy shifted his weight off of his hurt leg. "No, it doesn't, but it's knocking at the front door of it and we've only started to scratch the surface."

She smiled slightly, took a sip of her coffee, and whispered to him. "You know that old saying: where there's smoke there's fire? I like to think that where there's smoke there's somebody starting fires – and we need to know the name of that somebody."

"How about we get started on that right now? Mrs. Rhoden can probably point us in the right direction."

"Wait a minute," she said as she grabbed his left elbow. "What about Max? All of you guys said you started this whole thing to find out why Max was on that road near Avon Park – or have you forgotten?"

"We haven't forgotten – believe me we haven't forgotten. Someone wants us to forget about it, but that's one question that will be answered by the time the dust settles."